STEPHEN HUNTER

SOFT TARGET

A BOB LEE SWAGGER NOVEL

D0003905

POCKET BOOKS

New York   London   Toronto   Sydney   New Delhi

Pocket Books
An Imprint of Simon & Schuster, Inc.
1230 Avenue of the Americas
New York, NY 10020

This book is a work of fiction. Any references to historical events, real people, or real places are used fictitiously. Other names, characters, places, and events are products of the author's imagination, and any resemblance to actual events or places or persons, living or dead, is entirely coincidental.

This Pocket Books paperback edition August 2023

POCKET and colophon are registered trademarks of Simon & Schuster, Inc.

For information about special discounts for bulk purchases, please contact Simon & Schuster Special Sales at 1-866-506-1949 or business@simonandschuster.com.

The Simon & Schuster Speakers Bureau can bring authors to your live event. For more information or to book an event, contact the Simon & Schuster Speakers Bureau at 1-866-248-3049 or visit our website at www.simonspeakers.com.

Manufactured in the United States of America

10 9 8 7 6 5 4 3 2 1

ISBN 978-1-6680-1913-9
ISBN 978-1-4391-4994-2 (ebook)

Critics can't stop raving about
New York Times and *USA Today* bestseller

STEPHEN HUNTER

"Master of the modern gunfighter tale, he isn't
just the best action writer of this generation,
but the best of any."
—*The Providence Journal*

"A cinematic sense of story and combat."
—*The Oregonian*

"Hunter passes almost everybody else in the thriller-
writing trade as if they were standing still."
—*New York Daily News*

"The best writer of straight-out thrillers working today."
—*Rocky Mountain News*

"A great entertainer."
—*The Washington Post*

"I'm a fanatical reader of thrillers, and Stephen Hunter
has always been one of my favorites."
—Malcolm Gladwell, *Salon*

"What a good thing it is that the apple hasn't fallen far
from the tree" (*Kirkus Reviews*) in Stephen Hunter's
breakneck new adventure starring Bob Lee Swagger's
son, fearless marksman Ray Cruz

SOFT TARGET

"Combining elements of the locked-room mystery, the
disaster novel, and the lock-and-load thriller, Hunter
produces a remarkably gripping tale, building character
(the captives, the bureaucrats, and the 'terrorists' all get
compelling backstories) every bit as convincingly as he
drives the narrative to its *High Noon*–style finale."

—*Booklist* (starred review)

"Fast-paced . . . fearsome."

—*Publishers Weekly*

"Any thriller in which Middle Eastern terrorists whack Santa on the first page is bound to be exciting. As always, Hunter has crafted a fast-paced and all-too-plausible telling of our worst nightmares coming true. Ray Cruz is a worthy successor to Swagger. Hunter's fans, along with new readers, will enjoy the violent battle between Cruz and the bad guys."

—*Library Journal*

"Black Friday [is] on the cusp of becoming blood-soaked Friday."

—*Kirkus Reviews*

"A solid addition to Stephen Hunter's sniper series, made more engaging by its invocation of current events and political posturing. I join Hunter's other fans in hoping he has another one already in the works."

—*The Washington Times*

Praise for

DEAD ZERO,

the thriller that introduced Marine sniper Ray Cruz

"*Dead Zero* is at its best when Hunter has Cruz in the novel's crosshairs."

—*The Oregonian*

"The only book better than a new Jack Reacher novel is a new Bob Lee Swagger adventure. *Dead Zero*, with a dynamite plot and riveting characters, is everything any action fan could want as Swagger pits his wits against a man who could be a younger version of himself."

—*Toronto Globe and Mail*

"A juicy premise. . . . A top-notch thriller."

—*Booklist* (starred review)

*To the writing teachers who made an otherwise
unspecial kid feel special all the way through.*

Mr. Aita

Mr. Gregory

Dr. Guest

Mr. Byrne

Mr. Hungerford

Mr. Jacobi

Mr. Baldwin

Feathers flew like a turkey! Well, they shouldna run,
they shouldna run.

—CRAZY LEE, *THE WILD BUNCH,* 1969

The bullet hit Santa Claus beneath the left eye. It shattered his skull, blew a large exit wound from the rear of that vessel, and drove a bright red spatter pattern across the pale satin of his throne like some sort of twisted abstract painting. Worse still, the ballistic energy unleashed an upper-body spasm that shook his hat comically askew, and it slipped off his face and caught on his ear and hung there like a large red sock.

The four-year-old girl sitting in his lap stared not so much in horror but in fascination. She understood that this was "different" but had no larger context against which to compare it. She had no acquaintance yet with the concept of horror and the human fear of seeing the body's vaults penetrated and eviscerated, but she picked up immediately on the appropriate response from her mother, who grabbed her and started screaming as the hundreds of others clustered around Santa's throne began to do the same.

A FEW MINUTES EARLIER

It was like combat, except the food wasn't as good. It was . . . shopping . . . in a mall . . . on the day after Thanksgiving, the blackest of black Fridays.

Ray Cruz decided that he would never take an IQ test again, for the results, after he had agreed to this adventure, would prove suicidally depressing.

He shook his head, even as someone in the crowd jostled his shoulder. That person was outbound down the corridor called Colorado—after the river, not the state—while he was inbound. His fault? Maybe, maybe not, and courteous as ever, he shot a look to his victim, issued a tiny smile of contrition, noted that it was a she and that she was under twenty and concluded that he did not register as a carbon-based life form, and turned back to what lay ahead.

What lay ahead was people, confusion, greed, stuff, the despair of the holidays, the crunch of families that did not get along, duties and responsibilities only half-articulated but completely felt, guilt and regret, endless and passionate. All that was evident in the tableaux before him, the long corridor of mall America, a place he hardly knew, lined on each side by mercantile units offering the usual treasure—jewelry, clothes, shoes, ladies' undies, toys, a stop here and there for junk food or hooch—all of it lit through the daylight by the red-green-yellow spectrum of holiday illumination, though the temp was a steady seventy-two and the echoes that amplified the ambient noise level testified also to its indoorness. So much data, so many splendors, a multitude of faces and costumes, the range from beauty to grotesque, from health to sickness, from the very young to the very old. It was like a village bazaar he'd once seen in Afghanistan, except for the Afghanistan part. It sucked the energy out of him. He wanted to take cover. It was incoming, like an artillery barrage to the senses, 24/7. He felt his normally impassive face collapse in unwilled but undeniable melancholy.

"Hey, Marine, don't fade on me," Molly Chan said.

"I'm about to call a corpsman," he said.

"Big tough guy like you? You can get through this. We'll show up with packages and make them so happy and you'll feel good. The nephews will all worship you, the sisters will wonder why you took me over them, my father will offer to make you a partner in his business, and my mom . . . well, who knows about my mom?"

It sounded pretty good to Ray. Family. It was something that had been taken from him years ago, on a highway outside Manila when a drunken truck driver hit his mother and father as they drove home from a visit with her relatives. Even discovering that his biological father still lived hadn't quite filled the hole in his life; maybe the sprawling, argumentative, rambunctious Chan clan would.

He was forty-two now, a few months past twenty-two years of gung ho, Semper Fi USMC lifestyle, mostly shooting and getting shot at. Ray had many scars from distant, dry or cold places, and he had many memories that sometimes—less now than before—flooded over him: men and boys bleeding out or torn to pieces, the dysentery of fear, the yoke of duty, his own need to press on and finish, even if it finished him. What're you trying to prove, Ray? Achilles died a million years ago. Someone's going to put an arrow in your heel too, if you don't watch out.

I'm Hector, not Achilles, Ray had replied, knowing the difference.

But then, in the Washington area for a talk at one of the alphabet-soup agencies that sought his post-retirement employment, he had met Molly Chan, and maybe it would all change, maybe it would be better after all. It had been, of all places, another gigantic mall, one out in Northern Virginia.

"You look like you're about to cry," someone had said to him as he stood at the corner of Macy's and Lord & Taylor's, baffled as to direction and destination.

He turned; she was more Asian than he was, shorter than he was, and unlike his dead flat desert of a face, adept primarily at staying neutral while people tried to kill him, hers was lively, lit from within by intelligence and wit. And she had—

"You have cheekbones," he said.

"One on each side. They won't go away no matter how much I eat."

"I'm half-Asian," he said.

"I noticed both halves," she said. "I bet it's a long story."

"Longer than Tolkien. Denser too. But at least—no hobbits. Anyhow, yeah, I am about to cry. Why did I come here? It's like the end of the world. I just need some underpants."

"You've never been in a mall before?"

"Possibly. I'm not sure. I'm just out of the Marine Corps, twenty-two years. They may get you killed, but they do hand out free underpants."

She laughed at his little joke, and that was a kind of start. It turned out they got along, their rhythms were right, they agreed on who the world's assholes were, they didn't like pompous, overbearing, self-important people, they believed in hard work, modesty, repression, and honesty. Neither drank a lot, both drank a little. Both were embarrassingly smart. What could possibly go wrong?

First it was coffee, then it was a couple of meals, a number of enjoyably merry e-mails, then a really bad movie, and then some interesting stuff happened and here he was in suburban Minnesota, at the biggest mall in America—America, the Mall, it called itself, and everywhere you looked stood the three letters AtM—on the biggest shopping day of the year. He was visiting her parents and family, headquartered in nearby Saint Paul, and on this day, the Chans went shopping en masse.

The family was Hmong, that is, formerly mountain tribal Vietnamese, honorable and ferocious allies of the American war effort of the '60s and '70s, since (by political necessity) decamped to the upper Midwest. She was second-generation, had only been to Asia as a tourist. She was thirty-four and an attorney in Washington, at the Department of Energy. She was beautiful, too good for any man she'd ever met, and even now unsure why she had spoken to the trim guy in the mall looking for underpants but glad she had. He remained vague about his past, not knowing that at a certain time, before she got in too deep, Molly had called in a DC favor and had received a synopsis of his career highlights, all five tours in the suck, and the last, crazy ride to hell and glory that ended in that famous missile detonation at the Rose Garden.

"Now," he said, as they were carried along by the current of the torrential second-floor Colorado corridor, "are we at this spot by random drift or is there a conscious destination ahead?" On either side, stores came and went: Ann Taylor, InvisibleSHIELD by Zagg, LEGO Imagination Center, Impulse, Lee's Video Gallery. And everywhere lights, green and red, Christmas trees, elves, Santas, the whole nine yards of Christmas cheer braying psychotically at the innocent and the easily disturbed.

"I think there's a skateboard place up ahead. My nephew George needs tape, it has been explained to me. Thus tape. We get the tape and we are on the homeward bound."

"I guess I can handle that," he said.

"You'll prevail. You always have. Why wouldn't you now?" she said with a smile.

But the going wasn't easy, not by any means, and en masse the normally polite and melancholy Minnesotans became somewhat bellicose. Christmas was do-or-die for them, a full-contact sport, played more vigorously than their beloved if sad-boy Minnesota Vikings had played again this season, and two exotics like Ray—Reyes Fidencio Cruz, Filipino by culture if not by birth—and Molly Chan weren't going to stand in anybody's way.

They came to Skate City and he followed her

in and watched mutely as she purchased a spool of bright red grit tape so that her nephew could whistle around the streets off Central Avenue aboard a mini-surfboard on jet aircraft landing gear. One look at the shaky conveyance, built for speed, guts, stamina, strong legs, and a fourteen-year-old's lack of capacity to imagine disaster, and Ray faced his own advanced age. He'd been shot at several thousand times but a skateboard scared him to death. He'd rather face a brace of hadjis than something so lethal.

"See, wasn't that easy?" Molly asked.

"Not bad," he said. "I feel myself rallying. We are done now, no?"

"We are done now, yes."

"So we can move on to other things?"

"Unless," she said, "you want to ride the Wild Mouse."

"I'd rather do another combat tour than ride that thing," he said, as, not twenty-five yards away, the corridor called Colorado yielded to an amazing splurge of space under a wash of late-afternoon sunlight, and in the forefront of that space the single car of a roller coaster called the Wild Mouse slalomed by, shaking screams from its teenaged inhabitants. This spectacle was sited just beyond the rail of the balcony, for the mall at that location opened its central space to provide area enough for an amusement park under a vast skylight shaped to resemble a prominent map icon.

The conceit of America, the Mall of Indian Falls, Minnesota, and the stroke of marketing genius, was that it was no simple doughnut-shaped fabrication. Its designers had contrived it to more or less resemble the shape of the continental United States, a stylized pentagon whose morphic resonance would instantly conjure the association to America in the collective unconscious. It was correctly oriented to the compass, moreover, so that a flat, straight border was actually its northern extremity. Then a Washington-Oregon-California coastline angled downward to a San Diego corner before jutting eastward via a long, long wall engineered to form two crescents, which signified the swoops of the Mexican border and the coast of the Gulf of Mexico. At that terminus, roughly where Tallahassee was located in the real world, its outer wall trekked southeasterly to form a peninsular outcrop that stood in for Florida; to complete the fantasy, from the tip of the Sunshine State to the tip of frosty Maine, a wall ran with only one bend, to honor the Atlantic-side convergence of Florida and Georgia. This of course meant that the amusement park was in the "Midwest" or center of the 750,000-square-foot immensity, and above it the skylights were patterned across the vast roof in the configuration of the Great Lakes.

From the ground, the view yielded nothing of interest: no matter from which direction you chose to examine AtM, it looked more or less like an aircraft carrier hull dumped in the middle of the frozen Minnesota plains. That wasn't the point, however. The whole thing had been located on the primary flight path to the Twin Cities' great multihub international airport, so thousands saw it in its full glory every day, from 30,000 feet, as it had been imagined by its builders. Like the Pyramids, it only made sense from the sky.

Inside, besides the corridors designated by river names and zones by compass location, it continued with a zealot's intensity to have fun with geography.

Some wit had been allowed: the multiplex movie theater—fifteen screens—was on the fourth floor of "California," the higher-end, more sophisticated men's and women's shops in the NE, in "Manhattan." "Florida" contained vacationware shops; around the "Midwestern" amusement park had been clustered most of the many, many food stalls, snack bars, and restaurants; and so on and so on.

Most hellish was the amusement park. It sported not only the Wild Mouse but a batch of other thrill rides, one that whirled seats about at the end of tethered wires, another that replicated somebody's idea of a log waterway that shunted screamers down aquamarine, chlorine-infused liquid, more like Scope than actual H2O. The yells of the riders, the clack of the vehicles on their tracks, the blur of motion, the whoosh of disturbed currents filling the air of the huge place, all amplified under a roof of skylights designed to let in the wan November Minnesota sun and combined with the din of shoppers, made the place pretty much unbearable. It was all there, the two great things that befit a place calling itself America, the Mall: shopping and speed.

"Okay," she said. "Then let's get out of here."

"I am so gone," he said.

"Oh wait," she said. "Now, if you really want to make Molly happy, let me point you in the proper direction," and she twisted him forty-five degrees until he came to bear on a place called Boardwalk Fries.

"I smell potato," she said. "Potato is good. Potato, grease, salt, crispy exterior."

"Well," he said, "I have to say, they smell good."

"They do, but that's probably not the actual

frying-potato odor but rather some chemical product from Monsanto. It probably comes out of an aerosol can."

"Well, it worked on me. Let's get some french fries and—"

That was a sound he knew. One, loud.

Then lots of them. Percussions, sharp and hurtful, flashing back among the corridors and crannies, too loud, earsplittingly loud, replicating themselves in the echo unto multiplicity, and drawing the crowd into silence in a frozen instant before panic, screams, and chaos.

"Somebody's shooting," Ray said.

The man who shot Santa Claus was named Maahir; he was an unusually large Somali soldier from the militia Hizbul Islam, under command of General Hassan Dahir Aweys, opposed to the brigands and false believers of the militia al Shbaab. The policy differences between them were immense, and one could list them easily if given a year and a half to do so. The shot was about 150 feet, but for him it was nothing. Maahir had taken many other long shots in his time, making most; he'd also taken many close shots, and the spectacle of death as released upon a body by bullet wound was nothing new to him.

But everything else was new. This place, this strange structure, these people in their comfort, their wealth, their fear, the unbearable smells of food, the beauty of the young girls, the data so overwhelmed him he had almost fallen into enchantment.

But Allah had kept him rigorously devoted to mission.

After the shot, which signaled the beginning of

this great martyrdom operation, one that would see him happily arrived in paradise before the day finished, he looked around as people fled him in horror. It was so funny. Ha ha, the look of terror on their faces. In wars, you seldom saw such fear because you were always moving. Not so here.

He stood in the center of the collection of crazed speed apparatuses and listened as the gunshots arose from his brothers, as they engaged the infidels for the first time. Before him panic and fear but mostly collision as some ran this way and some that and many went sprawling in the crack-ups that ensued.

He edged backward a bit, to get out of the rush of the masses, and knew that if he wanted, he could fire and fire and kill and kill, but after all, there was no hurry, and there would be ample time for those pleasures.

On the large video screen displaying the SCADA icons, MEMTAC 6.2 purred away placidly, cyber-testimony to the fact that all was tidy in the kingdom of AtM.

You could be forgiven for not looking, but Phil Deakins watched anyway. SCADA stood for Supervisory Control and Data Acquisition, and it was the technology by which the mall was ruled, through the auspices of its software program, as designed by Siemens, in Germany, called MEMTAC 6.2. SCADA ran access controls, HVAC, energy consumption, life safety, and all other operational aspects of the mall. It "supervised" through the computer and it "acquired" data needed to tell the computers what to do. It could do the simple (unlock doors at a certain time) or the complex (reroute cash register transactions if the satellite processing system went down). It had no preferences, idiosyncrasies, quirks, glitches, charm, or moodiness and represented the dull, systemized perfection of the German engineering mind. You wouldn't want to go drinking with it; you'd end up barfing beer in a gutter while yearning to invade Poland.

It set the temperature, regulated the lighting, informed security when an alarm went off, controlled the credit card verification process, monitored the fire control system, determined that the cameras and the recording equipment worked at all times. What was so cool about it—those nutsy Germans!—was that its user interface was pictorial and user-intuitive.

Thus what dominated the wall of the security office of America, the Mall, was a glowing representation against an azure blue background of a large flow chart that looked a lot like a family tree from the planet Dune. Chunks of info, identifying labels, holding pens, all arranged by a grid of lines and accessed by an operator with a good mouse hand. The system itself, when it needed petting by humans (rare enough), was controlled by the technique called drag and drop or sometimes "dragon drop," whereby the operator made things happen via nesting the cursor on something and mousing it to another zone where it was deposited, and somewhere far-off, air-conditioning went down two degrees, the janitors were notified that someone had stuffed cotton underpants in the urinal in the men's at Hudson 3-122, the log flume chlorine fluoridation program was cranked down by twenty parts per million so that lab smell wasn't nearly so offensive to older people with oversensitive olfactory glands.

But until that afternoon, nobody had ever shot Santa Claus.

"Jesus, somebody just shot Santa," someone shouted. It was a security geek tasked with monitoring the camera displays on another wall as one of his too-many duties. "Jesus Christ, I am not kidding, they blew his head wide open—"

"Call the police," said Deakins. "God, I can't imagine what kind of sick—"

"Phil, look at nine!"

Phil, commander of the afternoon watch for America, the Mall, security, looked and saw chaos, speed, blur, panic spreading into a plague of indistinct animal movement on the monitor marked nine, which he knew to represent the NW Colorado corridor floor one camera, which gazed from its Plexiglas encasement down the thoroughfare toward, in the distance 150 yards, Area Z, as the Silli-Land amusement complex was professionally known. In fact by the crazed magic of closed circuit security television, he could watch the panic spread from nine to eight (Area Z, entryway east) while lights began to blink on phone lines and two-way radios barked as various security personnel called in.

Meanwhile the big board began to send signals of distress; it monitored pedestrian traffic density and noted drily an overload and backup at three exits.

"Oh, shit," called Thomason, number two in command at the fourth-floor security headquarters, "look at fifteen!"

Phil felt a cold edge of hurt slice his solar plexus and actually had to take a deep breath to keep from hyperventilating into collapse. Fifteen betrayed the same symptoms: panic, flight, mass movement, chaos, fear, people running, people falling, children being knocked over, old people pushed aside. The horror bled from monitor to monitor across the vast wall of security views into the mall from all angles—thirty-six of them total. In the background the hazy image of a gun muzzle issuing a white-hot spurt of blast drew all eyes, even if, packed in here, no outside noise reached them.

"I'm getting shooters," Thomason was screaming over the phone. "We have active shooters in the mall, first floor, people down and bleeding, Jesus Christ."

It was their ultimate nightmare, the one that everyone said would never come. But it had come. It was here. It was happening. Phil swallowed, dwarfed by it. He looked from monitor to monitor, seeing the armed men moving down the corridors, driving before them the unarmed civilians in the hundreds. Of course: drive them to the center, to Area Z, and hold them there or turn it into a slaughterhouse. He had a moment of remorse at the complexity of the mall and how hard a puzzle it would be for responders to engage: the amusement park at the center with its jungle of attractions and its loops and swirls of track spread across all altitudes. Of course the whole thing was equally riven by corridors and stairways running behind the stores; it was like an immense game of 3-D Chutes and Ladders.

His mind clarified. He picked up the red phone on his console, the direct line to state police headquarters, bypassing local suburban yokels. When he picked up the red line, no dial was necessary, as instantly a pipelined voice responded, "Daywatch Emergency, do you have an incident, AtM?"

Phil hung together. "Daywatch Emergency, we

have active shooters in the mall. As far as I can make it out, we have one, no, two of them, in each main corridor. I can't see who they are but I've got a massive panic situation here, I need relief fast. Someone even shot Santa Claus."

"Could this be some kind of a drill? Or a movie scene—?"

"No, *no*, it's for real, goddammit, people shooting, people down." Hysteria snuck into the margins of his voice.

Daywatch Emergency got it together, or maybe now it was an older guy, more experienced.

"Do not move from your command position, Officer," he said. "We are dispatching units immediately. We need you on the monitors, Security, do you hear me?"

"Affirmative," said Phil, who had fifteen good years on the Saint Paul Metropolitan Police force under his belt and had been in emergencies before. He turned, cooler now, to the number two guy.

"Inform our people, they are not to attempt apprehension unarmed. They'll just be gunned down. Jesus, we have no weapons, we—"

"Phil, I got Indian Falls Metro, they're sending cars, we have people all over the mall calling 911, we have cops inbound from all over the place."

"Man, this is a real basketfuck," said Phil. Then, again with the calm of a serious professional in the crisis of his life, he picked up his earphones and throat mike, slipped them on, went to override on the communications grid of the console, and spoke to his men spread throughout the mall, some on Segways, some on foot. "Listen, all personnel, we have a ten thirty-two, man with gun, maybe multiple. I repeat, a ten thirty-two, man with gun, multiple, shots fired. Do not try to apprehend armed personnel, you will only get yourself hurt. Move people away from the line of fire if possible, provide medical attention and traffic control to open exits. I am putting mall evacuation plan A in effect, I have alerted local LE, we have big help inbound. Come on, guys, stay with me on this, do your jobs, hang in there. We will get you help as quickly as possible, we have cavalry coming from all directions, and—"

With the sound of a vacuum tin being opened, power died in the room. Darkness fell, replaced in seconds by emergency red lighting. But the big board plasma screen with its gleaming representation of Germanic efficiency was black, all the security monitors were down, and the radio net had gone belly-up. The electrical backup system had not cut over and there were no comforting sounds of well-running technology.

"What the fuck?" Phil said, and he wasn't the only one, as all six men in the command office began to curse immediately, flipping buttons, hitting toggles, banging screens, twisting radio dials, yelling at handsets.

"Cool it, *cool it!*" yelled Phil. In seconds his team had gotten hold of themselves.

"He's taken over our security system," someone said. "Motherfucker has cut us out of it."

"Okay, okay," said Phil, "stay calm, nothing is helped if we panic. We—"

"The fucking doors are locked," someone said.

The men sat there for a second, amid dead security monitors, lightless communications equipment, air-conditioningless rising temps, feeling nausea.

They were trapped. They were in lockdown. The electromagnets concealed within each door had been directed by MEMTAC 6.2 to clamp them closed, using the full power of the lodestone, which was beyond influence by any force less than a well-planted explosive.

"Oh shit," someone said. "Smell that?"

Yes, it was an odor. Something chemical in nature had just popped in the air vent. The smell of fresh-mown hay filled the air. It reminded Phil of the farm he'd grown up on in Iowa, even as he recalled from a class on some long-forgotten law enforcement seminar twenty years ago that the smell of new-mown hay or grass was an indicator of a substance called phosgene.

It was a poison gas.

Asad thought, Look at the white sheep run.

Oh, how they ran. What sorts of men were these? They had no courage, no heart of lion, no belief in Allah. A little pop from the gun and they ran.

"What cowards," he said to Saalim.

Saalim's job was to cover the rear. He was not happy about it. It wasn't fair. Was he not a fighter like Asad, perhaps more so even? Had he not stood in the high desert with Hizbul Islam against the city usurpers of al Shbaab, near Wabra? Had he not burned their houses and executed their men and herded their women and children into the stockades? He had done it all, praise be to Allah, may peace be upon you, brother.

But now he was the rear security chap while this miscreant Asad reaped Allah's glory on the rifle, the cracks of the gunfire knifing through, then echoing off the profane walls of this grotesque temple of infidel faith, with its nude women in windows, its temptations, its—

Then a man appeared in a white shirt on some kind of insane upright motorcycle, his head clasped in a helmet, and certainly he was armed, for he had what appeared to be police wires running to communications plugs in his ears, as had the Iranian advisor in the high, bright desert, who'd talked them through the campaign and led them in their vengeance upon the false believers of al Shbaab.

The rifle was there, cradled in his arms against his shoulder, and with a surge of joy and glory, he fired, loving the drama of the baby Kalashnikov, and in the smear of flash at the muzzle he saw darkness blossom upon his enemy's chest, and down the infidel went, sprawling lifelessly in a heap beyond grace as if his legs had been turned to wet clay beneath him. That is how they die, no? Without dignity or sense of courage, just brought down like animals.

"I killed one, Asad," he said.

"Hah," said Asad, "I have killed many," but stung by the boastfulness in Saalim's voice, he felt that to retain warrior face he must kill again, and so he selected a cow from the herd and fired. She was a big one, black like himself, but slow, which is why she lingered at the rear of the fleeing crowd, but he had no mercy this day. The rifle cracked and spurt, spinning hot brass, and though he could not see the hit, she went down with the heavy flop of a large dead animal. Next to her, behind her, two more, a man and a child, went down, but the man got up, got the child up, and the two raced off, trailing slicks of blood, easy to track. He looked back at his kill. She lay in a sprawl, her face fat and slack, and next to her a child knelt, crying for his downed mother, unaware that today would be a day without pity.

"We will kill them all!" he exulted, feeling the power of God's will move through his body, the aphrodisiacal smell of the fired powder, the satisfying recoil of the baby Kalashnikov.

Before him, with even more urgency if such could be imagined, the crowd seemed to speed up, all the mothers and daughters and fathers and sons of the West, all of them, cursed unto damnation and eternal fire by Allah, and he, Asad, was the deliverer, the living embodiment of Allah's will on earth. Oh, it so fit with his imagery of the end of times—the scale of it, the fury of it, the blood of it, his own pitiless relentlessness like an angel from on high, sent by Our Lord to cleanse the earth of those who would not submit to the Faith. He was so lucky, he did not know how to contain himself. This day he would sit with Allah and feel his warmth and benevolence, and he would have sexual congress with any young women he cared so to select. And the best part: he didn't have to be dead to enjoy the sex. He had been promised a live Western girl.

To celebrate he decided to shoot up a ladies' shop. He turned, faced it directly, and began to pump the trigger at the big display window. The baby Kalashnikov danced in his hands, breathing hell's breath of smoke and flame and spent casings, as before him the glass yielded into punctures, then shattered in a sleet of delirious reflection, and behind that dummies that wore those garments that decent women kept hidden under their burkas and only showed to their husbands splintered and fell in puffs of white dust and snapping ribbon as the bullets pierced them and—in the metaphorical immensity of Asad's mind—pierced the West too, with its temptation, its licentiousness, its sultry ardor and appeal. It reminded him of a strip club in Toronto he'd visited and had wanted to shoot up as well, though it had been explained to him then that his rage was best controlled until it could be unleashed.

Then on his radio set came the stern voice of authority.

"You two," he heard the imam command, "we see you on the television screens. Asad and Saalim, correct? You were told not to wantonly destroy property with your limited amounts of ammunition. This is not a party, it is a serious martyr operation. Treat it seriously or be banished. All you boys, you listen. You are martyrs, not brigands. The mission is to drive the people forward into the center and hold them, penned under your guns. You cannot give in to temptation and random impulse. The Koran forbids it. Verse twenty-three, directive eleven: 'Know the wisdom of thy elders.'"

Throughout America, the Mall, there was frenzy. People scurried desperately to comply, to escape, or to hide. Their minds focused on a single thing and that was to survive. Yet they were not inhumane, and some were quite heroic. Goth teenagers helped old ladies. Black gangbangers helped white Republican mothers. Gay waiters helped high school football players. Old white men helped young white women without thinking about having sex with them, at least for a little while. Somali grandmothers helped Scandinavian grandmothers, who helped them back.

Fallen children were gathered and shielded and comforted by complete strangers. Doctors went to the wounded, tried to stanch the blood flow without bandages and placed their own bodies in the way of bullets. Dead Santa's teenaged elves tried to keep some panicked mothers from racing off, and one even threw herself on a child who had fallen in the crush, got the girl up, and helped her to—well, there was no place to go, but helped her to her screaming mother, who hadn't found her yet. No one hit anyone or trampled anyone to escape. None of them committed an I-must-live-above-all-else sin worthy of punishment. Manhood was in flower down there on the killing floor and so was womanhood, and fellowhood, until there was nothing to be done but to sit down under the guns of the attackers and hope that they had grown bored with slaughter.

But in all this motion, there was one figure of motionlessness. He was a gangly young man of an age perhaps between eighteen and twenty-five, more or less lounging against the fourth-floor railing of the balcony overlooking the amusement park area from the terminus of the corridor called Colorado.

He wore jeans over New Balance hiking boots, a hoodie that actually said HARVA-D, the *R* having flaked off after numerous washings, and an old Vikings cap backward on his head. From his coloring and the perfect shape of his nose, most would have assumed a shock of blond hair lay under his cap, and they would have assumed rightly. His legs were crossed and he slouched against the railing, his arms crossed as he supported himself upon it. He looked like he was watching a baseball game or a parade or something. No tension showed in the muscles of his body under the clothes, no shock, no fear, nothing except the utmost in relaxed viewing.

He was recognizing patterns. It was interesting to him that the Rio Grande team had been the most aggressive, and so they forced their flock into the center of the mall the soonest; meanwhile, the Colorado and Hudson driven reached almost simultaneously, and both mobs crushed together with much bumping and shoving. Finally, the laggards at Mississippi produced, and those folks were the most unfortunate, as all the prime real estate had been seized and they were left to the margins, which put them closest to the gunmen, the most apt to incur the whimsical displeasure and hair-trigger temper of the shooters, and therefore most at risk.

Then he switched his attention to the throne in the center, where Santa had been whacked. From four stories, he could just barely make out the man's ruined face and the pattern of blood spray across the satin plush of the throne. He was struck, nonetheless, by the considerable if de trop amusement factor in seeing the familiar icon so completely, comprehensively dead. It seemed to make up for a lot. He hoped someone got a good picture of it, because as an image of his ambition, it seemed to say it all. It was one of those casual artifacts that nonetheless are freighted with communication, a piece of spontaneous art.

He saw the image on the cover of a box: "*Dead Santa,* the Christmas Mall Carnage Game, for Microsoft Xbox Only." It was pretty damn funny.

The game had begun.

3:2O P.M. —4:OO P.M.

The shooting had stopped. Ray lay with Molly and several other women in the rear of a Frederick's of Hollywood store on the second floor. Generic women's bodies, truncated at neck and thigh, stood around in bikinis, leather corsets, underpants, pasties, but nobody thought there was anything remotely funny about it. Outside, the pedestrian traffic had disappeared.

"Oh God," said a girl. "Oh God, oh God, oh God, I can't believe this is happening."

"I don't want to die," said another woman. "I have children. I can't die. It's not right."

"Please, ladies," Ray said, "I'm no expert but you'll be better off if you hold it down and get a grip. You can worry about how unfair it is later."

"He's right, Phyllis," someone said. "Shut up. Just be glad Milt and the kids aren't here."

"I'm here to buy something to wear for his goddamn birthday! He *should* be here."

"It's probably some freak with a gun," said another. "The cops will get him. Don't you think they'll get him, mister?"

"I heard more than one gun," said Ray. "That's what bothers me."

"I can't get through. I have to call my husband. The phones are—"

"It's all jammed up," Ray said. "Everyone in this mall who isn't dead is trying to call home. Please, you'd be much better off not to worry about making contact now. Just try and stay calm and relax. I didn't hear any firing on the upper floors. I think this is restricted to downstairs, so if you'll just try and stay calm and still, in the long run that's the best course."

"We just lie here and they come kill us."

"If they were into slaughter, they'd still be shooting. Now I'm going to slip out and see what I can see. Stay here, stay down. Don't get curious."

Molly pulled him close.

"My mother and sister are downstairs," she said.

"Let me see what's going on," he said. Then, louder, "Is there a manager or a clerk here?"

A young woman crawled over to him.

"Mrs. Renfels is the manager, but she's in pretty bad shape. My name is Rose. I work here."

"Listen, Rose, I need to know about the security cameras here in the mall. Are they everywhere? If I sneak out, will someone watching them in the security headquarters see me? Maybe they've taken that over. That would be their logical first step."

"I don't think there are any in the corridors, you know, I mean, what I mean is—"

"Settle down, Rose. Take a deep breath. No rush. You're doing fine."

"Okay. Mostly they're at the intersections and they look down the corridors. They don't have them every twenty-five feet or anything, that's what I mean. They make you take a tour when you start working here and I was in that room. The views don't have a lot of details, you know. It's a long look down the corridor, there's a lot of shadows. I wouldn't stand up. If you stand up and someone's looking at that camera, they'll know you're there."

"Good, very good." He considered. "Okay," he said, "I'm going to crawl out and try and get a feel for what's happening. Ladies, please stay here. Like Rose said, if you try and get out by running, they may see you."

"What are you going to do, Ray?" Molly asked.

"Well, I guess I ought to scout around. I can't just sit here."

"Ray, you *can* just sit here. Follow your own advice. Just sit here. Wait. Help will come."

"I heard that one about a thousand times in the suck. It never did. I'm just going to slide out and see what's what. You ladies, you just stay still."

Slowly, Ray snaked forward. He eased his head around the threshold of the doorway. The corridor was empty, though signs of rapid abandonment were everywhere, dropped purses and bags of goods, upturned baby carts, some of the windows of the stores broken. He saw no bodies and no shell casings on the floor. But he heard moans, din, the sound of many people shifting in place. That noise came from the space of the atrium, seventy-five feet away, its openness and height guarded by railings. Incomprehensibly, Christmas music still filled the air and the lights from the amusement park still blinked remorselessly on. No, it wasn't a silent night; it was a loud afternoon.

He looked up and down the hallway for a sign of gunmen, saw nothing. Everything told him to get in the back of the store. Block the doors. Wait it out.

There can't be that many, even now law enforcement is responding in a big way, there will be an assault, and you do not want to be running around in the middle of that kind of shitstorm.

Fuck, he thought. I thought I was done with this stuff. He had been shot at a whole lot in his life, and for the most part, he was fine by that. It went with the territory, it was the avenue by which he expressed his odd, powerful, even self-defining gift to put a bullet where he wanted no matter the position, the distance, the angle, the firearm, to be the dark figure known as the Sniper. Someone wanted him to enjoy that talent, and it was the centerpiece of his life that he not blow the mission, whatever the mission was, whoever gave it to him, and now he knew that it tracked back over generations to an odd family of men with similar gifts, some greater, some smaller, but who had always gone beyond the edge with their possibly autistic (how else to explain it?) coordination of front sight and target and sometimes not even front sight.

But . . . now? Here? He thought he was home free from the suck, but the suck had followed him home and he was not free. Someone had given him another mission, and though his bones ached and his breath came in hard spurts, he had some obligation to . . . well, he knew the obligation more than he knew the name of the force that had generated it. So he pushed on.

Again, checking the hallway and seeing no signs of movement, he edged out and slithered in the low crawl. He stuck close to the wall, figuring that he was in a zone of shadow, and unless one were looking carefully at the feed from a particular camera, itself mounted a good hundred feet down the corridor at the intersection, he ought to be okay. He got by several stores and became aware that each contained people as well. The smart ones, the lucky ones, the strong ones, the young ones had beat it to the exitways and gotten out to the parking areas.

He could see the balcony ahead and, beyond it, the looming strutwork of various thrill rides, the buttresses of the coaster tracks, the log chute, the top of the whirling two-seat swings. The noise from just beyond had gotten more intense. He had to know what was going on below.

He slid forward just a few feet to the very edge of the balcony, lifted his head, and took a quick scan, then withdrew.

Shit.

First, of course, in the center of the park, dead Santa atop his throne of blood presided, head tilted, inert as the earth itself. He was the king of death. Beneath His Majesty, sitting disconsolately on the pathways that crosscut the amusement park, were at least a thousand people, packed closely, most in a state of shock. He saw what had happened. The gunmen had begun at the outer ring and, shooting wildly, killing enough to compel instant, terrified obedience, had driven shoppers forward to converge in the amusement park in the center. A thousand hostages, under the struts and buttresses of the roller coasters, under the vastness of glass above shaped like Lake Michigan. He hadn't time to check closely, but he imagined they were now circled by gunmen. That was two gunmen per corridor, eight gunmen at least, a team for each "river," in the wacky scheme of the mall, the Colorado, the Hudson, the Rio Grande, and the Mississippi.

He scooted low along the balcony railing, out of view from beneath, and popped up again for a look at the shooters. He could see them as if from his own nightmares: the insouciant postures, the raffish *she-maghs* thrown loosely around the neck in gaudy variations, otherwise in jeans and hoodies and sneaks. All carried some kind of AK, though from the distance and given the time he had, he couldn't tell if it was a 47 or a 74. They carried the guns with that movie-driven stylishness of the young jihadi, aware how cool and badass they looked, self-consciously modeled on the same figure they had worshipped for years on television. Thin-hipped, sexy, anonymous, deadly: the warrior of the East come to slay in the West.

And he saw what a mess they had crafted. The situation instantly became clear in Ray's tactical mind. Those on the upper floors will be abandoned there, too terrified to move downward, basically not a part of the equation. The young, the spry, the brave: they had escaped, running crazily past the gunmen, getting out of ground-floor exits, climbing, finding other ways out or secure hides. Who was left? The weakest of the weak, the most defenseless of the defenseless. The old. The very young. Mothers and fathers tethered to children.

At any sign of an assault, the gunmen could open fire. Even with semiautomatics, as his ears told him their weapons were, they could kill hundreds, while at each corridor their brothers held off the assaulters for a few minutes more. Ray looked up, saw the lake-shaped skylights. They appeared deserted, but at any moment snipers would station themselves there. Could they get shots through the heavy glass? Probably not. They'd have to blow the glass to have any effectiveness, and that would give away any surprise element. Military operators, Delta people or SEALs, could blow the glass and rappel down, but they'd be sitting ducks as they descended and they couldn't fire downward for fear of hitting the innocent. They could, Ray supposed, just keep coming, like the Marines at Iwo, but that kind of dying for an objective was definitely out of fashion. On top of that, operators at that tactical level were mostly deployed overseas; where would the Minnesota authorities, even with FBI assistance, get such men on short notice? And this whole op had the look of something planned for maximum outrage over a short window of time.

He remembered something similar in Russia, with Chechens. Didn't they take over a theater? Hundreds of hostages, lots of explosives and gunmen, no way in. The Russian authorities had gassed the place. But the gas was tricky, and although it incapacitated the Chechens, it killed half the hostages. There was no way Americans would be willing to run that risk. And with so many hostages children and the elderly, with undeveloped or overworked, inefficient respiratory systems, the gas would be doubly risky, perhaps doubly lethal. And who said the gunmen didn't have gas masks? They seemed to have everything else.

Fuck, Ray thought. He suddenly felt him. *Him?* Yes, the one, the guy, what'shisname, Beelzebub, Lucifer, whoever he was, the fellow who'd thought this thing up. In his mind, he saw some Osama variant, possibly with time in America, who knew American vanities and vulnerabilities, a guy with a special, malevolent cunning and a great deal, damn his damned soul, of creativity. He'd thought it through very carefully, for maximum impact, maximum drama, maximum casualties, at a site comprising entirely the innocent, at the start of the West's most precious holiday. He knew who his hostages would be; he knew where to place his assets for maximum utility; he had both a strategic and a tactical gift. Already, Ray knew, this was worldwide news, and in every department in the world, pointy-heads were trying to figure out its meaning. Nobody anywhere was talking about anything else.

Would I ever like to get that guy in my crosshairs, he thought.

Molly looked up as Ray slid back in the door.

"Did you see my mother and Sally?" she asked.

"No, I didn't have time. Ladies, listen up, I'm going to tell you what I think is best."

Quickly he narrated his discoveries, the situation, his estimation of the difficulties law enforcement would face.

"How soon will they come?" one of the women asked.

"Not soon. They have to get their best people in here; they have to acquire detailed plans for the mall; they have to try and penetrate the security system, which these people may already control and which was designed by geniuses to keep people out. They have to decide their best course. On top of that, these invaders, they may have demands, which will put further complications into the situation. They seem professional and this operation appears well planned. And nobody outside wants to make a hasty decision that could get a thousand civilians killed, believe me. So I'm telling you right now, you have to commit to the long haul. You can't pin your hopes on this being done quickly."

"So do we just sit here?"

He turned to the young clerk, Rose.

"Rose, what about a back way out?"

"There's a loading corridor that runs through each of the sections. That's how we receive our merchandise."

"Where would that take us?"

"Well, there's an elevator to the basement, which leads to the subterranean receiving level."

"First thing they'd do would be to turn off the elevators. What about a stairwell?"

"Yes, there's a stairwell."

"We could escape through the stairwell!" someone said joyously.

"No, not quite. See, I'm thinking that for now they're not going to pay attention to the upper floors. But as time goes by, they may send teams upstairs to root people out and herd them down to join the hostages. The more hostages they have, the more power to negotiate. So I'd go up one floor to three and find refuge there. Because when they come for us, one team will start at the top and work their way down. And another will come up to the second and work up. So the middle floor is the safest in the long run. Plus, if the cops do assault, they may drive some gunmen up here, to this floor, and have a shootout here, and trust me, you don't want to be in the middle of it. Does that make sense?"

A surge of good cheer arose and Ray noticed that all the women were buoyed at the prospect of doing something to help their chances. Except for Rose.

"Rose, what's wrong?"

"When the shooting started, I had the same idea. I ran out the back and tried the stairwell. See, all the locks in the building are part of the software. He's locked it. We're stuck here."

"Are the doors heavy?"

"They're not as heavy as the outside doors. Those are metal, sunk in metal. But these are tough, heavy wood and you'd have to batter and kick an hour to get them down. Or shoot your way through."

Ray didn't say anything, but he knew what that meant. Yes, it confirmed that somehow the attack team had taken over the security program that underlay the mall operations protocols. They had locked the doors remotely. They were in complete control.

He looked carefully at the SCADA representation of MEMTAC 6.2 where its captured images blazed from his own monitors. Quickly he checked off the key points.

LOCKDOWN ENABLED
ELEVATORS DISABLED
ESCALATORS DISABLED

No surprises there. Once you get in, you learn the culture of the system, the assumptions it's built on, how the German geniuses at Siemens think, how thorough they were, how they swept up their sandwich crumbs after lunch, and how shiny the bathroom fixtures were.

He continued to monitor, examining the eco-system of the empire.

AIR-CONDITIONING ON
TEMPERATURE CONTROL 72
FIRE SPRINKLERS ENABLED
FLUORESCENT LIGHTING SYSTEM
    ENABLED
AREA Z FUSES FUNCTION 100 PERCENT
POWER GRID STABLE
SANTA CLAUS DEAD

No, no, it didn't say that, but he had a morbid sense of humor and he saw it in his imagination, as he also thought about what he could do with his power. Since the owners of this mall owned dozens of other malls in the US and Canada, all using the MEMTAC-driven SCADA, all linked, he could really raise hell if he wanted by refusing credit cards, turning cash registers insane, locking out and in, freezing elevators, directing the Coke machines to urge customers to buy Pepsi all across the land. But really. That wasn't the point. The point was . . . the game.

And then as an afterthought, his pièce de résistance.

INTERNET CONNECTION DISABLED

Ha. I hear you knocking but you can't come in.

Well actually, there was one way in. It would be interesting to see if there was anybody out there smart enough to figure it out.

————————————

"I can't get in," said a computer technician from the Minnesota State Police. "Whoever he is, he's taken the thing off line. It's internally sealed. I've run all my conventional link search programs and I'm not getting a thing. It's a vault."

"Keep trying," said Douglas Obobo, who was the newly appointed commandant of the state cops. "I know you won't let me down."

A special warmth came into Colonel Obobo's voice on the last sentence. *I know you won't let me down.* That was the Obobo touch, known in its limited way and possibly about to become more famous. He had the gift of inspiration, of making people believe, first in him, second in the mission, third in the larger program that sustained the mission, and finally in the administrative entity that embraced all. It was why he was the youngest man in history, at forty-four, to become a superintendent of state police, and the first African American. It had been national news.

"Sir, we need more sophisticated programs and more sophisticated IT guys. The federal people will have that; maybe they can get in."

Obobo said, "I understand and that's why I have federal people on the way. I know if we all work together, we can get this done with a minimum of loss." He spoke with the confidence of the man who knew the truth.

And why shouldn't he? His success had been pretty much a certainty. The son of a Kenyan graduate student at Harvard and a Radcliffe anthropology major, he'd graduated from both Harvard and Harvard Law. But instead of taking the conventional path to whatever the American Dream was, he'd joined the Boston Police Department as a beat cop. He was quickly absorbed into the Homicide Bureau and had been the front man on a series of highly publicized cases, where he revealed himself to be a mellifluous speaker and a quick wit and to exude a kind of enlightened law enforcement attitude that could console the races, even in a tough town like Boston.

Despite the fact that he never broke a case, arrested a suspect, won a gunfight, led a raid, or testified in court, in five years he left the department to become the lead investigator for the Senate Subcommittee on Government Fraud, where again his charisma made him a star and got him noticed on the national level. Run for office, many said. You have the gift.

But he was a cop, he said, and committed to the healing of America by progressive law enforcement policy. The old days of kick-ass and coerced confession were gone; the new day of respect for all had arrived.

He became, quickly, the assistant commissioner of the Baltimore Police Department, then the chief of the Omaha Police Department, though he cared little for the snowy plains far from the national media. But they kept dropping by anyway, and he made the national news more than any other police executive in the country, in 2008, 2009, and 2010. Finally, his big move, to head the Minnesota State Police with the idea of bringing it into the twenty-first century, making it the premier investigative agency in the state while aiming to cut traffic fatalities to a new low. That hadn't happened yet and in fact no stated goal had been accomplished, but it was hard to hold that against a man struggling against the old culture and the old ways. The media loved him for his effort. Somehow, he'd ended up on the cover of the *New York Times Magazine,* subject of a gushing profile by David Banjax.

Now, his first real crisis. He understood that America, the Mall, was a mess. First responders had had a nightmare approaching, as shoppers fled in the thousands, most in cars, gridlocking the place so that incoming LE simply added to the confusion. Meanwhile, the reports were sketchy. Mall security was not answering and had not communicated since the first 10-32 alert went out. Thousands of 911 calls crowded the circuits, all some variety on the theme "Machine gunners are in the mall," or "I lost my grandma in the mess, help me find my grandma."

Grandma was going to have to wait, unless she was already dead.

But he also understood that this was an opportunity beyond measure, in some way a gift. The national spotlight would again shine on him and the decisions he made, the leadership he showed—the resolution coupled with fairness, the fortitude coupled with compassion, the eloquence coupled with wisdom—would be on fine display. It wasn't about ambition, he always said; it was about gifts. He had been given many; it was mandated, therefore, that he give back.

"You know," his longtime civilian advisor and public affairs guru David Renfro had whispered in his ear on the thunderous ride over, "few men get a chance like this. This is an opportunity we have to seize by the throat."

Obobo and his senior command team—including Mr. Renfro—were in a state police communication van parked across the highway from the huge structure of the mall. They were roughly in the position of Bermuda, about 250 yards out from the Middle Atlantic states, directly to the east.

He had made some early organizational decisions: one major was liaising with incoming SWAT teams from the local area, assigning the men positions on the perimeter. But the colonel had authorized no entry or engagement. The situation was too unclear; he had no idea what he was up against, who these people were, what they wanted. The last thing he needed was an out-of-control gunfight between his heavily armed operators and equally heavily armed terrorists or whatever in the middle of a crowd of civilians. Hundreds would die. But he also knew that people inside were bleeding out with wounds, suffering heart attacks, anxiety overloads, had been separated from children or other siblings or relatives, were hiding in stores, panicking, maybe plotting a rebellion of their own.

Then he had a major running communications, trying to get everybody on the same met and organizing the inflow of information.

"Any news on the feds?"

"A skeleton team is inbound from Minneapolis fast under siren. They're still collecting their SWAT people. They've got their HRT team gearing up at Quantico, but they're still three hours out, and then when they land, they've got to get here. It's going to take a while. Colonel, are we going in? I've got people in body armor at every exit now. Maybe we shouldn't wait. Reports are that there's a lot of wounded inside. Those folks need medical attention."

"Ah," he said. An issue of jurisdiction was looming. By federal law, the FBI took charge in any situation that was defined as "terrorism" and ran the show. But things at America, the Mall, were still unclear: despite reports of terrorist-like gunmen and terrorist-like tactics and ruthlessness, he thought it could still be some crazed white militia, some NRA offshoot, some screwball Tea Party gone berserk. In his mind, one never could tell about the right in this country, particularly deep in the glowering Midwest, where men clung to guns and religion, cursed bitterly as America changed, and still believed, fundamentally, in the old ways.

Renfro said, "Colonel, you cannot let the FBI people run this show. It can't be a Washington thing. There are sound policy reasons for it—harder for them to coordinate with the locals, unfamiliarity with the territory, lack of intelligence on the local scene— but the politics count here too. Washington will want in, but you've got to hold Washington at bay."

"I know, I know," said the colonel. "I've got a plan."

Obobo's idea was to use the FBI as the primary investigative tool of this operation. They would interview witnesses, run the databases, check the photo IDs and the fingerprint files; they would liaise with ATF on ballistics. That would be plenty for them. But in no way was he prepared to relinquish command. This one was his.

"Negative, negative on any kind of assault," he announced to his gathered majors. "I am not going to tell the governor that he has presided over the largest bloodbath in American history. Establish the perimeter, hold the medical people and the ambulance in a zone, keep the media in the loop because we do have a responsibility to inform a panicked public, and try and set up some kind of contact with these people. They must want something, and I know I can influence them positively, given the chance."

"Maybe they just want to kill a lot of folks," someone said. "Maybe the longer we wait . . ."

This was Mike Jefferson, another major, head of SWAT and by nature aggressive; he'd won three gunfights and could be a pain in the ass. Obobo mistrusted him, as he mistrusted that kind of man, bodacious, body-proud, thick-armed, tattooed, and a little too hungry to go to guns. If you went to guns, he knew, all kinds of craziness was loosed upon the earth and nobody knew which way the bullets would ricochet. He would *never* go to guns. On the other hand, it was not his way to crush underlings.

"Major Jefferson, that's a great point. Therefore I want you to begin to assemble an assault plan and be ready to deploy and implement. At present, I feel we must hold until federal reinforcement arrives, and then we will see where we are and consider our options. But we have to have other options and that's your job."

Jefferson understood he'd just gotten a no that sounded like a yes; he muttered something and backed off.

Someone else said, "Mike, the doors are locked from the inside. To even get in for an assault, you'd have to blow fifty doors simultaneously and we don't have the technology or the explosives to do that. Only the feds have stuff like that."

"The feds don't even have it, not in their shop in Minneapolis," said Jefferson. "Get the governor to authorize the National Guard to the site. Isn't there a Special Forces unit part of the Minnesota

National Guard? Maybe they have the expertise. Also, DOJ, maybe DOD. We may need some Army commandos."

"Major, it'll take hours, maybe days, to get commandos in here."

"I got Minnetonka SWAT incoming. Where should I put them?" asked one of the radio operators.

"I think we're weak at California," said the major in charge of logistics. His job was to decide where to place the various units, determine their areas of responsibility, keep them from stumbling into each other or being assigned redundant tasks, and also managing food, coffee, blankets, and other support for the men on the line.

"Dispatch them to holding positions at the California entrance," said Obobo, once again reiterating his major theme, on the management theory that you tell them, then you tell them again, and when you're finished, then you tell them again. "No contact, no initiatives, stay off the air unless there's an emergency. Their job is to help late stragglers get to medical aid, not to be heroes. The last thing we need is a hero. Now let's have a quick press conference. We have to start putting information out. Mr. Renfro, you're on top of this?"

"I am, sir," said Renfro.

It was difficult to determine who died first, Mrs. Goldbine, from her heart attack, or Mr. Graffick, from his lower-back wound. The sixty-seven-year-old woman certainly died the loudest. She gripped her chest and began to breath harshly, coughing now and then. The woman sitting next to her, a Somali waitress who worked in a restaurant in the mall, tried to comfort her and held her hand. The woman turned gray. The waitress stood, raising her hand desperately to attract the attention of one of the gunmen, who pushed his way through the crowd with the familiar arrogance of the armed among the unarmed.

"This lady is very sick," said the waitress in Somali.

"Too bad for her," said the boy.

"She will die," said the girl.

"Then that is what Allah has decreed, sister. Do not take up with these white devils. All are going to die sooner or later. If you are nice to me, maybe I can spare you."

"Go fuck yourself," said the young woman in English.

The boy laughed and turned away.

"What did he say, what did he say?" a dozen nearby hostages had to know. She decided not to tell them what he had told her.

"He says he doesn't care. He thinks he is God. He will find out different."

She bent over Mrs. Goldbine and saw that it was too late. She had passed.

In another sector of the crowd, Graffick lay in the arms of his wife. He had taken a bullet meant for and aimed at her. It had hit him in the lower back and initially didn't produce much blood or even pain. He'd stumbled but continued to push her ahead in the mad scramble toward the middle of the mall, not that there was safety there. There was safety nowhere. But the law of least resistance produced the inward rush.

He lay, looking up at the lake-shaped spread of skylights four stories up. He was not a religious man, for driving eight hundred miles a day in the cab of an eighteen-wheeler for forty years does not incline one toward the more spiritual things in life, nor was he ever in any one place long enough for church to present itself as an option. If he worshipped anything, it was a goddess: his wife.

"You must fight," he told her. He knew about fighting: 1st Marine Division, An Loc, RVN, '65–'66, Purple Heart, Silver Star.

"Jerry," she said, "just be still."

"Sweetie, listen. These bastards, don't let 'em see you crying. Don't give 'em nothing. Don't give 'em no satisfaction at all. When I go, just put on your steel face and don't show a thing. Remember that time I got busted in that vice sting in Ohio? You didn't talk to me for a year. Honey, that's the face. I know you got it. You give it to them and make them fear you."

"Please, please, Jerry."

She was sitting in a lake of blood. He was bleeding out, and the warm fluid ran from his wound into her dress and puddled around them on the floor.

"God, I love you so much," he said, and then went still.

Not far from him a man named Charles Dougan was concerned about a bowel movement he could not prevent from occurring. He was ashamed. It was one thing to die, it was another to die with your pants full of shit. He didn't realize that incontinence of one sort or another was a crucial feature of hostage situations, because no media ever dealt with it honestly. But the significant commonality among a large number of people held against their will was lack of sanitation for bodily fluids and that was simply an unfortunate biological reality.

He raised his hand.

A boy shoved his way over, roughly.

"I have to go to the bathroom," he said.

"Shit in pants," the boy said and turned away.

And so to his shame and horror, that's what Charles Dougan did.

"I'm sorry," he said to the young woman next to him.

"That's okay," said Sally Chan. "It doesn't matter."

There were at least a thousand, sitting cross-legged and head-down on the brick pathways of the Silli-Land amusement park. The rides, now still, towered over them. Absurd contrivances, they seemed yet more insane given the circumstances, but no one in the crowd much cared about the irony of being surrounded by thrill rides while being held at gunpoint under threat of death. And there was dead Santa on his throne, his body twisted, his hat on his ear, his head so askew only a corpse could sustain it, and that red spatter of blood V-shaped by the exit of the bullet on the satin plush of his chair. A loudspeaker issued the words "Jingle bells, jingle bells, jingle all the way," but nobody paid much attention.

The armed boys wandered the perimeter, sometimes kicking their way into crowds to deal with issues. Their faces were impassive, but the guns, sinister black with ventilated barrels and wicked curved magazines, were terrifying. Nearly everyone had seen such weapons on the TV news and knew them to be the tool of the subhuman category of merciless terrorists, of which their owners were surely members.

The boys occasionally came together and laughed. Or one would vanish into the mall and return with, say, taffy apples or french fries, and all would eat.

They drank a lot of Cokes and pretty much looted the Silli-Land refreshment center for shakes and hot dogs. One of them put a cowboy hat on, squishing it down over his *shemagh* headdress, and all helped themselves to new jeans and high-end New Balance or Nike sneakers.

Who was in charge? There didn't seem to be a leader, but the boys weren't quite random in their movement and more or less obeyed the rules of sound security, each knot of two hanging in that quadrant of the perimeter, keeping their guns oriented toward the seated hostages. At any time there were a great many guns bearing on the hostages, and all fingers on all triggers. Most of the hostages also believed the guns were "machine guns" and that a single pull would send a squirt of bullets out to take them down in batches. That concept alone was enough to keep them seated and quiet.

There was no chance at heroism. Any kind of mass rush toward a gunman was precluded by the impossibility of coordinating it and the immediacy of mass death it would ensure. The smell of burned powder still hung in the air. It was like an anti-aphrodisiac to dreams of action. To rise against the guns would be to die pointlessly in a mall, even while outside the rescuers accumulated.

From above it looked somewhat like the Bristol Speedway, Nikki Swagger thought. A huge, absurd structure decreed into the middle of nowhere, its odd shape touching automatically on chords of patriotism and sacrifice in all who saw it from the sky, serviced by a mesh of highways that came to it from the vague hinterlands. Now it seemed like race day:

activity, activity, activity. Trucks kept pulling up, all of them spurting illumination that lit the twilight in incoherent splash patterns. From them spilled urgent men in black, with strange devices, who ran to cover and took up positions. The whole portrait pulsed with energy, purpose, dedication, high training, sophisticated deployment, yet nothing was happening. A fleet of red-white ambulances and other emergency service vehicles had gathered in one of the parking lots. Outside the ring, the highways were jammed with cars and trucks, even as more public safety teams tried to fight the rush and get through them to get close enough to assist.

Over her earphones she heard Marty back at the station.

"Nikki, the great Obobo is giving a briefing."

"The first of many, I'm sure."

"He didn't say much, only that this appears to be some kind of violent takeover, shots have been fired, some people have been wounded, and the mall has been evacuated."

"Duh," said Nikki, "who didn't know that? Does he have a time frame?"

"He just said law enforcement from all over the state is gathering on site, the feds are pitching in, but the situation is still hazy. He has no casualty numbers, no time frame, no declarations of policy, nothing but your usual tight-lipped five-oh bullshit."

Nikki knew 5-0 bullshit—she'd covered cops in Bristol, Virginia, for five years—but this guy Obobo was a bullshitter beyond any she'd encountered. He was handsome, smooth, learned the reporters' names, knew which cameras and what lights were used, and how to apply his own makeup. Her joke:

"For a cop, he knows more about makeup than Lady Gaga."

But this was her big op too, she knew, just as it was the ambitious Obobo's. She'd worked as a news producer in Cape Coral, Florida, for a bit, and now she was a producer for WUFF-TV, Saint Paul. Scoops here, on this day, could get her to a network, to Washington or New York.

She gazed down on the scene from about two thousand feet in the WUFFcopter, as it was called on the air, the WUSScopter by station personnel, because everybody was scared to fly in it. Usually it covered traffic, but today, with Cap'n Tom at the controls, it orbited over the mall, while in the rear, Larry Soames and Jim Diehl worked cameras to send the images back to the station and thence to the greater Minneapolis area. She hoped Cap'n Tom wasn't drinking today and cursed the United States Marine Corps, for whom he had once flown, because it was that connection that got him the job with the station manager, another ex-Marine, and she chose not to acknowledge the fact that it was her connection to the Corps, via her father, that had probably gotten her the job too. In fact, the station was a kind of Marine outpost in the chilly upper Midwest.

"Nikki, I'd like to go up a couple thousand. It's tricky this low," said Cap'n Tom. Her paranoia tried to convince her that there was a slur to his words, but she couldn't be positive.

"Tom, let's hold it a little longer. We need good pictures for the feed and up higher it's just blurs and lights. People need to *see* the damned place."

"Nik, I agree with Tom. If we crash into KPOP we'll be the lead on someone else's live feed. You'd hate that." That was Larry, older of the two camera jocks. He knew how fragile and precious life was, even if the concept hadn't yet dawned on Nikki.

But she would hate to lead anybody else's feed: she was ferociously competitive, so much so that it scared many people. In the station, she was called "Mary Tyler Moore from Hell."

She looked out the window and saw a fleet, a mob, a density of news choppers hovering about her same altitude over America, the country, and America, the Mall. It was a tricky thing; the birds had to avoid updrafts and couldn't predict blasts of prairie wind, so they tried to keep a good three hundred feet apart, but nearly everyone wanted the money shot, which was the state police communications trailer a few hundred yards east of the mall, itself surrounded by police and other official vehicles, in the same shot with the south entrance of the mall, with its famous AtM sign, plastered four stories tall, that was based on a cartoony simplification of the mall's Americanized shape.

"Just a few seconds more, guys," she commanded. "Marty. Are you getting good pix?"

"The best, Nik, but don't get yourself killed yet. If we need you to die for ratings, we'll let you know."

"Ha ha," she said humorlessly. "Okay, let's get out of here—"

"Something's coming through," said Cap'n Tom, and he plugged the emergency general aviation channel into the radio system.

"This is State Police HQ, I am asking all news helicopters to rise to and not wander below three thousand feet. We have incoming to the mall and I need you people out of the way so you don't get hurt."

"Hey, maybe something's finally going to happen," Jim, the younger, the more eager cameraman, said.

"We won't be able to see jack from three," said Nikki. "Larry, what lens are you using? Can you go to something zoomier?"

"You really lose a lot of resolution," Larry said. "It'll look like plastic toys in split-pea soup. But no one else will have much anyway."

"Damn," she said. "Okay, let's do it."

She felt the bottomless-pit sensation as Cap'n Tom elevated the craft against the pull of gravity and the structure beneath got smaller. From altitude, the mall stood in gigantic isolation, a wounded America whose sundered arteries spurted illuminated blood into the purple haze of the lowering sun.

It felt so strange, this proximity thing of the media. There they were, safe and toasty at 3,000 feet above the place, and inside, terrible dramas of life and death were being played out. Nikki and her cohort were there to witness and report, yet it was real life and real death at stake, nothing neat or melodramatic about it. And of course they knew that if they did well—what was the line from some old movie? "I think it's safe to say you men are in for some promotions, medals, and positive recommendations in your personnel files!"

Then she saw it.

The cavalry? Not quite.

"Is that all?" Jim asked.

"Clearly, that's not an assault," said Nikki.

It was just the state police Bell JetRanger, rising from a parking lot and veering on the tilt toward the mall, all lights running hot and red and blinking.

"What are they going to do, scare the bad guys with the noise?" Larry said.

The bird, painted in the maroon-brown scheme of the Minnesota State Police, took a direct line to the mall and hovered six feet off its roof. Six young men in dark suits jumped out and began to deploy at the edges of the lake-shaped glass skylights that topped the atrium over the center of the mall.

"Six guys?" said Jim.

"Those aren't guys," said Nikki. "They're snipers."

"Don't have too much fun in there," someone yelled merrily at Special Agent Jeffrey Neal.

He was one of the bright guys, tech-style, who worked in the Hoover Building, detecting mainly on a computer. He was an unbuttoner, a penetrator, a second-story man, a slippery little shadow in the night of cyberspace. It was said he'd get the department if he didn't fuck up but that he would fuck up, as guys with his IQ could be counted on to get busted for falling in love with escorts or acquiring a drug habit or coming to believe Ancient Grecians were communicating with him through his Grecian Formula hair coloring brush, something self-destructive that for some reason always draws the hyperintelligent into its flame.

"Ha ha," he commented from within the shroud.

The shroud was a canopy draped over his second computer, which was connected to the Internet. It was next to his unshrouded non-Internet-connected computer, and the two machines and two monitors crowded his small cubicle in the Computer Services Division of the Pennsylvania Avenue monstrosity. The shroud on the net beast kept inquiring eyes out and political correctness at its highest level, for one had to dip inside it and only in dark secrecy encounter the very special hell known as the universe of child pornography.

It was dues you had to pay, even if nobody wanted to.

But Neal had three months left to go on his six-month tour on the Child Porn Task Force, which meant he went home each night feeling like a used condom. His own sex life, mild as it was, had been destroyed. The things people did to kids, the sick worms in their heads that compelled them to conjure new variations in torment, abuse, piercing, and posture. You wanted to reach through the screen and crush skulls, watch the bastards—not just fat white guys in their forties, but amazingly handsome people of all races, ages, demo groups, normal-looking people, even distinguished-looking people—bleed out in the gutter, whimpering. But he soldiered on, knowing that at the end of—

"Neal, hey, wake up in there, hot one in from HQ. There's some kind of mall takedown in Minneapolis and we have to get into the computer system." It was his supervisor, Dr. Bob Benson, SA and PhD.

"He's in the system?" Neal asked.

"Is he ever. He's got a thousand hostages, he's locked down the mall, no local agencies have been able to penetrate. Guess on whose plate it is now."

"On it," said Neal.

"Get upstairs ASAP for the briefing, then get down here and get your action into gear. This baby's so hot it's steaming. No more kiddie rape."

Neal rose quickly, started to dash out. But he turned back, reached out, grabbed the shroud of his enforced disgust, and ripped it down. It was sort of like John Wayne throwing off the rifle scabbard as he saw the burning ranch before him in *The Searchers*. It meant he was going to war.

On the way over, Kemp had been on the phone with Washington the whole time. Subject: politics. Tone: unpleasant. Reality: discouraging.

"You have to play this very well, Will," said Assistant Director Nick Memphis. "He will not want to give up command, and if you backstreet him, he will go to the media and they love him, you know that."

"So how the hell do I play it?" said Kemp.

"I wouldn't buck him," said Nick. "Let him come to you. He has to."

"He better come to me, goddammit," said Kemp, the SAIC of the Minneapolis Office, a vet of several task forces including a long spell in Texas with ATF and Drug Enforcement that got him shot in the leg. "He doesn't know a goddamn thing."

It was true. Colonel Douglas Obobo really hadn't done anything. His career was primarily a phenomenon of showing up, giving speeches, accepting awards, then moving up to the next level, as assisted by the superb public relations and career advisor David Renfro, who'd spent years working the trade, fronting at various times for the New York chief of police, the San Francisco police commissioner. Renfro had met Obobo when both worked for the Senate committee and had been with him ever since.

"Don't say that to anybody," counseled Nick. "Keep it to yourself. Publicly you love and respect him as does everyone in the Bureau. He's the One, we all know that."

"What a mess," said Kemp, and both men knew

what he was talking about. Rumors were rife in Washington that Obobo's next big job would be as director of the FBI, the first black man, the youngest to ever get the job. So both Memphis and Kemp knew that whatever decisions they made today might come back to shadow them if they ended up working for the guy somewhere down the road.

"Assistant Director Memphis, if I think he's endangering people, I have to act. I *have* to. That's the bottom line, you know that."

"Look, all this may be premature. The situation may not be as bad as we think or it may resolve itself peacefully without force, and everybody will walk away unscathed. If the worst comes, he has good people in the Minnesota State Police to advise him."

"If he listens to them."

Three Ford Ranger XLT modified trucks, black with black glass, pulled into the area under the on-off rhythm of red-blue and rolled to the state police trailer.

Kemp leaped out, in black Nomex SWAT gear, with an MP5 submachine gun on a sling across his chest and a Glock .40 in a shoulder holster strapped across his body armor. Three of the other seven men were equally equipped, but the four snipers unlimbered large, awkward gun cases from the back of each big SUV.

"Special Agent Kemp, I'm surprised you don't have more manpower," said Obobo, in full uniform, with his shadow Renfro close at hand.

"Colonel Obobo, we've got all our people coming in. But it's a tough thing, logistically. More will arrive shortly."

"Of course," said Obobo. "Now, let me brief you quickly. I've got Jefferson on assault planning, I've got Carmody handling logistics, I've got Neimeyer trying to coordinate with the medical people. I will be handling negotiations myself. But of course we need to get an investigation going and that's where I see the Bureau making its contribution. I've decided to turn over the investigation—the witness interviews, the collation of evidence, the records and forensic database checks, all that—to the Bureau."

"Sir, I'm sure you realize by federal statute the Bureau is obligated to take over any incidents involving terrorism."

"Of course and absolutely," said Obobo, smiling broadly, putting a big hand on Kemp's shoulder. He was tall, towering over most, and had an especially beguiling style, even in disagreement, so it was hard to dislike him. "But this situation has not clarified, I think you'll agree, and we're not sure with whom we're dealing. There is no operative intelligence suggesting foreign involvement, other than unsubstantiated reports of some Arabic-styled scarves. I'm sure you agree, that's not enough to make a determination. This could be any group of nuts. As I've already organized my teams, I think it's more sound for me to retain command. Of course if and when evidence develops that clarifies the situation, and if it's within parameters, I'd be happy to make another disposition. But you understand, of course, and I know you agree, that turf is less important than teamwork. I know I can count on you to work with our initiatives and within our framework."

"Yes sir. I'm hoping you're open to advice from

my people. We do have a lot of experience in these matters."

"Of course, Special Agent. You'll get your more detailed briefing from Major Carmody, and if you have any suggestions, we'd love to hear them. But let me tell you up front, I am not about to launch an assault. Even with your additions, I don't have the people, the expertise, or the equipment. We've asked the governor to get us some National Guard people to take over the perimeter and that will free up our SWAT personnel for possible deployment."

Kemp suspected the chances of a SWAT deployment order from Obobo were somewhere between ze-fucking-ro and na-fucking-da; he kept his face that administrative blank that long government service teaches.

"You know the drill," said Obobo. "Perimeter security, establish commo with the hostage takers, and begin to negotiate. Time is on our side. They'll get tired, hungry, and scared. We'll play them out over their demands as long as possible. If I might suggest, I'd like you to get on the horn to Defense and see if we could get some advice on chemical agents that might come into play."

"I will, Colonel Obobo. I also brought in some very good snipers. I'd like to deploy them on the roof."

"Of course, and we'll combine forces with some state police marksmen. But I'm advised the roof skylights are heavy Plexiglas sealed in concrete. I don't know how we get through them. Yes, we'll send snipers, but no shooting without permission of course, and they have to understand their primary mission is observation."

"Yes sir," said Kemp.

Standing nearby was the rogue state police commander Mike Jefferson. His take was different, but he had fewer people to answer to, and if he lost his job, his status as a famous police gunfighter and SWAT warrior would get him rehired anywhere in America on a moment's notice. He'd been thinking about Idaho, as a matter of fact.

But his warrior's instincts were all lit up now. His idea: assault the gunmen, have a gunfight, take the casualties and the press bashing that would occur, and to hell with it. Kill all the bad guys, that was the basic idea. He was Custer, always moving to the sound of the guns. He had no patience for the Obobo school of psychobabble bullshit, for that faction of police psychology that required "negotiators" well-trained in making empathetic connection to the hostage takers, understanding their pain, and cajoling them to a peaceful resolution. He knew that Obobo, by long reputation not afraid of the sound of his own voice, would assume that responsibility for himself. But Jefferson knew how fragile these things could be and had seen it all go down. His idea was to end the bad guys' pain by shooting them in the head.

But he saw now nobody wanted to listen to him or entertain his speculations. Jefferson thought these gunmen were here simply because they wanted to kill people. That's what would make the biggest splash. If they killed five hundred people on the day after Thanksgiving to the greater glory of Allah and the Islamic Faith—no, no confirmation that Islamists were involved—in a mall called America that looked like America, then that would be their victory. Hell, they'd already killed Santa Claus! There was no evidence this wasn't a suicide thing, and suicide—martyrdom, the goatfuckers called it—was a part of their mind-set.

The truth was, Jefferson really shouldn't have been a cop. He should have been an old-time marshal with a six-gun on his belt, not a Sig Sauer. That was his mentality. He felt fully alive when he faced armed men, and his solution to all problems tended to angle the situation toward man-on-man violence. The team play aspect of law enforcement had never meant much to him, not since he was twenty-one and faced three armed robbers in a Saint Paul bank and shot it out face to face (to face to face) with them, took two .38s in the left arm and hand but dropped all three, two fatally, with his own .38, it being the day of the revolver. Nothing since had quite matched that moment of maximum life/maximum risk. He was a gunfighter, that was all, and love him or hate him, he'd never be another thing as long as he lived, which might not, given his personality and lack of fear of anything, be very long.

"Mike," another major yelled, "we have detailed mall plans, just arrived from the construction firm that built the place. An engineer is here too."

"Bring him along. Maybe he knows the back way in."

Meanwhile, Obobo and Renfro conferred briefly in the corner.

"You handled that well," said Renfro. "Decent, smooth, no macho bullshit."

"That goddamned Jefferson, though. He has been a pain since the start. I can tell, he doesn't buy me, never has, never will. The tough guys hate me, think I'm too fine a lady. I'd love to push him up to

International Falls, in charge of taking the temperature."

"You were fine with him, Colonel. Yes, he's a pain, all the SWAT people are. Kill 'em all, let God sort 'em out. But you handled him. Here's my advice: Keep him busy. Keep him running around, making reports, checking this way and that. You don't want him here at Command, sowing doubts, collecting allies. Make him your little errand boy and bury him in praise. That's a weapon he can't overcome."

Saalim had his eye on the Somali girl in the crowd. "Fuck you," she had said in English to him, the two words he knew. Ha ha. She was spirited. She was proud. She had bright eyes and fine, straight white teeth and a rich crop of hair. She would make a good wife. He wondered how many goats her father would charge. Probably many.

Sitting there in the mall, his baby Kalashnikov across his lap, his pistol dangling from his holster, the *shemagh* tight around his face, he had a brief fantasy that reflected on a childhood he never had. He was the son of the tribal chief in the high desert. He was a fierce warrior, a killer of men and lions. He was favored by Allah, and the mullahs agreed he was destined for greatness. He would have many wives and many concubines and many goats. He would lead his people in many battles and that one, that proud African girl, she would be his.

Actually, he had been born in a slum of Mogadishu; his mother was a whore. He lived the life of an unclean, wild pig for some years, scrapping and fighting for survival. Finally, when he was big enough to hold a Kalashnikov, General Hassan Dahir Aweys's

Hizbul Islam militia took him in. That was his family, boy soldiers and brutal leaders, and enemies to be slain in the name of Allah.

"Fuck you," she said! What spirit, what—

"Saalim, I can tell by the glaze in your eyes you are dreaming," said Asad, next to him. "If the imam catches you with a faraway look on your face, he'll cane you and make you sleep with the goats."

"There are no goats here," said Saalim. "This is America. They keep the goats outside. No goats, no goatshit in a fine American place."

"That is why we came so far. To destroy it and spread the will of Allah—"

"And to bring the goats inside, where they belong!"

Both boys laughed. They were lounging on a park bench on the southeast side of the Silli-Land Park, near the ticket office for the Ride-a-Log flume shoot, a twisty tube of water that enabled Americans the thrill of a downward thunder of a splashing ride, now vacant and unattended. From where they were, they were spared the disagreeable sight of Dead Man in Red upon His Throne. But they did see, everywhere, desultory Americans sitting crunched together, supposedly with their hands on their heads, though this imposed discipline had soon disappeared.

They were teenaged boys: their own discipline was not superb. They were supposed to keep iron eyes on their captives, to make certain little cliques didn't form and plot some kind of revolution. But the Americans seemed to have no spirit for that kind of work and mostly just sat there, in a kind of stupor that both Saalim and Asad had seen among the struggling citizens of Wabra. Thus, Saalim and Asad found themselves occupied with chitchat, petty teasing, attraction to various girls, shows of adolescent bravado, and hunger for fast food, which was abundant in the now largely empty mall. That sometime soon soldiers or police officers would surely crash the place, guns firing, and probably kill them was of utterly no concern. Given the toughness of their lives, death held little sting.

But suddenly a crackle came over the earphones they wore under their *shemaghs.* It was the imam.

"You, Asad, that is your name, correct?"

"Yes, Imam," said Asad, jumping alert.

"You remember what we discussed, you and I?"

It was true. He had a special mission.

"I do, Imam," he said into the throat mike.

"Well, it's time. You can find this place?"

He remembered. Second floor, NW Colorado, C-2-145. That was the destination. The imam had shown him on the bright-colored brochures with maps that guided them through the mall.

"I can, Imam," he said.

"Good," said the imam. "It's time to go and get the babies."

Humbly, Mr. and Mrs. Girardi approached the police officer at the farthest extreme from the mall. In fact, they could see it almost a mile away in the twilight, looking like a big tub upside down, surrounded by police cars and fire engines.

"Folks," said the cop, "sorry, I can't let you in any closer."

"Sir," said Mr. Girardi, "we're looking for our son. He's fourteen."

"It's the first time I've ever let him go to the mall

alone," said Mrs. Girardi. "I usually take him or he goes with friends. But he wanted to do his Christmas shopping."

"Yes, ma'am."

"We haven't heard from him. Should we call him?"

"He hasn't called you?"

"We haven't heard anything. We just know what's on the TV."

"No, I wouldn't advise that," said the officer. "He may be hiding or something, or hurt or—well, you just don't know what his circumstance is and it's probably better to wait until he reaches out to you."

"Is there any information available?"

"No, sir. We're trying to get a command structure set up and get organized. It's a terrible problem and nobody is clear on what to do. To be honest, it'll be several hours before we really get what's going on, and even longer before we have information. I'm sure your son is okay. He's young, he's strong, he's quick."

"He's not really. He has asthma. He's very thin and frail."

"Well," said the cop, stuck for an answer. "Maybe the best thing for you to do is find the Red Cross tent. I think they're set up on the western side. You can rest there and you'll get information there sooner."

"I never should have let him come to the mall by himself," said Mrs. Girardi, as her husband led her away.

Lavelva Oates shushed the redheaded one. He was a handful. Maybe it was because he was a redhead, he seemed to want a lot of attention and had tendencies toward disruption. He kept picking on a little Asian girl who would do nothing but sit and weep when he addressed her. Smack him hard on his burry little pipsqueak head? That's what Lavelva wanted to do, but she knew it was a mistake. Jobs were hard enough to come by these days and no one went around hitting damn babies.

"Okay, boys and girls, now let's play a new game," she said brightly. "In this game, I want you all to be playing Hide from the monster. When I say go, you go hide. We'll pretend the bad monsters are here. But they won't see you, and you'll be all right. We can hide from the monsters together."

"That's a scary game," said Robert. She knew he was named Robert because he had a big name tag pinned on: ROBERT 3-4. But it was past four o'clock and Robert's mom hadn't shown up. Maybe she was dead.

"I want to go home. Where's my mom?" asked Robert.

"I'm sure she's on her way," Lavelva said.

"I have to go to the bathroom," Linda said.

"Peepee or the other?" asked Lavelva.

"Both," said the child.

"All right," said Lavelva. "Anybody else?"

A few hands came up.

"I'm going to take you back there"—the lavatory was in the rear of the room—"but we have to go on tippy-toes."

"I don't like tippy-toes," said Larry. "It's for babies."

Lavelva was the day care service coordinator, afternoon shift, second floor. She had seventeen unruly kids, three through eight, under her charge. This was her first day! Goddamn!

She wasn't sure what was going on. She was trapped in the day care center, a large room full of beat-up toys and pissed-on dolls, on the second floor. About an hour ago, she'd heard the shooting—loud sharp cracks, echoing eerily along the walls, the nooks and crannies of the mall, very frightening—and herded her kids to the back of the room and told them to lie down. She went to the doorway and watched as the crowded corridor outside seemed to drain itself in a couple of minutes. People ran crazily, screaming, "They're shooting, they're shooting, they have machine guns." She knew there was no way she could get seventeen kids through that mob and that the kids would be knocked down, separated, even hurt. Where was her supervisor? Mrs. Watney, head of mall day care, didn't answer her calls or her texts. Maybe she'd raced out the door too. She tried her mom; couldn't get through. She tried her brother Ralphie installing carpets, even though he'd told her never to call while he was on the job. It didn't matter; couldn't get through. She tried 911. No response. She was alone.

Lavelva knew two things immediately: the first was that she'd be much better holding the children here until someone in authority—a cop, a fireman, someone—came with instructions, and second that if there were men with guns around, she had to have a weapon. In her universe, inner-city Minneapolis, Twenty-Eighth and Washington, it was a tough life and all the young men carried. She'd seen them lying on the streets, bled out, eyes blank. That was the world. There was no other. All the newspapers were always jabbering about the tragedy of it, blah blah and blah, but words like *tragedy* held little meaning for Lavelva; hers was a more practical turn of mind, and it had to do with dealing with what was instead of dreaming about what could be.

She herded the kids back to the rear of the room and sent Linda in to do peepee and the other one. Suzanne, Mindy, Jessica, and Marsha went too. In fact all the girls went.

"Everybody gets a turn. No shoving. Stand in line. Make Miss Lavelva proud," she instructed, knowing these passive little white girls would do exactly that. She couldn't go with them, of course; policy was that no childcare coordinator could be alone in a bathroom with a child of either sex. But perhaps, on a day such as today, the rules had gone out the window. Still, it was better to obey policy, no matter what was happening outside. Here in the second-floor Mall Service Childcare Center, policies would be obeyed.

Well, all but one.

She said to the boys, "You all line up against the wall. We're still going to play Hide from the monster. You lie down, you be quiet. You don't let no monster spot you. This is going to be a long game, so best get used to it. I don't want crying or whining. Y'all have to be brave little boys today, you hear?"

They nodded. The redheaded one, CHARLES 3-5, said, "What's brave?"

"Like a big old football player. Ain't scared of nothing."

"I am scared," said Charles. "It's different now."

"Yes it is," said Lavelva. "It is very different. But Charles, you are so feisty I want you to be the leader, okay? You be the bravest."

"Yes, Miss Lavelva," said Charles.

Lavelva turned, went to her desk, or rather *the*

desk, as it was generic to the center, owned by none of the coordinators. She saw nothing that could be altered to be dangerous, no letter openers, no files, no spikes for spearing paper notices, nothing. Not even a ruler. Obviously, with nimble-fingered little brutes around, thought had been exercised on keeping the space free of dangerous implements.

Then she saw the daily schedule notebook, a three-ring binder volume. She opened it, realized that a steel or at least metal slat ran up its spine. She pulled apart the three rings, and dumped the papers out, then used her strength to rip the slat from the spine of the book. It tore messily, taking some cardboard binding with it, but it was eleven inches of sharp steel, albeit flawed by three rings, which she snapped shut. She slipped it into her jeans, in the small of her back. Then she turned back to the boys.

CHARLES 3-5 was standing and pointing.

"I see a monster," he said.

She turned, and through the glass block wall that divided the center from the pedestrian corridor, she saw the shadow of a gunman.

There were six of them, but the manager, Mrs. Renfels, had broken down: all women, all terrified, except for Molly, who was more concerned for her mother and her sister Sally than she was for herself. Even tough little Rose, the assistant manager, had quieted down as apprehension gripped her.

"You won't find out soon," Ray told Molly. "You have to worry about Molly first. You have to commit yourself to staying put, locking down, waiting them out. That is how you win." There was no privacy, as all of them were jammed in the rear storeroom, under racks of bustiers and negligees and all the scanties of the male imagination that now seemed quite alien to their world.

"I have to know," she said, trying to quell the anxiety. Sally was impossibly cute at fifteen, with smart, vivid eyes, a thin girl's body, and grace just easing into a woman's radiance, and Mom was still feisty even if she had never quite adjusted to American ways. It sickened Molly that the two most vulnerable members of her family were in the greatest danger. The last she'd spoken to them on her cell, they had in fact been on the first floor where the roundup had taken place. But if they'd been luckily in the outer ring, they might have made it to an exit. She wanted to call, but she was terrified that if they were in the mob of hostages Ray had described, the ringing cell might have attracted attention.

"I wish they'd turn that goddamn music off," Milt's wife said. "If I hear 'Jingle Bells' one more time I will puke."

"Not on me, please," said the blonde, the one who clearly considered herself a hot number.

"Why is this happening?" Mrs. Renfels asked, her first words since the crisis had begun.

"It's because we should have used the atom bomb on them after nine-eleven," said the hot blonde, obviously the sort used to issuing opinions and by her beauty banishing responses. "If we'd have burned them all, this wouldn't be going on."

"You can't kill a billion people because, what, thirteen men are crazy assholes," responded Milt's wife.

"Oh yes you can. You push a button and they are in flames."

"That is the craziest—"

"All right, all right," said Ray. "I am not trying to be a boss or take over or anything, but it's better if you don't get in squabbles until this thing is over. You may have to work together and you have to see the person beside you as a family member. You can fight all you want when you're advising on the set of the TV movie or something."

"He's right," said Rose. "Just keep a cork in it, it's better for all of us."

"It's easy for you to say," said Mrs. Renfels. "You're young, you're in this for yourself. I have three kids. If something happens to me—oh, why is this happening?"

"Ma'am," said Ray, "I don't mean to tell you how to think, but I am a former Marine and I have been in some fights. If you'll allow me, I would advise you never to use the W-word today. The W-word is why. Sometimes there is no why, and if you get hung up on why, you lose your effectiveness. I've seen it happen. The men who die are the men who can't believe they're in a fight and can't believe that someone is trying to kill them. It seems so unfair to them and they're so busy feeling sorry for themselves, they don't seek cover, they don't return fire, they don't scan the horizon, they forget how to use their expensive equipment. The men who live get it right away; they understand they're in a different world and they have to deal with exactly what is before them with maximum concentration."

"That's very good advice," said Rose.

"Maybe we should surrender," said the blonde.

"No, ma'am," said Ray. "You should instead consider how lucky you are. Some people are dead, some people, maybe a thousand, are under the gun. You are, for the time being, safe. No one knows you're here and no one, that I can tell, is looking for you. Just stay put and trust in God and the public safety people who are, I guarantee you, working very hard right this second to set us free."

"Great job," said Obobo. "Major Jefferson, this is a fabulous plan. I'm very impressed."

Jefferson amplified: "We don't blow all doors simultaneously and move down the corridors into the crowd, unable to engage until we reach the amusement park. That's a no go, because it gives them however long it takes our people to advance down the corridors to open fire on hostages. One guy at each corridor shooting at SWAT could hold up the advance for six or eight minutes. Way too much time."

"Go on, Major."

"So we take the six best shooters with gunfight experience, all armed with red dot MP5s on semi-auto. And we've got these guys. Some of our people are good, some of the FBI guys are really good, and Phil Mason of Edina SWAT is the Area Seven three-gun champion. I've shot against him and he is damned good and damned cool. So we six, we go underground through a shaft that runs from parking lot seven to the mall central. That puts us right underneath Area Z. I have a guy from Bloomington SWAT who was an army engineer in the sandbox. We rig six detonations to blow through the floor. At a given moment, we turn off the power, the place goes dark. It'll be a few seconds before the emergency gen kicks in. But the gunmen immediately see the holes and assume men will come from them. No, uh-uh, that's the diversion. We've quietly come up through the ducts under the Area Z concessionaire stand here"—he pointed to it on the chart—"and have only floor boarding and linoleum at a certain locality that the engineer has specified. Once the gunmen commit to the assault from the ground, we hit 'em. They will have moved to cover the openings we've just blown. Head shots, targets marked, we can take 'em down fast, before the crowd has a chance to panic. But Colonel, we have to move now. It'll take time to get men through the ducts into the space under Area Z, it'll take time to locate and plant the explosives, and it'll take time to—"

"Again, I can't tell you how impressed I am," Colonel Obobo said, explaining his reasons. "It's thorough, it's creative, it takes all the variables into consideration. I'm very pleased to take it under advisement." He touched the intense major on the shoulder as if to confer a blessing. Then he turned away, leaving an incredulous look on the major's face and the awareness that he'd just gotten another no that sounded even more like a yes.

"They're shooting inside the mall," one of the radio techs announced. "FBI snipers say they're shooting inside the mall."

McElroy was first off the chopper, first into position. From the air, the lake shape of the glass was apparent and he had raced to what must have been the tip of Lake Michigan, right at Chicago, but now that he was here, it was simply Lake Glass, or Lake Plastic, an immensity of transparent, thick plastic that would somehow have to be penetrated. But first he had to equip.

He unzipped the rifle bag and laid out a Remington 700 with a Leupold 10× tactical scope, the whole thing anodized forest green. Carefully he removed a long green tube, which a Velcro strap had secured inside the bag, and brought it close to his eyes for an examination. It was a Gemtech suppressor, about eight inches long and an inch and a half in diameter, and under the tubing it consisted mainly of baffles and chambers and holes, the point of which was to elongate the time of escape for the rapidly expanding gases of a shot so that when they reached the atmosphere, they were slowed down and exited with a kind of snap instead of a terrible, earsplitting crack. With the suppressor screwed carefully on the threaded muzzle, he inserted the bolt into the receiver, reached into an ammo compartment to remove a box of Federal 175-grain match cartridges in .308, and slid five into the rifle's magazine, closing the bolt on and chambering the fifth. He flicked the safety on, not that he believed in safeties, looped the sling around his shoulder, and stood to examine the scene.

What lay before him was a wall about five feet tall that formed the well of the vast skylight that was Lake Michigan. It was of course not a single sheet of Plexiglas but divided into cells about 20 by 20 feet. Peering over the edge of this southernmost cell, he was rewarded with a vision from five stories up of a crowd of disconsolate Christmas shoppers jammed into the walkways and open areas of a Technicolor amusement park and seen from ninety degrees at an altitude of about 125 feet through heavy plastic; details were hard to pick out. In time he recognized what had to be a gunman, mainly by the black object carried under one arm and the black-green rag on his head. Details emerged: pistol, knife, throat mike. With access, it would have been an easy shot, and he prayed to the sniper god that he would get a chance to take it.

He radio-checked.

"Sniper Five, set up, in position," speaking to a state police sergeant in the headquarters van.

"I have you, Five. Sitrep, please."

"I have a good angle on the scene, almost straight down. I'm at site Chicago at the bottom of Michigan and therefore have a good view of the balconies on the opposite, that is, the eastward side. No activity there. I do not have a shot, repeat, do not have a shot. The glass or plastic or whatever it is is very thick, I don't think I could get through it if I had a fucking hammer."

"Be advised, no shooting, that is our call. You stay on position and call in periodically with intelligence and we will take that under advisement."

"May I talk with FBI supervisor?"

"Negative, Five, he is in conference with incident commander and others. The governor is expected momentarily."

"Request conference with him when available, over."

"Noted, will try and make that happen, Five, but no promises, out."

So that was it. All dressed up and no one to shoot. Or rather, no way to shoot, although, given the angle, the bad boys would literally represent the idealized fish in a barrel.

Dear Sniper God, your humble servant Dave here, please let me take one of these motherfuckers before the day is done. But he also knew the ways of the sniper god, and the sniper god would only help those who help themselves.

McElroy, thirty-two and a Bureau lifer who loved the SWAT life and had been on a hundred raids and on the periphery of two or three gunfights but had yet to fire a shot in anger, looked around him. Beyond, of course, was Minnesota, turning dark and pierced with an ever-increasing array of lights as the sun was setting. Far off he could see highways streaming with cars, the illumination of suburbs and strip malls, just regular American stuff. Then there was the roof itself, the flat, black-asphalt stage upon which this drama was playing out. The flatness was vast, way out of human scale, easily bigger than an aircraft carrier's deck or a football stadium's parking area, reaching to infinity. About a mile away, or so it seemed, was a rack of industrial-looking apparatuses, presumably part of the cooling and heating system. There were at least six little sheds—they looked comically like the ice-fishing hutches these Minnesotans built on their frozen lakes in winter—that presumably held doors that opened onto stairways into the interior. He guessed they were all locked, but it occurred to him that a good B-and-E man could probably get through, and operators could be fed into play that way. But surely they would know that at Command.

Then, more immediately, these goddamned lake-shaped skylights, here at the center of the vastness. Regularly spaced around the perimeter of Michigan, he saw a fellow such as himself, all Tommy-Tacticaled up in Nomex jumpsuit with Glock .40 in shoulder holster, with a big bad rifle, a black watch cap or Kevlar helmet, and a posture of utter helplessness with reference to the thick wall of impenetrable glass between himself and his potential targets.

He thought, I will get through this fucking glass. I will, I will, I will.

But how? This wasn't one of those absurd movies where the guy reaches into his kit and just happens to have exactly the right tool, a computer-driven microdiamond buzz saw that was also miniaturized and could cut through the stuff like butter and makes a hell of an old-fashioned. No, darn, he'd left that at home. Nor did he have Gatorade and cough medicine that could be instantly combined into sulfuric acid and melt the glass. He didn't have a goddamned thing.

He walked the edge of the skylight, finding it uniform in its precision. Why had the developers built it so sturdily? Couldn't they have cut corners, couldn't a worker have faked the effort, couldn't there be some way the thing wasn't up to spec and a hole could be bored through the joinery of glass and building, giving him a shooting lane? No, no such luck, it was all solid and tight to the finger. Okay, so—

His eye caught movement below.

What was—

Looking down from God's-eye view, he could tell that two of the gunmen had kicked their way into the center of the crowd, covered by other gunmen. They cleared a space. Then they grabbed five people, apparently two women, two men, and a teenager, and dragged them to the center of the opening and made them kneel.

It looked like an execution.

Please, Sniper God, give me a shot!

But he had no shot. He was sealed off by thick glass.

One of the gunmen walked behind the kneeling five and with his rifle shot each in the back of the head. McElroy felt the vibration of the gunshot meeting the glass, giving it a little buzz. He wished he could look away but he could not.

Executed, each victim fell forward without grace and hit the floor face-first and hard. They lay sprawled, loose as ragdolls. In a bit of time one, then another, and finally all began to spew a blackish puddle from the head, and these multiple lakes of plasma reached out, found and followed fissures on the floor, and joined in a large wetland of blood, though leaving the odd island of high spot.

"Control, this is Five, directly below me the gunmen just executed five hostages, shot 'em dead through the head."

"I have that," said the radio.

"Jesus Christ, let us blow this goddamn glass and take these pricks down. They don't know we're here; if we get through the glass we can do them all in under thirty seconds."

"Negative, negative, Five, you are advised to do nothing but stand and observe. If we go tactical, you will be notified and assigned targets."

"Goddammit, they are killing people and—"

"Five, this is Command, commo space is at a premium and we don't want you using it up on a rant. Tactical discipline."

"Sir, please put Special Agent Kemp on—"

"Any information must be channeled through Command," said the frosted voice.

This is very disturbing," said Colonel Obobo.

He stood unbelieving in the center of the state police Incident Command van, surrounded by several majors and the FBI executive, Kemp, as they dealt with the news from the snipers that five people had just been executed. Mr. Renfro stood immediately to the left of the colonel, saying nothing.

"Could it be a phony?" someone asked. "Maybe those are actors or something, or his own volunteers previously put in place, and—"

"They're real," said Mike Jefferson, the aggressive SWAT commander. "And he is talking to us—in blood."

"I just—"

"Look at the time, Colonel Obobo. It's five o'clock. He killed five people at five o'clock. He'll kill six people at six o'clock, seven at seven o'clock, and on through the night. There aren't any demands, except that we get a lot of body bags. This is just a straight murder job. We have to get our assault units in position, issue orders, distribute the proper breaching equipment, and get ready to jump."

"He will talk to us," said the colonel. "This is just his way of getting our attention."

"He had our attention, for God's sake!" shouted Jefferson. "For Christ's fucking sake, men with AKs shooting everything that moves, he *has* our fucking attention."

"No," said Obobo, ever courteous, ever unflappably astute and collected. "He has to demonstrate that he is capable of ordering executions. That is his baseline. All our negotiations will now have to take that into consideration. He's laying down the rules, that's what he's doing. He will talk to us, before six. Well before six. And he knows that to assault, we have a massive job of logistics, planning, equipping, moving, and coordinating, and he's putting something before us to slow us down, baffle us, make us inefficient at that very tough job."

"Ah," said Jefferson in immense frustration. "Colonel, let me begin to put people in play under the mall. We've got to be able to breach that floor, it's the only way, and we have to have them there now in order to do it anytime in the future. We can't just blow the doors and charge into the place."

"Can we chopper people to the roof? Aren't there doorways, they could come down from above somehow?" someone asked.

"No," said Kemp, "at least not as a main strike. It would take a dozen choppers to get men in force. He'd know. If they blew the doors, it would take ten minutes for them to work their way down. If they rappelled, they'd be sitting ducks for the riflemen. You'd just get a lot of highly trained men killed for nothing, and maybe fifty or sixty hostages."

Obobo tuned it all out. He made eye contact with Mr. Renfro and the two exchanged listen-to-these-idiots-talk expressions. The advisor then nodded, communicating his sublime confidence in Colonel Obobo's abilities. He knew that if the colonel could just talk to these people and make them see the hope-lessness of their position, the inevitability of what lay ahead, he could make this thing go away. He had that power. He was a convincer, an inspirer.

"Gentlemen, for now I'd like you to hold your positions," Obobo finally said. "Commo, continue to monitor the channels to see if he's trying to talk to us. We have to know his demands. When we learn his demands—"

"His demands are that a lot of people die; those are his demands," said Jefferson. "This is a straight murder raid, like Mumbai or the World Trade Cen-ter. He just wants a lot of people off the earth and his own glory and ascension to heaven guaranteed. He thinks when this is over, he's going to get himself fucked royally by seventy-two—"

"Major Jefferson," said Obobo, showing a whis-per of irritation, "I think you've made your point. In the meantime, I want a written assault plan from you, a list of assets you currently have and those that you will need before I can authorize any kind of a strike. I hope to hell I never have to issue that order. Nichols, get on the phone to the Justice Department and see how our request for Army engineers, Delta, and SEAL people is playing at Defense. Special Agent Kemp, I want an update on your investigative efforts in Minneapolis as well as our requests to BATF for support in the firearms investigation."

"Sir," said Jefferson, "this isn't an investigation, it's a war."

"Major Jefferson, you've made your point fifty times over. Please follow my orders or be relieved of duty. I can't fight him and you."

"Yes sir."

"Sir," someone said, "do we release to media?"

"No," said Mr. Renfro, who rarely addressed tactical or operational issues but this time couldn't help himself. "If word gets out he's shooting hostages, it'll add pressure to an already pressurized decision."

"Good point," said the colonel. "Do you concur, Special Agent Kemp?"

Kemp, thanking God he had no dog in this fight, said, "Yes, Colonel."

"Sir," someone said, "the governor is here."

"Oh fuck," said somebody.

It happened that Nikki was watching a particular sniper whom she had nicknamed Chicago with her binoculars from three thousand feet up at a particular moment as the WUSScopter hovered at that height. Though from there he was a tiny, almost blurred figure and the light was quickly diminishing, she saw him suddenly bolt upward, then lean forward, tense radically as if he were willing himself somehow to penetrate the glass of the skylight and fly down into the atrium; instantly, his finger flew to the radio unit at his belt—she knew where to look because she'd covered cops in Bristol—and presumably switched it on. He began jabbering into the throat mike. She zapped around the margins of the lake of Plexiglas until she'd located all five snipers and noted that all five were on their mikes.

"Something just happened," she said.

"How can you tell?" asked Jim, the cameraman.

"I saw the snipers jerk up, and now all are reporting in."

She switched to Marty back at the station.

"Is Command saying anything?"

"No, nothing. We've had reports the governor is incoming. We might want to put you on the ground and get over there in case he has a presser."

"Marty, no presser means anything tonight. They'll use the press to put out reassuring bullshit, knowing that whoever's doing this is monitoring. Pressers are a waste of time and it pisses me off that His Eminence puts his big fat mug on camera tonight."

"Settle down, Mary Richards, it was only a suggestion."

"Well, something's happened here and—"

She had an idea. Two weeks ago she'd been to the mall and had bought a pocketbook from a shop called Purses, Bags and Whatnot, one of those cutesy places that smelled of potpourri but had very nice leather bags. She pulled out that very same pocketbook now and began to riffle through it, because she remembered that's where she'd stuffed the bill of sale. Yes, indeed, there it was, amid a scruffy collection of receipts for $100 from Bank of America, $35.47 for gas at Sheetz, and $22.75 from Safeway.

Remembering the very pleasant young woman who had run the transaction for her, she looked at the bottom of the bill of sale and saw a handwritten note, "Thanks so much, Amanda Birkowsky."

"Marty," she said, "real quick, run the name Birkowsky through AnyWho.com and see what you come up with."

"Nikki—"

"Just do it, Marty. I don't have time to explain.

It's a rare enough name so there probably aren't too many of them."

There were, as it turned out, only three in the three Minneapolis–Saint Paul area codes. She dialed the first, got no answer, and then hit on the second.

"Yes," she said. "This is WUFF-TV. May I speak with Amanda, please."

A woman said, brokenly, "Amanda is in the mall."

"I am so sorry, Mrs. Birkowsky," Nikki said, guessing from the voice that it was a mom, not a sister.

"She's all right," said Mrs. Birkowsky. "For now. She's upstairs in the—who did you say you were?"

Nikki explained the connection.

"What is it you want?"

"I'm trying to reach Amanda. She's called you? I guess she has a cell, she called you to tell you she's all right, she's in no danger, or no immediate danger."

"I can't give you her number."

"I understand. But . . . can you call her, give her my number, and if she decides, she can call me? I just think people have a right to know what's going on. It's my job. There's next to no information available and that's never a good thing."

Amanda called Nikki three minutes later. She and two customers and two other staff were hiding in the rear room of Purses, Bags and Whatnot on the first floor of the mall, in the dark. They felt themselves all right for the time being as no one had begun to search the stores for hiding shoppers.

"Did anything happen at five?" Nikki asked.

"We heard five shots. Bang. Bang. Bang. Bang. Bang. Not a machine gun, not like that, but five individual shots. Then we heard the crowd—it makes noise, like an animal, all those people—we heard what

I would call some kind of uproar, I don't know, then barking from the voices of the guards, I guess. It was very unclear but something bad must have happened."

"Five shots?" said Nikki.

"Yes, exactly. I could try and sneak out there and—"

"No, no, no, no, you just stay where you are."

"Are they going to come get us soon? The police."

"There are police all over the place, but in truth, I don't see any signs of an attack or an entry or anything."

"This is so awful."

"Listen, if something happens and you want to, and it seems safe, can you call me back? And if I think the cops are going to go, I'll give you a heads-up through your mom, okay, and you can get low to the floor behind cover. I'll never call you, because I won't know what situation you'll be in. Is that fair?"

"Thank you," said Amanda.

"Sweetie, don't thank me. You're the brave one here."

One minute later, Nikki was on the air with the news that five shots had been fired within the atrium and that possibly the gunmen had begun to shoot hostages.

"They just shot five people," Ray said.

"You don't know that," Molly said.

"Yes, I do," said Ray.

It seemed that the sound of the shots still echoed through the weird acoustics of the gigantic space. Everyone in the Frederick's had stiffened when the sounds reached them, and in the several minutes since, nobody had said a thing until Ray broke the silence.

"Maybe some kid raised his rifle and pulled the trigger five times because he thought it was a cool thing to do," Molly said.

"No," said Ray. "That would have been faster shooting, onetwothreefourfive. This was deliberate fire. One shot, move to the next, shoot, move to the next. He just shot five people."

Nobody said a thing. Ray, Molly, Rose the clerk, the broken-down manager of the store, and the three customers just lay there in the dark, in the storeroom.

"You could go check, like last time," Rose finally said.

Ray didn't answer right away. Then he said, "No. No, if I go out there, I'm not coming back. Somebody's got to do something and I'm probably the only man with training who's close enough to the situation to act and the police have no idea of how to get in here."

"Ray—" said Molly, but Rose cut her off.

"If you go, what do we do? Do we just lie here? Six women, and there's guys out there with machine guns? What do we do? What happens to us?"

"I think you're okay," said Ray. "You don't need help. The people down there do."

"There's nothing you can do," said Rose. "There's a bunch of them, with army weapons. What can one guy do? You'll just get yourself killed. You don't even have a gun, much less a machine gun."

Molly said, "She's right. If they see you, they'll kill you. That's all. After all you've done, some punk kills you in the Payless shoe store or the Best Buy and you haven't helped a thing and in six hours the hostage takers make a deal with the cops and fly to

Cuba with a million dollars and what has your death accomplished?"

"If I hide in the ladies' underwear store, what has my life accomplished?" Ray said. "You'll be all right. As I said, you stay here, you commit psychologically to the long term, you don't expect help now or in an hour or a day or a week, and you will survive."

"He thinks he's John Wayne," said Molly, bitterly. "John Wayne was a fantasy. He never existed. He's a dream, a phantom, a ghost."

"He existed," said Ray, "and his name was Bob Lee Swagger. He's my father."

"You don't even have a gun," said Rose.

"Then I will have to get a gun," said Ray.

"Okay," said Lavelva quietly. "Now, boys and girls, let's go back to the bathroom, all right? The name of this game is Let's hide in the bathroom."

"Miss Lavelva," said DAVID 3-4, "I'm scared."

"David, don't you be scared now. No one's going to hurt you, you trust Miss Lavelva on this, sweetie, okay? Now, kids, come on now, let's put on our quiet shoes and our quiet voices and go back to the bathroom and it will be all right."

Somehow—she could feel their fear in the drop-off of energy, the quiet that overtook them, the lassitude that seemed to creep through their small bones—she got them back and into the room.

"Larry," she said to the eldest, "you be in charge here, you hear? You stay till Miss Lavelva comes back. Y'all stay quiet now and listen to Larry."

"Miss Lavelva, I'm scared too," said SHERRY 4-6.

"It's okay, Sherry," said Miss Lavelva. "And when

this is over, Miss Lavelva goin' take you to get something nice to eat, maybe french fries or frosties, whatever you want, a nice treat, from Miss Lavelva."

That seemed to quiet them down.

Lavelva slipped out. She was alone in the bigger room. She looked at the translucent glass blocks that marked off the day care center and saw nothing. Maybe he'd missed her. Maybe he was gone.

Asad could not read the English in the mall directory pamphlet, but he got the representation of the map well enough, and the imam had drawn a circle around the location of the day care center. Yes, this was the Colorado corridor, yes, COLORADO 2-145, the numbers were right. It seemed that helpfully each store had an address that indexed it to the map, and even though he had little English, he recognized the address NE C-2-145. He divined practically that it meant Colorado corridor, second floor, 145 retail designation, and since evens were on the left and odds on the right, it had to be on his left. Even though he assumed that he had free range, he was careful. He was aware that many of the stores still hid customers. What if some of them came rushing out and jumped him? Then he laughed. No Americans would do that. They were a soft and decadent people, and here, in this palace of luxury and greed, their reflexes and warrior minds, if they even had them, would be shoved way down by shock and fear. They would lie in the dark weeping, praying to their absurd man on the cross, saying to him pleasepleasepleaseplease.

He missed it. He looked at a store and saw an address that read COLORADO 2-157. He turned back, began to edge his way down the corridor. It was quiet and dark, strewn with abandoned bags, tipped carriages, shoes, hats, jackets, all signs of the intensity of the panic. A few windows had been broken but no looting appeared to have taken place.

Slowly he tracked the stores, stopping every once in a while to check for signs of threat. He saw none. And then he came to it. For about thirty feet, the gaudy glass windows of the storefronts yielded to glass brick, and a double door stood in the center. Above, a sign must have announced the purpose of the location, though he could not read it. He slid to the glass doors and peered in, and soon his eyes made out toys on the floor, children's furniture tilted sideways, that sort of thing. This had to be where the babies were. But it was quiet. Maybe they had moved the babies, but he didn't see how. Maybe they were inside, in hiding.

He slipped in, his eyes in full search mode, scanning what lay before him in semidarkness, and everywhere he looked, he swept with the muzzle of the baby Kalashnikov, his finger on the trigger, a full orange magazine clicked solidly in place.

Then he saw her.

She was dark, like him. She stood, facing him, twenty-five feet away. Her face was a stone mask. He read her bones and saw that she was not Somali, thin-nosed and -lipped, high-foreheaded, like him, but still of Africa, with that stoic face of the sub-Saharan peoples, broad of nose. She wore her hair in the African style, in tiny ringlets all over her head.

"Sister," he said in Somali, and she replied in English, two words he knew.

"Fuck you," she said.

——————————

Nothing worked. When you busted kiddie porn, you pierced. You fought your way through pretty elementary protection schemes, worms, predatory malware, you looked for back doors, baited and phished, you ran decoding or password-finding programs, and eventually, with stamina and creativity and a strong stomach, you got in. Then the deal was trying to put a network together, finding out who was buying the stuff, who was distributing the stuff, who was producing the stuff. Then you penetrated, playing the role of John A. Smith, corporate lawyer, father of five, country club member, Kiwanis, Rotary, bar association vice president with a hunger for watching children violated, and you put all that together, documented the linkages, and you took it to whichever fed or state prosecutor in whichever state had the most juice and eagerness and you pounced. Yes, you got dirty but you took down someone much dirtier.

But none of those programs worked. Whoever was playing this game had a brain or two in his head.

Neal had tried everything, had madly improvised program improvements, had written enough code to start a new social network, yet SCADA was impenetrable by virtue of the tough defenses built into MEMTAC 6.2 and its resolute steadfastness in avoiding temptations to jump to online status.

"How's it coming, Jeff?" asked Dr. Benson.

"This guy's good. He tightened up their protocols so I can't even get the SCADA meme up, just to get a rope on the culture. I've been to the Siemens website and it's clear what this guy has come up with is even beyond them. Jesus, he could be making a billion a year writing code for Steve or Bill and getting laid by nerd-babes left and right, and he's doing this shit?"

"Maybe he doesn't like nerd-babes," Benson said. "So what are you going to do?"

"Pray."

"Swell. I'll tell them that—"

"Pray, as in, 'talk to God.' God being the engineer at Siemens who designed it. You better get me a translator fast, Bob, because I don't speak one word of German."

Lavelva looked at him. This was it, then. Somali, like so many Somalis in the area, thin, arrogant, reeking of narcissism because he considered himself so beautiful with the thin nose and the thin lips. Presumably the hair was that thick froth so Somali in its wiriness, but she could not tell for he wore a patterned scarf tied tightly to his head, held in place by a band. He wore baggy jeans and a hoodie, like any banger she had seen, and she'd seen a lot of them, Somali and otherwise, and he carried a Kalashnikov and he had a handgun dangling in a holster. He was all warred-up. His eyes seemed slightly crazed, all Nubian-warrior-lion-killing bullshit in his mind, and that was what made the Somali gangs so feared on the East Side and anywhere they left their signs.

He called to her in his jive.

"Fuck you," she replied. No way she backed down to this sucker, no way she gave him the kids. No way, no way, no way.

He smiled, showing bright teeth. He walked to her, full of bravado and confidence, lion-proud with his big guns and a knife. He spoke again to her in his gibberish. She held her ground.

He approached.

"Babies," he said. "You give me babies," in poor English. "Now, give me the babies."

"Ain't no way I'm giving you nothing, Jack," she said.

"Babies. I want babies. Imam want babies. Downstairs, bring babies. *Now.*"

He poked her with the muzzle of the Kalash. Then he poked her again, this time hard enough to bruise.

"Want to die, sister? I kill, no problem. Bangbang, shoot dead black sister, then take babies. Maybe I kill a baby. No problem, no problem."

He poked her again but did not see the thing in her hand that now flew at him and struck him with a sword's cut across the face and drove a flash of light and pain up through his head, and he stepped back, feeling the tremendous hurt of it, the gun muzzle dropping as he pivoted, and then his pain alchemized into rage and he flew on her, wanting to kill her with his hands and the two grappled awkwardly, spinning this way or that and she cracked him another time in the head with her weapon, another slicing gouge that shot off lights behind his eyes. But he was stronger and he leaned into her and twisted her down and was on her. He would kill the bitch with his own hands, choke the life out of her, and then get the babies.

The press loved him. They always had. They projected their dreams upon him, he knew, and he had no problem internalizing that emotion and building it into his persona. After a brief sum-up by the governor's public affairs idiot, the governor uttered a few bromides about his confidence in Minnesota's first responders and announced that he had activated the Minnesota Guard and that units would be arriving within five hours. Then FBI Special Agent Kemp, repping the feds, said aid was on the way from DC and all over America, and back on Pennsylvania Avenue in the Hoover Building, analysts and intelligence experts were applying their full energy to the crisis. And then the gov's idiot turned things over to Colonel Obobo, and everyone smiled and took reassurance from his collected calmness, his radiant charisma.

He stood at a podium outside the Incident Command van, lit by a thousand TV lights, to say nothing of the mercury vapors on aluminum supports already in place thanks to the site's origin as a parking lot. Behind them, blank and gigantic and without detail in the gloaming, the mall itself loomed one hundred or so feet tall. It was ringed by emergency vehicles and police units, all lit to hell with their flashers going, so that its darkness was jabbed by the red-blue cop lights. Above, a fleet of choppers held in steady formation at three thousand feet, the roar of their engines undercutting the press conference.

"As you all know, we have a terrible situation here. I simply want to echo the words of the governor and our friends in the FBI. The Minnesota State Police have assumed primary responsibility for resolving this situation, under my command, and we are moving quickly to secure the mall. But we are not cowboys and this is not Dodge City. Our enemy isn't so much these deluded men but violence itself. We have no intentions of getting into a showdown and demonstrating that we are capable of more violence than they are. Violence is death and death is unacceptable. So we will pursue alternative means of de-escalating the situation, all the while hoping that as time passes, tempers cool and justice, rather than vengeance, becomes the order of the day. That I promise you."

"Are they executing hostages?"

Goddammit! Somehow, some TV reporter had gotten through to someone in the mall, reporting that witnesses were claiming that five shots had been fired. Already, Mr. Renfro was on the line to the station, complaining bitterly about unauthorized news reports, even if accurate, and how they jeopardized operations.

But clearly five shots would not signify a head-on assault; the only conclusion was hostage execution, and this drama held a particularly ugly fascination for the reporters. Americans put on their knees and shot in the head in a mall in middle America on the opening of the Christmas season, the day after Thanksgiving, the most family—some might say, too much family—of family days.

"I cannot confirm or deny reports that hostages have been shot," was all that Obobo could say. But he was extremely annoyed at the abruptness and the hostility with which the question had been launched at him. It was not the sort of treatment he was used to.

"But there *was* shooting in the mall?"

It was a thin line, but he stuck to it.

"I cannot confirm or deny there has been shooting in the mall. Obviously, we prefer to keep tactical details to ourselves as we deal with this situation."

"If they start executing hostages, don't you *have* to attack?"

"We don't have to do anything," said the colonel. "It's when we permit ourselves to be locked into 'have to' situations that tragedy ensues."

Hmm. No, he didn't like this tone of hostility. In fact, all of a sudden, he decided he was sick of them. He looked out on a hundred faces. Where was the love? Where had it gone? It began to needle him. He would have to discuss this with Renfro.

"I did not say they were killing hostages. I will not be announcing tactical plans here. Presumably, these folks are monitoring our public announcements."

"Who are they?"

"We do not know yet. As I said, they have yet to make contact or issue demands. I can say we have secured the mall and nobody is going anywhere. At this time we are studying various options. As you might suspect, this is a tremendously complex undertaking, and we don't want to do anything hasty and stupid."

"At Columbine, didn't they decide they should have moved immediately on the shooters? All they did was set up guard posts outside while people bled to death. Is that what you're doing?"

Another ridiculous question! Who did these assholes think they were? Where was Renfro?

"This is not Columbine. This is an entity that is far more than a high school, the number of gunmen is as yet unknown, thought to be ten or more, extremely well informed, working with a well-thought-out plan, heavily armed with professional-quality weapons. As Special Agent Kemp said, we do have Army and Navy commando types inbound, and they are far better suited to this kind of tactical work than we are. I have at least twenty teams ready to go in, but I have to get them coordinated, I have to get them inside, I have to get them moving in step with each other, and they have to have clear targets guided by intelligence. None of those conditions exist at this time, so we are in a wait-and-see mode."

"Ladies and gentlemen," interrupted the governor, "although it's true that shots were fired, we have no evidence that people were executed. It could have been just some kid shooting his gun."

Great! The stupid bastard had just put the shots on the table.

"Colonel Obobo, Tom Kiefaver, NBC News." Handsome national haircut, sometimes anchored the big show. "Are you comfortable in established positions while people may be a few dozen feet away dying?"

"I think we all need to get back to work, folks. You'll forgive us," and he turned manfully and walked back toward the trailer. As he went back to the van, Obobo saw the governor giving one-on-ones to the national news and the big Minneapolis channels, each team waiting patiently. The governor seemed to be enjoying himself.

It went all fuzzy on Lavelva. The Somali pressed his thumbs into her larynx, grinning wildly, his gashed face bleeding, the blood falling into her face. She bucked and fought and twice again swacked him hard with the steel spine of the notebook, but each time he saw it coming and turned, flinching down, and the blade bit into his hairline and across his ear, cutting shallowly but not hurting him bad enough. He had her now. It was over. She felt herself in the whirlpool as the oxygen debt turned her lungs into broken balloons.

Then he relented. His fingers came slightly out of her throat, and he let a desperately sought gush of air into her throat. But his fingers did not come off her neck. He spoke in Somali, not that she understood anything but the emotional gist.

"Hah, girl, see what Asad does to you! Hah, now I send you to the fiery noplace of infidel hell you who stand against Allah must go. I am your killer, your ruler. You defy me and die as do all peoples everywhere soon to know the power of Islam."

What bullshit! He was all lit up, so proud of his mighty victory, unwilling to let the moment go, savoring the kill. She whacked him again, but he blinked only a bit, shook his head, and said, "Now, die, bitch."

The thumbs went hard into her, and her air supply drained quickly and she sucked at dry nothingness, bucking against him but feeling her will vanish and wishing she'd been able to save the babies, she tried so hard to save the babies and—

And someone broke his neck.

Broke it clean and hard, and she heard the snap as the vertebrae cracked into two pieces, and his tongue came into his skinny-ass lips and his eyes went all cue ball on him and his head hung at a broken-spring angle and his thumbs lost their power and he was lifted from her like a sack of potatoes and laid on a floor from which he would never again rise.

Some Asian-like dude looked down at her.

"You okay?" he said.

"Man, he like to choke the fuck out of me."

"Just relax, rest. He's not going to choke anybody ever again, okay?"

The guy, she now saw, was some kind of thin, hardball type, had warrior written all over him in the leanness under his sweatshirt and the veins thick with blood on his wrists. He turned and quickly began to loot the fallen Somali, separating first the AK from the boy, then quickly unbuckling the bandolier of ammunition—the clips were all weird *orange,* you know, like popsicles—then slipped the kid's belt with knife and pistol off. He checked the pistol expertly, pinching back the slide to see if it held a chambered round, and then he began to reassemble himself in the image of the man he'd just killed. Finally, finished, he turned back to her.

"Feeling better? You'll be bruised for a month, but I think you'll be all right. Sweetie, I can't believe you cracked him with that shiv. You can play ball on my team anytime, the guts you must have."

"Who you?" she asked.

"The name's Ray. Spent some time in the Marines, that's why I'm all going-to-war now. Nobody else is. Anyhow, I saw this joker slide in here as I was stalking him. Sorry I didn't get here sooner."

She looked at the dead boy. She'd seen the gaze before, on the streets. That I'm-asleep look, the eyes blank, seeing nothing, the I-ain't-nothing-no-more look of extinction. Someone run into a bullet or a blade with his name on it, down he go, his face come all moony nothingness, like this sucker. She could still gut him, cut his slimy insides out and hang 'em up to dry. But no. He dead.

She turned back to see the Chinese Marine studying a mall pamphlet, which must have come from Mr. Dead Ass.

"You have kids here?"

"Seventeen of them. In back. That boy said he'd come to get the babies."

"Yeah, the place is marked. So they want children,

they need 'em as hostages, and they sent this joker. Okay, we're going to move the kids a little ways down the hall into the ladies' underwear place. There are some women in there and they can help you take care of them. Does that seem like a good idea?"

"It does."

"You want them in a single file, hugging the walls, make it a game. See, that way those TV cameras can't pick them out of the shadow. You get that?"

"I do."

"Let's get this done fast. I don't know how long it'll be before they notice war hero here didn't come back with the babies."

It made as much sense as anything. It was the first positive thing that had happened since the shooting started.

"I also want to hide this guy," he said. "If they find him, it may piss them off and they may take it out on the hostages. They have about a thousand people down in the amusement park."

"Yes sir," she said.

"Hey, what is your name?"

"I am Lavelva Oates."

"Well, Miss Lavelva. I say again, you did real good. If I had it, I'd give you a medal. Stand up to the killer with the gun. Not many have the sand."

"Yes sir," she said, secretly so very pleased.

Next she went back, got the kids out of the bathroom on the pretext of a new game: Creep down the hall. Be a kitty cat or a doggy. All fours.

By the time she got them organized, the body was gone, and so was the Chinese Marine. And so was the AK rifle.

Bet he know how to run that, she thought.

It took a while before anyone at the Red Cross tent paid attention to Mr. and Mrs. Girardi, and it was not their personality type, either as individuals or as a couple, to demand notice. They simply stood there and watched while nurses bandaged the odd escapees from the mall who'd fallen and cut themselves, bruised, torn, twisted something, and handed out glasses of juice and cookies. Meanwhile, uniformed policemen moved among those on the cots or waiting to see a physician or a nurse to interview the escapees, hoping to pick up that one new piece of information that might matter. But it was a sloppy process, the cops were under great pressure to produce, and when witnesses turned out to have nothing, they were quickly abandoned, raising hard feelings and complaints. All this frenzy took place under the open-walled canvas structure lit by fluorescents, and enough insects remained to buzz and hum around the lights, which themselves were so harsh they showed everything in vivid clarity, the red of the many Red Cross insignias, the blue and gray of the police uniforms, the white smocks of the doctors.

Finally, a woman came to them.

"Have you been helped?"

"No, ma'am," said Mr. Girardi. He was fifty-two, stooped, balding. He was an unimpressive man by any standards and in no crowd would he stand out.

"What's the problem?"

"The policeman over there suggested you might have some information. Our son Jimmy, he's fourteen, he went to the mall today by himself for the first time. We haven't heard from him."

"Ah," said the woman.

"We wondered if there was any information. We thought they might have released a list or something. They might know who had escaped and where they were."

"He's small for his age," said Mrs. Girardi. "I never let him go alone, but he was so insistent that he wanted to get his shopping done early."

"Gosh," the woman, a volunteer from an upscale suburb, said, "that's a tough one. But no, I'm sorry, they haven't released any information or names. We just really got set up a little while ago, and we're really here to deal with seriously hurt people if and when there's a battle and people need fast medical help. I can't help you. I can get you a cookie and a juice. Does that interest you?"

"No, ma'am. Thank you very much."

"You might try the media tent. It's where all the reporters and TV people are. That's probably where they'd release information."

"Thank you," said Mrs. Girardi. "You've been very kind."

T he Geeks had spoken. That is, the first Behavioral Sciences report had come in, BeSci being the forensic psychology unit of the Bureau tasked with inferring personality of perpetrator from evidence, originally begun in response to various colorful serial killers of depraved sexual impulse, then glorified in novel, film, and TV. However, despite their glory, the boys seldom got out of the office, a bunker in a nondescript building on the FBI campus at Quantico. Since their duty was basically riding the net 24/7, putting together personalities from what they uncovered, and then offering their work product to whomever was interested, and not many were, they were known as the Geeks. They looked mostly like the excitable guys who try and sell you televisions at RealDeal.

"It's a very interesting set of attributes," said Kemp to his second in command as they both looked at the document just e-mailed to them. "The Geeks point out that he's clearly got intimate familiarity with this mall, which, after all, isn't just any mall. That means he's worked here, he knows it forwards and backwards, and this thing began as a fantasy that became a temptation so overwhelming he couldn't resist it. It's probably been at the core of his secret life for three or four years now."

"If that's the core, I think we can assume further," said number two Jake Webley, "he doesn't have a real life. So I'm seeing some techno-nerd full of resentments and grudges, working alone in a little corner of the mall, probably convinced that no one gets how special he is."

"Very good," said Kemp. "So we have to find that guy. He's probably been fired or he has a record of near firings, disciplinary problems, and everybody says, 'Joey, you're so smart, why on earth can't you get along?' and they don't get that the reason he can't get along is that Joey's so smart."

"Agh," said Webley, who'd seen that dynamic in play more than a few times. "So our first move is to begin to search the records for that profile. I will get teams in contact with every corporate HQ of all shops who—"

"Wait," said Kemp. "There's more."

"There's always more," said Webley.

"Ain't it the truth? Okay, he's got computer chops and has been able to take command of the mall security protocols. That means he's penetrated several layers of obstacles, evaded several firewalls, avoided setting off countermeasures, all in all a world-class job of hacking, perhaps on a WikiLeaks level."

"I hope our geniuses are smart enough to fight him. I hate the smart ones," said Webley, "they make all the trouble in the world. They get so teched-up they think they're supermen and we normal one-thirty-IQ drones have to clean up after them."

Both men, all geared up in their combat style

and decorated with automatic weapons and tear gas grenades, huddled a hundred or so feet from the big state police Incident Command trailer in their own recently arrived HQ, a smallish commo van, which put them in private contact with the Bureau and its assets.

"Okay," Kemp said, "add to the profile a dense immersion in computer science. There must be twenty computer or computer game shops in the mall. They must employ a hundred bitter grinds. Maybe one of those guys got fired or disciplined or lost his girlfriend or something. And one of his buddies would know that. And that would lead us to him, and when we know who he is, we'll have leverage of some sort on him."

"I will inform our teams."

"And yet, the Geeks also point out that despite his brilliance, he's got some odd, perhaps revealing gaps in his knowledge. Even, possibly, subtler strategy. I'm talking about the phones."

"It is strange. He could but he hasn't cut off the cell phone usage in his little empire."

"So . . . did he not do it because he's stupid and didn't think of it? Unlikely. Did he not do it because he doesn't know how to do it? It's pretty easy, actually. All you have to do is override the frequency with white noise and you could do that with a microwave oven. Or did he not do it because he knew that a major thing like this is going to produce megamultigazillion phone calls and he thought that would impact our communications big-time? And maybe he also wanted all the bad information, the chaff, that would produce?"

"Good question."

"Then there's the power," said Webley, clearly on a riff, leaping through mental gymnastics with super agility, seeing things clearly for the first time. "He must have shut it down in the security office when he iced the place. But he left the main lines on. We haven't shut 'em down because it'll terrify the hostages. But we can shut 'em down easily, plus, maybe we'll want to do that as a prelude to an assault."

"Doesn't this mall have an emergency generator?"

"It does, on the roof," said Webley. "Now the issue is, what does he know about power? Has he anticipated action in the dark? Do they have night vision? If so, and we think we're all state-of-the-art with our night goggles, we could be walking into a killer ambush. Or has it just not crossed his mind? Or maybe he's aware of that vulnerability and the vulnerability of the emergency generator. We can shut down the power and light in thirty seconds, or so we think. But this guy has tech chops, this guy has the profile of a bomber. He likes to express himself through his mastery of tech. I'm surprised he hasn't planted explosives. The little fucks at Columbine did, maybe it's the same mentality. When we go to blow the emergency gen, it may be booby-trapped. Maybe we ought to get a team on that now."

"Good idea. Make it happen."

"I will. But what I'm seeing doesn't sound like a terrorist of the turban-wearing, Koran-spouting kind. You know, *that* guy. Nothing in this whatsoever suggests Islam or international terrorism. Despite the reports of the scarves. Fuck, anybody can buy those scarves mail order. You see 'em on chicks these days. No, I see another guy: some twisted computer freak with a hard-on against authority," said Webley.

"I agree. And yet—"

"And yet?"

"And yet there's still another component that doesn't really fit with this first diagram," said Kemp, as if it was his turn to be the brilliant one. "What is wrong with the picture? I'll tell you: how does this guy, bitter techie, the IT man from hell, how does *he* of all people round up hard-core gunmen and send them down hallways machine-gunning little girls?"

"Good question."

"He needs manpower, firepower, fire-and-move small-unit training, communications setup, all the sorts of things a Green Beret or some kind of SEAL pro could handle. Not the president of the chess club who's angry because he got fired from Computers-R-Us."

"So maybe it's a partnership. Two of 'em. The bright kid, somehow the seasoned combat operator. Highly unlikely, I know."

"Those aren't types that hang together, no way."

"Okay," said Kemp, "maybe you ought to put people in DC on professional soldiers, contractors, Graywolf vets, ex-Berets, or SEALs in the greater Minneapolis area. Also, maybe get somebody local digging into very smart but screwed-up kids. Arsonists, bomb threateners, maybe commies or socialists, you know, 'activists' they call them. I'm thinking University of Minnesota would be a good place to start looking, plus if there are any 'gifted and talented' high schools in the area, and I'm guessing there are."

"I'll get right on it," said Webley. "If we could find a convergence, we might find our guy, or our guys."

"I'll bring this to Obobo. Maybe he's got state

police investigators to toss in, plus we ought to be able to get metros from Saint Paul and Minneapolis."

"That's a good idea, Will," said Webley. "But the thing is, even if we figure out who is doing this, how does that help us stop him? I mean, if we put his crying mommy on the bullhorn, it could just as easily set him off as break him down."

"I know," said Kemp disconsolately. "I have a terrible feeling we're going to lose a lot more civilians on this one and I don't think there's a goddamn thing we can do about it."

McElroy found something. He found it by tracing with his fingers around the joinery of glass to stucco of the entire loop of lower Lake Michigan, from Milwaukee, past Chicago and Gary, on up into Michigan, halfway to Canada. It was a subtle thing, a sort of give in the surface as though the stucco wasn't quite set.

He pulled out his SureFire, put a bright beam on it, and decided that what he saw revealed under the harshness of the illumination was a subtly different coloration in the stucco, the concrete, the whatever it was that comprised the window well. Next he took out the wicked long Spyderco he carried clipped into his thigh cargo pocket, flicked it open to reveal a blade bad enough for killing, for getting deep into blood-bearing organs if the need arose. The need was not present now, but the sharpness of point and blade certainly looked promising, and he set at the patch of whatever it was and began to chip and dig away. The surface yielded swiftly, and McElroy realized that this zone here must have been somehow damaged, water damage maybe, a broken pipe or something, maybe a lightning strike, but anyway the mall's engineering staff had done a quick repair, not with hard-set concrete or whatever but with putty, and had then painted over it. A cheap repair, cost-saving—the recession, remember.

That's what he wanted. Just what the doctor ordered, he thought, and began to dig aggressively, soon revealing the heavy metal of the window frame itself. Couldn't get through that with a knife blade, of course, but beneath it, more of the soft stuff, and he was so heated with energy over the enormity of his discovery, he worked with renewed dedication, feeling himself a Superman. The sniper god had answered his prayer.

He lost track of time, but it seemed to be only seconds. In that period he scooped out an actual channel through the material, being sure as he dug to draw the stuff toward him so that debris didn't fall upon the crowd and the gunmen five stories below. But it was gloppy, somehow, and the moisture provided an adhesive factor; the knife scraped off not particles of dust but gobbets of mucus, clay, something unpleasant.

It wasn't much, but he had opened an oblong gap alongside a section of the steel frame of the sky light. He peered through it, and no glass obstructed his view. He fished out his binocs and saw what he could see, now jacked up by an optical factor of ten.

He had an angle onto a few feet of major corridor leading to the balcony overlooking the amusement park, about two hundred feet away at roughly 135 degrees. Not a lot of range, not a lot of elevation or windage, but he had the view into one of the corridors—Colorado, it had to be, based on his familiarity with the place—with nothing but air between him and his theoretical target. Could he get a shot? That was the first issue, and it had to be solved before What would the target be? even came up.

He picked the rifle up, eased the suppressor through the hole he'd opened, found a shooting position, his spotweld, and went to the scope and saw . . . nothing.

Goddamn.

There was clearance for the muzzle, but the scope was mounted higher than the muzzle by about an inch and it looked squarely into the metal frame.

He began to grind downward, trying to torque the suppressor deeper into the putty to lower the muzzle another inch or so, which would afford him the vantage of the Leupold tactical 10× he carried.

Nah. Couldn't get enough leverage. He withdrew the rifle, went back to the knife. He hoped he didn't have to cut any throats or cut open any tin cans, because he was blunting the crap out of the murderous sharpness of the blade, but he could afford a new knife.

Ugh. He ground, he scraped, he rubbed, he spit, he thought about pissing, anything to wear down the resistance of what opposed him, for it seemed he was beyond putty now and fighting the higher tensile strength of something hardened. It seemed to take hours, he felt the sweat running down his sides, he felt the ache in his wrists and fingers from the steady pressure he was applying to the structure through the medium of the blade.

He sat back at last, and it seemed he'd opened a loophole in the building material under the frame of the window. Would it be enough? Was he done?

He reacquired the rifle, repeated the shoulder-ing and inserting process, tried to gauge how far he'd come, how far he'd have to go, and finally peeked through the scope and saw lightness, blur, what-ever, realized he was focused at two hundred yards and this was much shorter, just seventy-five, and his finger flew to the focus knob, and he found himself staring with surprise into the face of a terrorist edg-ing down the corridor. He looked up, through the window, and confirmed. It was a man, stealing his way toward the balcony, and that was an AK in his grip, his head was blanketed in an Arabic tribal scarf, and a boom microphone came around to cover his lips from earphones inside the headgear.

McElroy went back to scope and saw the face quad-risected by the four pie slices of scope upon which the reticle was centered. He had the kill shot with his sup-pressor. He had to get the okay to shoot.

Amazingly, the guy looked not Arabic at all but sort of Chinese or something.

It was Webley again, Kemp's second in command, and this time he'd come up almost secretly to Kemp. He spoke in a whisper.

"One of our guys on the roof has managed to bore through a soft spot under the frame of the win-dow. He has a target."

"Tango?" asked Kemp.

"Affirmative. Dead center, moving down the hall-way. One guy, isolated, AK-74, don't know what he's doing up there. My shooter is suppressed, he's on him now, can take him down quietly, the others won't know."

"Interesting," said Kemp.

"Will, we have to take this guy."

"We ought to clear it with Obobo."

"He'll say no. I guarantee you, you know it, I know it. He's risk-averse, force-averse, kill-averse. I don't know what he's doing in this line of work."

"Jake, keep it down. You don't know who's listening."

"Will, let us take this guy. It's one less to deal with. Obobo doesn't need to know. It's our sniper, our operation, we have to take this chance."

Everything in Kemp warned him to say no, which is why he himself was surprised when he said, "Greenlight him. Drop the fucker hard."

"Sniper Five, cleared to engage," McElroy heard.

"Roger wilco," said McElroy, trying to fight the spasm of elation that it had finally come, the clearance to make the kill, the order he'd been waiting for his whole life. He almost pulled hard at that second but . . .

Some sniper wisdom from somewhere halted him, maybe the sniper god reaching down to calm him. He'd been in position too long, his body discipline was breaking down, the whole goddamn thing was pretty shaky because he wasn't set up on something to take the weight, the rifle wasn't on its bipod, he didn't have a bag or a tight left arm under the buttstock to eat up the tremble. This was all fucked up and nobody in sniper school had ever said a thing about an improvised position like this.

He stood half hunching, all weight centered on the small of his back, which was beginning to object. His legs were slightly spread but he couldn't lock his knees and instead had to keep them precisely folded to stay on target. He supported the rifle entirely on the strength of his arms, which deadened his trigger finger and sent telegrams of pain to wrists and gripping hands. The yips had begun to build, little random tremors that could come from nowhere and blow the shot he'd made ten thousand times. He stepped back, eased the rifle down, took a deep breath of cool air, felt it soothe his lungs and his dried throat, felt the oxygen send a squirt of strength to his much-troubled and overworked limbs, and he willed himself back together again.

He went into his hunch, drawing the rifle up, knowing that he wouldn't want to spend too much time on target but break the trigger at the first sight picture. He torqued his elbows inward even as his trigger finger snapped the safety forward, making him hot, good to go, ready to rock. He found the spotweld, watched the sight picture clarify, noted that his guy had moved just a bit and was possibly a foot closer to his objective—which had to be the balcony overlooking the hostages—and felt a little oddness.

Why was he so cautious? Why was he not striding about like he owned the place? Why was he kind of Asian?

McElroy had no answers.

But on the other hand: *He has an AK. He is dressed in the tribal headdress of Islamic, specifically Arab, persuasion. He has a throat mike, a pistol, a knife, as had all the others McElroy'd seen. He was a terrorist, he had to be, the only explanation that made sense.*

Kill him, he thought, *kill him quick before the yips break you down again.*

He made the slight adjustment to drop the muzzle to account for the slight forward progress of the man, felt the trigger strut against the softest push of his finger just exactly as the four right angles of the reticle settled on the blank of the forehead, and beheld the perfection.

The rifle fired itself.

First person shooter at its ultimate. First person shooter, for real. First person shooter, the logical destination. First person shooter, the end of the road.

He watched on number seven, the big screen. He knew he should be watching the other screens, should be scanning this corridor and that stairwell for all the signs of disturbance, for possible threat, for danger, for sloppiness on the part of the kids, but he could not stop watching.

The rifles, unnoticed by their users, had miniaturized vidcams clamped to the barrel with some fixture from GG&G or Bravo Company or LaRue Tactical just behind the muzzle, and each sent a streaming vid feed to him at his headquarters, via the mall's Wi-Fi network, and came up on the big screens adjacent to the wall that displayed his intercept of the security cam data. Images, images everywhere on the walls of this dark back room, which was filled with screenglow, turning everything a translucent gray white, yet more surrealism for this most surreal of enterprises.

The guncam imagery, of course, was sent to and recorded on the 6 TB memory card, but he was still able to hit replay at the local level and watch a designated sequence over and over again.

So now he watched number seven, for about the fourteenth time. The gunman was Maahir, the oldest and most reliable, the killer of Santa Claus. It took a while for the video to settle down, but even as the muzzle prodded the arbitrarily selected five and pried them out of the crowd in a dazzle of near-abstract shapes and black-white-gray imagery, certain lucid visions still arrived: the look in the eyes of the woman, the sullen downcast of the face of the old man, the simple dullness of the uncomprehending teenager. Then it all went to blur again as the gunman walked them to the cleared space, got them on their knees. They hadn't yet figured what was going to happen because of course it was so outside their imagination. This kind of thing, this wantonness, this jihadi contempt for life, it hadn't yet come to America. Oh, sure, 2,900 at the Trade Center, but those were meaningless numbers. The deaths of these five would be far more terrible and would live forever in the Western imagination when the data got into the world blogosphere. But that was still a few days off.

Okay, now. Five kneelers, hands at their sides. Maahir has settled down, the gun muzzle isn't flappity-flapping all over the joint, reducing the imagery to a smear of gaudy electrons, and the tiny camera peers down from its forearm mount, seeing the muzzle as a black prong in the upper right hand of the screen, eternally fixed in the image.

The woman is first. The camera closes on the back of her head as he presses the muzzle almost to her skull. She has no idea she's about to enter history and sits placidly awaiting a deliverance that isn't to be. Flash, jump, blur, a haze of smoke, and the image is still again and fills with light as she topples forward, twisted slightly, instantly extinct. With animal death comes the end of body discipline, as all the muscles let go at once and she lunges forward like a felled building, straight into the floor, not much damage visible because the bullet passed through hair, burning it, pushing it aside, but still hiding the fragility of the skull.

As the muzzle sweeps to the next in line, his eyes shoot back to the gunman, laced with bulgy fear. Flash, jump, blur, haze, stability. He topples sideways, out of the frame. The next is the younger woman, who appears to be knit up in desperate prayer, all bunched up, her jaw vibrating as she uncorks the various afterlife mantras and deity ass kissing that constitute formal address to the supreme, then flash, jump, blur, haze, stability. An eccentricity. She does not fall immediately but for some reason remains intact and upward for another second or so, then seems to melt from within, as if her core has turned liquid and imploded downward.

The fourth is the older man, who struggles in his anger to rise and fight, so we get a double jolt, the first from Maahir tomahawking him with the gun barrel to drive him back to his knees in pain, and then the flash, jump, blur, and haze of the shot itself, a disappointment because it hits him above the ear, disappearing again in hair.

The last is better, the teen, actually closer to a child. Small, frail skull. Thirteen-, fourteen-year-old boy, he thinks. Flash, jump, blur, haze, but the head detonates, becoming in an instant too swift to even record something called not-head, or unhead, a kind of broken, empty vessel, departed entirely from assumptions of human anatomy. It's deflated, emptied, eviscerated, but the boy's bones are so light and his musculature so unimposing that he falls to earth almost insignificantly.

Maahir steps back from his work and casually sweeps the carnage he has unleashed. Five bodies shorn of dignity on the floor in the cruel black/white videography of the guncam. Maahir walks around them, muzzle on them in case he needs to fire another shot, but all are quite dead in their loose-knit positions, and beyond them, on the pavement, a kind of communal blood pool has formed, fed by five tributaries.

In the screen room, Andrew toggles a button on his keyboard and restores the live-feed guncam data, which has, he has to admit, turned out to be rather useless except in special conditions, such as the one he's just witnessed. It's mostly blurs of floors, as the boys sweep this way and that, and occasionally you get a view of the cowed hostages sitting in misery and terror or a look down some deserted corridor as the boys are sent out on various errands.

He looks at his watch. It's almost time.

It was like being hit in the head by a snow shovel. The shock was more disconcerting than the pain, as the world went to crazed fractionality, his memory purged, the eternal sensation best described as *What the fuck?* commandeered his entire mind, and it seemed to take minutes before clarity finally restored itself, to the effect that *I've just been shot in the head.* The next logical question, *Why am I not dead?* somehow didn't follow. Instead, his knees gone all Jell-O-y, Ray threw himself back in primal panic and slipped into some kind of notch in the wall, where he shared a few square feet with a water fountain.

He fought for cognizance. First he remembered who he was, then he remembered squeezing Lisa Fong's left tit thirty-one years ago in the cloakroom of the Subic Bay Naval Base Elementary School No. 2, then he remembered that he was in a shopping mall taken over by the Huns, and only then did it occur to him that a sniper was shooting at him! *At him!* The nerve of some people! He sucked in his chest, just in case an inch or so of it extended beyond the edge of his little water fountain niche and invited another shot. But he also realized he was trapped.

He could risk a run but even now the guy was on

him from wherever, his reticle greedily massaging the edge of wall that shielded Ray from death. He tried to think: Can these guys have brought snipers along and salted them all over the mall in case there's some movement from the people hiding in the stores on the upper floors? But that seemed a little far-fetched. Yes, possible, but . . . also insane and therefore unlikely.

So, who the fuck was shooting at him? And why did he miss?

It didn't take a genius to make the next leap. Sure, it was a law enforcement sniper, maybe directly across the atrium, on the other second-floor expanse of balcony, maybe a part of a team the cops had somehow gotten into the mall who were even now moving into position for the assault. He's on his scope, he sees a guy with an AK and a head scarf and he figures he's got a target, he gets his authorization (or maybe not?). And then he puts a bullet in Ray's head, only for some reason, he misses.

Fuck you, Jack, Ray thought.

But telling Jack to fuck himself did nothing to solve his immediate problem. And the more he thought about it, the more he realized the guy probably wasn't across the way or even higher, on the third or fourth levels, but even higher than that. He had to be firing through or from the skylight. If he'd been right on Ray, he couldn't have missed, but the higher he was, the more extreme the angle was. If you're shooting downhill, the rule was you always hold low because the bullet's point of impact will be higher. He'd forgotten while putting the hairs on Ray's forehead, and the bullet had instead hit high, blitzing Ray's head right through the scarf and the crew cut, spilling red but not gray stuff. But fuck, it hurt.

Ray could feel blood sliding down through his hair. His ears rang still and he couldn't stop shaking. Man, that was a close sucker, that was as close as close gets without death being involved.

He tried to work out a move. Hmm, maybe a feint, to draw a shot, then a quick dash during the cocking sequence. But suppose Jack isn't shooting a bolt gun but is on some state-of-the-art semiauto rig, so the gun reloads itself in a one-hundredth of a second, and after his feint Ray steps out and catches the spine breaker.

The bastard has me dead-zero, he thought.

"Sniper Five, Sniper Five, come in," McElroy heard through his earphones.

Shit!

"Sniper Five, have you engaged, Sniper Five? Goddammit, McElroy, what the fuck is going on?"

McElroy recognized the voice of his immediate supervisor. He couldn't hide anymore.

"I have engaged," he said. "One shot."

"Can you confirm a kill?"

"Uh—"

"Oh, fuck, McElroy, you missed? Jesus Christ, I am going to have your ass for sure."

"No, I hit him, I saw his scarf blow up as the bullet impacted in the rear quadrant of the head, but he didn't prone out. I think I damaged him badly, but he slipped back in this niche in the wall. That's where he is now."

"You have him zeroed."

Did he ever, even if the weight was racking him. He'd now been in this awkward half-hunch off-hand standing for a good seven minutes, sweat was everywhere on him despite the forty-degree temp, the small of his back felt like it had taken the bullet, his arms and wrists were fighting those oncoming yips, and he kept squirming a little this way and that to find a more comfortable position even as the crosshairs had begun to widen in their tremble circle. He wasn't sure how much longer he could hold it and still have the confidence to squeeze one off if the guy made a sudden move.

On the other hand, he did not want to lose this. *I will not let up. I am strong enough. I will stay on this guy no matter what.*

"I have him zeroed," he said.

"Sitrep?"

"He's stuck in there. He's out of the fight. I'm guessing he's bleeding out. He'll be gone soon. You know, brain shots aren't always instantaneous, sometimes not even fatal. But he's not going to do much more today, that I guarantee you."

"Yeah, but while you're on him, who's on your window, sending us dope?"

"There is no dope, nothing's happening."

"You stay on him for a little while longer, but if I have to, I'm pulling you off and sending you back to general intelligence reporting."

"I will get him for you," said McElroy, thinking, *I will get him for me.*

The phone vibrated. Great. Trapped by a sniper, shot in the head, men with guns all over the joint, and the phone vibes.

Somehow Ray got the little rectangle of plastic genius out of his pocket, careful not to extend an elbow past the edge of the niche and invite a bullet into it, slid the answer icon to the right, and saw Molly's name announced as the caller.

"Are you all right?" she asked.

"Not really," he said. "Sort of stuck here."

"I heard from my sister. Ray, she's in with the hostages. My mother too."

"I can't do anything for them now."

"Ray, what should I tell her?"

"If there's an assault, get down. Don't run. Most of the firing will be at waist to chest level or higher. If they're down, they'll be much safer. Crawl slowly away from the area but be willing to play dead at any second. It'll be over quickly. There'll be a lot of firing, a lot of confusion, and they should be as innocuous as possible. If they panic and run, someone may target them as movers, our guys, their guys."

"Okay, I'll tell her."

"Did those kids get there?"

"Yes, the place is now crawling with them. All the women are helping. That day care girl is something."

"She'd make a hell of a Marine. Meanwhile, I've just had an idea. I have to get off the phone."

"Okay. Be careful."

Tell *him,* Ray thought.

But now that he had the phone out, he went quickly to his contacts screen and touched the call icon for the one man who might be able to help him, the strange, remote, laconic guy who was, they had both so recently learned, his biological father.

"This is Swagger," came the message. "Leave a number and maybe I'll call you back. But I probably won't."

Ha ha. Great for the dry humor the old bastard was known for, almost as much as his shooting, but it did his son no good now.

Ray swept his contacts and at last came upon another possibility.

Nick Memphis, FBI, the entry read.

Only a few people had his private number, so Nick was somewhat surprised to feel the phone tingling in his jacket. He picked it open, saw Ray's number, thought it odd that the man should be calling him at all, particularly now, today.

"Cruz, how are you? Long time no hear, nice to get a call. Actually, Ray, I'm kind of busy—"

"I am too. I'm betting you're watching reports come in of a terrorist deal in Minnesota. Well, I'm in the middle of it."

Memphis was stunned. He was indeed sitting in the FBI Incident Command Center in the Hoover Building in DC, actually not doing much except pitching in his comments on dealing not with the gunmen but with the phenomenon known as Douglas Obobo, a tricky character. On another floor, theoretically brilliant people on computer terminals tried to hack into the closed-off mall system; up here, others worked the phones, trying desperately to find some clue as to who was behind this, and others ran logistics, helping coordinate the problems by which law enforcement units continued to pour into Indian Falls, particularly the now airborne FBI HRT from Quantico, while still others were on the phone constantly to Will Kemp, the SAIC in Minnesota, giving him advice and handling his inquiries while also monitoring the situation and evaluating his performance.

Ray explained what was happening to him.

"Jesus," said Nick, thinking instantly how ugly a fate it would be for Cruz, after his legendary service, to get nailed by an FBI sniper in a bullshit friendly-fire incident.

He looked over, saw Ron Fields, head of the FBI's sniper school and a leading tactical guru within the institution, on the phone.

"Okay," he said. "Cruz, you stay put. I'm going to try and get you out of the kill zone."

He went over and said, "Ronnie, I have a situation."

Fields had the usual deadpan SWAT response to anything, even the fact that a Marine sniper was being targeted by an FBI sniper inside a terrorist takeover of a replica of America in the heart of the actual America on prime-time televison and that someone had shot Santa Claus. If anything in the fix seemed ironic or ridiculous or even unfortunate, he didn't register it. He solved it. He nodded, pushed some buttons, and handed a hardwired receiver to Nick, saying, "Webley, Kemp's number two, on site and helping Kemp."

"Webley," came a voice. "Webley, this is Nick Memphis."

"Yes, Mr. Memphis."

Nick heard Webley pop to immediately, aware that he was on the phone with a big DC player, probably for the first time in his life.

"Webley, you have snipers on the roof?"

"Yes sir," answered Webley. "One of them is engaging even as we—"

"That's the problem," said Nick. "The guy he's shooting at is a good guy. Ex-Marine, sniper himself. Call him off."

"Yes sir."

"And put me on the line."

"Yes sir."

Nick listened as someone did more connecting, and heard in a few seconds, "Sniper Five, this is Command. Disengage, that is an order, disengage."

"Goddammit, I have him. He's going to break out of there and I will nail him—"

"Sniper Five, I am advised you are firing on a friendly."

"What? He has an AK and a head scarf and—"

"Sniper Five, this is Assistant Director Memphis in DC. The man you are firing on is an ex-Marine with sniper experience himself. Do not engage. He could be our asset inside."

"Can he signal? Three fingers?"

Nick put down the phone, picked up his cell.

"Ray, hold out three fingers. I've got the guy on the line, actually."

"He's not some fucking kid who'll shoot 'em off, is he?"

"He sounds excited, yes, but he's under control."

There was a pause.

Then Sniper Five said, "I have acknowledgment. I see three. I am stepping down."

"Good, good," said Webley.

"Okay, Ray, you're clear now. At least Sniper Five won't be—"

It seemed to occur to all of them at once, and the jabber was impenetrable until finally all shut up and let Nick say what all had figured out.

"Webley, I'm going to give you Ray's number. His name is Ray Cruz, twenty-two years USMC, maybe their number one sniper, five tours in the sand, great, great operator. I don't know what he's doing there, but he's there and we're fools if we don't use him. Have Sniper Five contact him. Maybe the two of them can work together and deal with these guys in a way no one else is in position to."

"Got you, AD. Wilco."

Nick went back to Ray.

"The guy on the roof is going to call you. Sniper Five, don't know his name, but maybe you and he can see things we can't and help us."

"Got it," said Ray, clicking off to wait.

"Sir," said Webley, "should I alert SAIC Kemp about this contact?"

"You know Kemp, I don't. You make the call."

"Ah . . . he's not too anxious to get heavy into this one. It looks like it's going down bad for all involved and there could be big repercussions."

The Bureau culture. It was, as often as not, the true enemy. SAs learned that the route to promotion and retirement plus lucrative security industry positions afterward was a spotless run through their twenty years on the street, and that had the inevitable effect of drying out initiative. Nobody wanted to make the big mistake and get creamed. And no one seemed to notice that Nick had mavericked himself aloft, but even Nick knew he was the exception and that his connection to the even more maverick Bob Lee Swagger had been a fantastic aid. So these guys always played it cautious, and somehow career considerations came into play in command decisions in ways that couldn't be anticipated. It was nobody's fault, it was the culture.

So Nick said, "You know, he's got a lot on his mind, Webley. And I don't want him trying to conceal anything from Obobo. So until we see how this is going to work out, we'll keep it to ourselves, okay? If Ray moves, he may have to move fast, and I don't want him fighting Bureau culture and Command doubt among his many enemies."

"I am on board, sir," said Webley.

Nothing scared Mom. Her wrinkled old face had knitted up tight and now showed nothing but fighting rage. And she knew a little about fighting rage: she'd been born into the tribal mountain zones of a country that had been destroyed, into a war culture, and had grown up to the smell of aviation fuel from the coming and going of the American helicopters, the fluttery lights of illumination flares parachuting down outside the wire in the night, the far-off and sometimes not so far-off popping of small-arms fire. She knew how to fieldstrip both an AK-47 and a carbine. She knew how to lay a mine, cut a man's throat, read sign, and stay dead still when the northerners, in their ridiculous uniforms (were they monkeys? she thought they looked like monkeys) stalked her. She'd lost three brothers by the time she was fifteen, and her father, Gua-Mo Chan, had worked with a variety of young American commandos on missions against the same hated northerners. She married at seventeen to a fighter named Jang, the bravest of the brave. Then one day he didn't come back, and so she mourned for a year and a day, and at eighteen married another fighter, her current husband, Dang Yan, called Danny, now a travel agency owner on Central Avenue in Saint Paul.

She remembered the day when the world ended, and it was foretold that the northerners would win.

The Americans were not cruel; they did not abandon their loyal allies. But they were not gentle either, and in truth, what followed next was a mess coming close in its sloppiness to a tragedy. In a confusion of camps and helicopters and ships and more camps, she ended up with those of her family who still survived in the belly of a cold, far city. She began a new life and raised five daughters and nothing ever scared her.

This filth didn't scare her. Boys with guns, black boys with guns, just like the ones you sometimes saw in Saint Paul, with no respect for ancestors, for family or clan, no warrior ethic, not even an ability to read or write. They were nothing. She spat on creatures so low.

What scared her was her daughter Sally, who sat next to her under the blaze of windows in the roof high above, in an ocean of victims, somewhat like the camps where she had spent too many months. They sat, hands folded on heads, driven here by the panic of the crowd at the gunfire. Some had already died. Some were crying, some were breaking down, some sat with the dullness of the soon-to-be-dead, most prayed for deliverance or tried to hush frightened children, but all of them just hoped not to be noticed.

But someone had noticed Sally, Mom saw. He was the shooter, the one who'd killed the five. He was maybe a little bigger than the others, and there was something surly about him. He alone was—the Hmong word was *khav,* meaning "proud" or possibly "self-important," although she didn't know English well at all, even after these many years—in the way he carried his weapon with a certain deliberate coolness and disdain. The other filth saw nothing. Their eyes were blank, they had no appreciation for what lay in front of them, as if other lives had no meaning and other places had none either. They had no depth. Whatever had formed them—war, poverty, whatever—it had left them empty, incapable of paying attention to or feeling anything. They would take what was before them, life or death, beauty or ugliness, fate or luck, and do what they had been instructed. But they would not select. They would not consider, they did not winnow, they did not decide. This one had decided.

Sally, her youngest, was a fragrant blossom on a spring day, before the wet season arrived. She smelled of delicacy, sweetness, not-yet-ripeness. She was too young to have developed but you could tell from the way men looked at her that she had a rare, almost ethereal beauty. Molly, the eldest, so smart, went away to school and now was a lawyer for the Americans in their capital; Annie had married a Japanese dentist with a practice in the suburbs; Ginger was a softball coach and nationally ranked player who had almost made the Olympics and might still; and Jeannie was in first-year med at Bloomington. But Sally, a latecomer, a final surprise from God, was the baby of the family, with ears of porcelain and a perfect little nose and bright eyes and thick, lustrous hair gathered in a ponytail. She was her mother's prize.

But he had noticed her. She sat beside Mom, huddling, trying to comfort both Mom and herself. She wore Ugg boots in suede, black tights, a little blue jean skirt, a hoodie sweatshirt with ST. PAUL TRINITY stenciled on it, and a blue jean jacket, much too light for the weather, though Sally was a native Minnesotan, far hardier than her tropically raised mom, and normally shrugged off the cold, like the white people did.

The crowd parted as he bullied his way to them. About ten feet away, he stopped, bent down, and snatched up a woman's purse roughly. Opening it, he grabbed the wallet and pulled out a wad of bills. Then he tossed the purse and strode forcefully to Sally through the crowd of cowed hostages. He stood above her, looking down on her imperially, like the conqueror he believed himself to be. He smiled, showing broad white teeth. Then he took a step to Mom, bent down, and said, "I have no goats. Here, take this," and he threw the money at her.

"I buy her from you. Now she is mine. She will be my bride this day." He laughed heartily. Then he reached down, forced his hand inside her sweatshirt and bra, and enjoyed a fondle of her small left breast. Mom saw the pain and shame cross her daughter's face and the girl, violated, seemed to diminish before her. The large man laughed, winked at Mom, and stomped away.

Mom watched him go. She knew what she must do. She reached back, over a low stone arrangement that separated grass from garden in this mock outdoors, and surreptitiously, she snatched up a fistful of black soil. She dumped it into her purse. Then she did it again and again and again.

It seemed to take forever, setting up the phone connections, finding a special agent fluent in German, getting numbers from someone at a Siemens branch in New York, reaching finally a Siemens PR gal in Stuttgart, then finally a vice president, getting an authenticating call from the German Federal Police (they were so goddamned careful!), and now finally, Hans Jochim, fifty-four.

Yet it was not like talking to someone named Hans Jochim, fifty-four. It was like talking to someone named Holly Burbridge, thirty-two, who sat next to him. She was the translator and eventually the rhythms of the time lags seemed to disappear.

"Sir, I understand you were the design team leader on the MEMTAC 6.2 program that runs the SCADA system at several big malls in America."

"Well, not exactly team leader," Holly responded. "I was more of a coordinator. Policy is set by the executive branch, and, alas, vetted by marketing; then an environmental committee and a labor union committee have to file action reports, which of course must be responded to, in detail, and then there's the hearing where the arguments are made orally in front of a board composed of—"

Jesus Christ! How long would this take!

"Sir, we're in an emergency mode here. May I proceed, with all due respect, Herr Doktor Ingenieur?" the last a flourish he'd picked up from some World War II novel or something.

Grumpily—grumpiness came even into Holly's voice—Herr Jochim said, "I am not a Doktor Ingenieur, I am an Ingenieur. I may go back to Hamburg—"

"Sir, our perpetrator has taken the whole system off line and we can't penetrate. It is necessary, lives are at stake, for us to penetrate the system and regain control of the building's security system. I'm sure with your brilliance, sir, you can suggest another route in, a back door or something."

Wrong word.

"Back door!" exploded Holly in rage. "I do not forget things! I have no *back doors*. This is not a parlor game, it is one of the most sophisticated programs in the world. It controls *everything*. We wrote a million kilometers of code just for the cooling system. And—"

Neal took his headset off, waiting for the Teutonic typhoon to blow out to sea. Finally, hearing a pause, he jumped in with—

"I did not mean to imply accidental openings or sloppiness in any professional discipline. Obviously, you're smarter than I am because I can't get in and I need your help and—"

"The fire control system," said the German.

"The fire control system? It has guns?"

"No, no, as in fires, fire engines, firemen. We had to interface with another firm, very delicate business. Japanese. Very arrogant people. You cannot tell them anything."

"Can you be more specific?"

"They do have the best fire control hard- and software in the world, and they maintain their very high standard by retaining direct access to their system from Tokyo. They can monitor and troubleshoot anyplace in the world from their headquarters in Tokyo. All by nothing more sophisticated than— perhaps you have heard of this?—a telephone."

"My God," said Neal.

"Yes. Now I am going to give you a number to call and an engineer to talk to. They are very careful too, so I advise you to have your State Department run interference. You want to get into the system? This is how you get into the system."

Decisions. Obobo, with Mr. Renfro's shrewd advice, had a superb gift for making the right one. His confidence, only a little shaken by the hostility of the press conference, had reassembled itself, and now various people put various issues to him for disposition. But there were so many of them. Some could be put off or safely ignored.

Jefferson, the SWAT hotshot, wouldn't go anywhere, he was so desperate to get the nod from Obobo to go in shooting. Of course, shoot, shoot everyone, that's a good idea, a mall full of bodies with lakes of blood on the floor. But Jefferson, like other men of his ilk, was basically so obsessed he was stupid. He could be manipulated with flattery and attention and easily disposed of.

Other decisions: Should we leave food at the doors and pull back, in hopes that the gunmen, whoever they are, will take it in and distribute it? What about medical supplies, antidepressants or antianxiety drugs? Renfro agreed the answer to both: yes. Why not? The stress on the hostages must be godawful, not that anyone could do anything about it.

Then there was the pressure of the media. National correspondents were hammering Renfro for more info, and Renfro pointed out that if you let them feel like insiders, maybe they won't be so rough on you. But Renfro also knew it would be ill-considered and play to the strength of the colonel's enemies if he were seen giving one-on-ones in the crisis. So it was a thin line to be walked, and Renfro advised giving the networks brief one-on-ones but against a dynamic situation, all in standup so that it didn't have that public relations feel to it and was more cinema verité in nature. Renfro had also arranged for the colonel to suit up in tactical gear, and the man was now resplendent in a black jumpsuit with his Beretta in a midthigh tactical holster, as well as radio gear, flash-bangs, cuffs, and Danner tac boots. Now he looked the part as well.

And the frustrations! Why was he getting no meaningful intelligence? Where was the FBI on this? To get him some leverage, they had been tasked with running an investigation. They had the access to the various federal databases, and so far what had they come up with? A little something from the Geeks that Kemp had thrown at him but really constituted nothing but a big yawn, obvious stuff. So disappointing. They were supposed to set up an information central under command of a major, by which data from records, interviews of witnesses (many grabbed on the run), advice from other departments and police executives would all be collated, evaluated, prioritized, and then—the most important—brought to him, and of course it was an utter fiasco: too much information too fast, too much of it unreliable or hearsay or interpretation. So that enterprise had yet to produce anything.

Meanwhile, he was aware of the clock, spinning its inevitable way toward 6 p.m. That would make three hours since the thing had begun. Three *long* hours. Suppose the man inside shot six more people. Then he'd have to go before 7 p.m.; he couldn't stay on the outside for seven at 7 p.m., then eight at 8 p.m. Why didn't these people talk to him? Tell me what you want. Start a conversation. Let's see where we are. Nobody does something like this and then goes silent. It doesn't make any sense. He knew that if he could only start a dialogue, he could ultimately bring them to his side. That was one of his greatest gifts and it always served him well. His intellect, his humanity, his empathy, his compassion: those were his secret weapons; those would win the day.

"Sir," came another voice, one of many, and he said, "Yes, yes, what is it?" then turned, his attention caught because he saw Jefferson outside talking to a TV reporter and he didn't want to be criticized from within the command during the incident, and at the same time, he saw his PA hustling in, possibly with some new directive from the governor, and outside the window in the falling dark he saw reporters laughing and knew they were having a good one at his expense and—

"He wants to talk."

—and he himself had to go to the bathroom and he hadn't had dinner and couldn't stay sharp without food and—

"Who wants to talk?"

"Him," said the tech.

Suddenly it got very quiet.

"The fellow inside?"

"Sir, it's a call from Mall Security Command. I've verified it, it's the right number, it's from inside all right. It's from somebody who says he represents an outfit called Brigade Mumbai. He wants to talk, he says, or at six p.m. he'll kill six more people."

THREE MONTHS EARLIER

The Imam, Nadifa Aba, locked the door of his storefront mosque—Masjid Al-Taqwa—on Bedford Avenue and checked for his enemies before walking to his car.

He had many enemies. Of course the FBI, but at least they kept their distance. Then the young American black men, who thought he was a fool and mocked his dignity and laughed at his prayerfulness and liked to intimidate him with fantasy violence that ended with a blow halted an inch from his nose. When he ducked, they collapsed in laughter.

But worst of all was the Reverend Reed Hobart, of the Minnescola Avenue Baptist Church of the Redeemer, who one day decided that his God had spoken to him and it was his duty to drive the non-Christians from Minnesota. The reverend had a long history of crusades and himself was probably under FBI surveillance for links to a violent antiabortion underground, but he also had a nose for publicity and for two weeks had shown up at ten each morning for four hours of nonviolent but very loud protest outside the imam's modest mosque.

ISLAM IS THE BUNK one placard read, and GO BACK TO GOATLAND read another, and OSAMA IS TOAST, and the worst was KORAN +

MATCHES = HOME COOKIN'. To see the text desecrated like that! It filled him with rage and pain and hatred, pushing him further and further toward the violence that he felt deep in his heart. But he knew if he struck at the Reverend Hobart, with his mane of hair and his big head and his loud voice, he'd only be mocked and ridiculed. How could a believer keep his dignity in such a hellish circumstance?

But the reverend had taken the day off, and no one cursed at the imam as he walked to the car. To his right, as he passed a vacant lot, the vividly lit towers of downtown Minneapolis gleamed in the surprisingly chill August night like a nightmare. Metaphorically, of course, it was the West, hideous and tempting, all gloss, glitter, licentiousness and flesh, insolent black youth, bellowing white false holy men. He sniffed in disrespect, sending a snort of disapproving breath out into the air, purposefully not looking at the sky-line of decadence, a Babylon of infidel scum.

He was a bitter man, forty-two, tall and angular like many Somalis, with bright eyes, white teeth, cheekbones like razors, and a froth of beautiful hair. He yearned for dry heat, the solitude of the desert, for quiet brightness, for the path of God's will to be known to him, for a mission more potent than his current one, which was to enforce the Faith upon an ever-diminishing group of countrymen and observe in desolation as for every new arrival who joined, two older ones wandered off, away from the Faith, captivated by the temptation of America. Since the killing of Osama the Holy Warrior and the barbaric spectacle of celebration that ensued, the imam had been in a state of constant, fiery rage.

He shrugged, drawing his cheap coat tightly about him to keep the chill out. His circumstances might be severe but his spirit was not. He fancied himself a warrior, a mover of worlds and shaker of universes; he burned with zeal and urgency. He glanced about, checking for his FBI monitors. Sometimes they were there, sometimes they were not. Maybe they weren't even FBI, as he was on every Western terrorist watch list, mainly for his propensity to write angry essays in a small number of Somali-language community newspapers, such as his most recent, "Allah Demands Harshness, Yet Pity, in Attacking Homosexual Deviation," drawn from several Koranic sources yet given a certain modernistic oomph by the imam's relentless prose style and his merciful conclusion that the deviates should be defenestrated, not stoned. So much easier on everyone, including the transgressors, for whom he was not without compassion.

Tonight was a rare treat. Not only was the reverend blessedly absent, but as well there appeared to be no federal agents about. You could tell them because their sedans were inevitably dark in color, without American frill, and held two rather doughy-looking white men who appeared wracked with boredom. They followed at a respectful distance and sometimes they accompanied him all the way home and sometimes not, depending on who knew what indicators that suggested tonight would not be the night he blew up America.

So he had a free night. He checked his watch, saw that he still had an hour before his last prayers were expected, thought about this or that temptation—a small glass of wine, a trip through the pages of the latest *Hustler*, a rerun of the 9-11 video as Al Jazeera had reported it—but decided that tonight would be a pure and consecrated devotion.

He unlocked his Ford Tempo and climbed in, turned on the engine, waited for the moisture to clear from the windshield, and pulled into traffic, checking the mirrors to see if on either side of Bedford anybody pulled out behind him. No one did. However, in his own back seat, someone rose directly behind him and sat back, relaxed.

The imam's gut clenched. You always had this fear in America that some crazed follower of a maniac like the reverend would take it in hand to blow away Islam in the form of the imam, as if the imam himself were plotting to blow up America, although of course that *was* on his to-do list. He cursed his stupidity for not checking the back seat. He was at war, he had to be alert. He prayed to Allah that this was not his death. And then he heard an American voice say, "If you're worried about the FBI, they're not here tonight. They only come on odd-numbered days in odd-numbered months and even-numbered days in even months. On the odd months, the shift is the last twelve hours of the day, the evens the first twelve hours. It used to be 24/7 but, you know . . . budget cutbacks."

The imam swallowed drily.

"Who are you?" he asked, licking his lips. "Are you from the Reverend Hobart?"

"Not exactly."

"Who, sir? Please."

"Don't turn around. Drive to your home, the usual route. The car is bugged, but I've momentarily diverted their penetration."

"How do you know?"

"I've hacked into their computer net and examined their operating orders and their technical capacities. To get the car bugged, they hacked into the new MyFord Touch wireless connection. This lets them hear everything in the car, see out the rear window, track via GPS, turn it on and off, everything. I wrote an iPhone app to control the car and switched the FBI views to another vehicle. Currently, they're watching a soccer mom deliver her kids to practice. They think it's some kind of anomaly. So I will talk while you drive. You will park in your garage. Now listen hard and well and remember what I tell you."

"Are you of the Faith?"

"Shut up. Listen. My faith is of no importance and you would not understand it anyway. Accept my aid, consider me a messenger from your God, but for now, shut up and listen."

The imam swallowed again and kept his eyes straight ahead.

"I want to hurt them. Badly. Why? None of your beeswax, holy man. Maybe just because I love rock and roll. But I need gunmen. I want twelve Somali jihadis smuggled into Canada and held in a safe house near the border in mid-November. They should be true believers of low intelligence and profound impulses toward religious obedience. True believers, the seventy-two virgins, all that horseshit. If blooded, so much the better."

"It's impossible," said the imam.

"I told you, nothing's impossible. You have connections with half a dozen refugee organizations. As well, you have contacts with Hizbul Islam in Mogadishu, and the general will provide you what you need if you can convince him. And you will convince him."

"What is this all about?"

"America, that is, America, the Mall. You know the place? A hideous vulgarity a dozen or so miles out of town in Indian Falls. Busy, busy, busy. It will be jammed on the day after Thanksgiving. Your gunmen will unjam it."

"That's impossible."

"Nothing is impossible. I will provide weapons and access and plans. I will take over the mall security system. We will give them a lesson they will never forget to the glory of your God and mine. Your job is to get the men, hold them, and deliver them at a certain moment. The plan is not sophisticated and will require no rehearsal. These fellows will simply walk down a hallway, shooting. Then they will hold hostages for a short while. That's all. None of them will survive; it is a martyr's mission. I invite you to join me in death and glory. Together, we will punish them for their sins, and for the murder of the Holy Warrior in his bed."

"It costs money and permission. You cannot do such a thing without finances and a judgment from higher councils. We must examine to make sure such a course is correct and consider the political consequences. Ours is not simple nihilism but political policy."

"Bullshit. Listen to these rules and commit to them, or this will all go away and you will burn in your hell for eternity. No e-mails. E-mail has been penetrated. No phone calls, also penetrated. Nothing written. No Facebook or Twitter or any stupid teenaged thing that you guys always give yourself away on. Nothing amateur. There must be no physical or electronic acknowledgment of the planned event, no records. Everything recorded can be recovered. The imam himself must not deviate from his routine of the past few months except to handle communications with the great General Hassan Dahir Aweys in Somalia, solely by satellite phone, which will be provided. But he should contact no other units, no Al-Qaeda cells, nothing, as all communications must be presumed penetrated. He must never ask permission. Everything must be local and person to person, guaranteed by a handshake and mutual obedience to your faith."

The imam hardly knew what to say. Was this a dream, a phantom, a movie? But then he had an image of America, the Mall, consumed in flame, riven with blood, heaped with bodies of dogs, the smoke blowing its acrid perfume, an America blazing in the heart of middle America, and he was profoundly moved. The Holy Warrior avenged.

The imam arrived at his prosaic two-bedroom house in his prosaic neighborhood.

He pulled into his garage.

"Get out quickly, go inside, and say or write nothing. Cling exactly to your routine. Here is an envelope with ten thousand cash, to support your activities. It must never be banked because banks raise alarms. They are not on your side. Make plans to go to Somalia within the month to find and arrange for the boys. Nothing on paper, nothing by phone, nothing by e-mail. Be hard, disciplined, focused, and I will give you glory you haven't even dreamed of."

"Is this a trick? Are you an agent provocateur? Have you been sent here to gull me into a mistake? What is—"

"You want proof, is that it? You don't trust the white kid? You think I'm on some kind of prank or working for the assholes of five-oh? Hmm, what can I do to convince you?"

"You must convert to—"

"Not hardly. Oh, I know. I'll give you a nice present. That will convince you. Would you like some delicious candy? What about a gift certificate for Walmart? Possibly a new clock radio, one that goes ding-dong five times a day."

The imam said nothing in the face of such blasphemy.

"Okay, my friend. Reach down under the dashboard in front of the seat to your right. There's your present. Enjoy it in good health."

The imam thought this was another joke. But he looked and, indeed, in the darkness of the space beneath the dashboard thought he made out a shape. He bent, and his fingers closed around some kind of green plastic garbage bag. He pulled it up to the seat, feeling its four pounds of weight. He set it down, studied the drawstrings of bright yellow plastic, and pulled it open.

It was the large, florid, and quite excited head of the Reverend Reed Hobart.

"Won't that look great on the mantel?" said the boy as he slipped out the back and disappeared into the darkness. Then, suddenly, the dashboard display came alive and the radio blared.

Stones. "Paint It Black."

Ray slid the answer icon to the right and put the phone to his ear.

"This is Special Agent McElroy," he heard.

"No," he said, "it's Chucklehead McElroy. Dumbbell and dope. You ever shoot down-angle, McElroy?"

"I guess not," said McElroy.

"You have to hold low. If you hold straight on, you hit high. You owe me fifty."

"Dollars?"

"Push-ups."

"I'm a little busy now," said McElroy.

"And you're going to get busier. Put that rifle down, you're too dangerous with it. You find me isolated targets out of visual contact with their main force and I will put them down. We'll reduce their team one by one before they even notice it."

"Uh, Sergeant, that's against policy. I'd have to get some sort of higher approval on that, and to be honest, I don't think an agent has ever acted under such a wide license. It would definitely be against our policy."

"It's against *your* policy. It's not against *my* policy. My policy is stalk and kill, one-shot variety. It's what I do. It's all I do. I can shoot suppressed, so noise isn't an issue. Now I am going to move out and try and take these people down. Having you bird-dog for me from on high like my private satellite would be very helpful. Or I can do it on my own. Either way, it will happen, McElroy. You decide right now who you are with."

He heard McElroy pause and even imagined that the phone picked up the vibrations of a dry swallow. But then McElroy said, "Okay. I'm in. Nothing's happening here anyway." Then he said, "First, maybe you have some intel I can forward to Command. You got your gear from one of them, right?"

"He didn't seem to mind. Black male, age twenty-two or so. Somali, I'd guess, from what I've seen of them in Minnesota. Handsome dude, even with a broken neck. Didn't do an ID check."

"You took his stuff though. Equipment data?"

"Okay, the pistol is a Heckler and Koch P7, much battered, I'm guessing some European police department trade-in. You have to squeeze it to make it shoot, very unusual gun. The 9-mil ammo has a foreign head stamp, I don't have time to check it exactly. It looked grungy, as if it had been stored in tins for three decades. The AK is a 74, not a 47. It's overmarked WTI, Laredo, Texas. Looks to be a Bulgarian or Romanian clone, I can't really read the serial number. The ammo is 5.45×39, which is the Eastbloc variant on 5.56 NATO. Small, lethal, fast, 50–60-grain round, looks surplus too, no recognizable head stamp, crappy OD steel case, red band at base of bullet, copper gilding. The mags are sort of plum-orange color, and I saw that shade all over the Mideast and Afghanistan, so I'm guessing Eastbloc junk too. The commo shit is Radio Shack, low-end. The knife was some kind of surplus AK bayonet. The whole thing could have been supported out of some shit-city surplus store, so maybe that's a place for you to look."

"Got it. I'll get this to Command, we can get ATF hacking on it."

"You do that. Meanwhile, I'm on the stalk. The more we kill, the easier any kind of assault will be when the heavy hitters go in. And when that happens, I can provide distracting fire and then suppressive if they have to maneuver. You're my spotter, McElroy, clear on that?"

"Yes sir," said McElroy.

"Good. Now find me targets."

McElroy closed up the phone and pressed his radio. He got Webley's assistant on the wave and fed him the weapon info he had just acquired. Then he signed off, eased over the edge of Lake Michigan, and went to work through his binoculars. Nothing much had changed one hundred feet below. From his nine-zero-degree perspective, he could see a mass of humanity gathered on the walkways of the amusement park, shaded here and there by the foliage of trees, plastic or real unknown. Santa, still dead, still on his throne. Why didn't somebody throw a blanket over the guy? The people were crowded together so tightly it was hard to make out the individual from the herd. Most were on their haunches, some still with hands on head or behind necks, looking nowhere except straight ahead. Many were trying to talk inconspicuously on their cell phones. On their outskirts he could make out the more vigorous movements of the gunmen, who strolled about the perimeter, AKs showily in hand. They were easy to spot because of the bright tribal scarves, which made excellent target markers. Someone either hadn't thought that one through or had thought it through very carefully and didn't particularly care that if the assault came, targeting the gunmen would be much easier. McElroy himself didn't know what to make of it, nor did he know what to make of a situation in which so few controlled so many so completely.

He thought about it: yes, indeed, if all the hostages rose and ran at one of the gunmen—say that dude there, who lounged against a mall pillar, smoking an illegal cigarette, looking not particularly terrorist but more teen punk—they could almost certainly overcome him and flee en masse down the corridor. But to do that they'd have to act as one, and the first twenty-five or so would have had to have made friends with their own death. No twenty-five middle-class Americans were about to do that; whatever, that spirit was gone and nobody down there today would die of crazed courage. They would sit, try to wait it out, pray for the authorities to run the rescue, and pray that they'd be spared when that happened. The guy behind this puppy knew his victim psychology à la America, the Mall, and America, the country.

He looked for evidence of explosives rigging, canisters of gas, maybe tanks of ignitable propane, all emblems of weapons of mass destruction mall-style, and saw nothing: just men—young, if he read their rangy, undisciplined postures correctly—and their rifles. The five executed hostages had been dragged over to the railing that separated the Wild Mouse ride from the public areas.

Targets? None to be had. If the Marine sniper pegged one of the gunmen, he'd go down in full view; the crowd would react, the other gunmen would see, and the whole game would be up. They'd shoot ten more, then ten again until he gave himself up; that was the message in the first five deaths.

But then—yes. Okay, maybe, yes.

On the second floor, three jihadis had emerged from their posts below and now overlooked the crowd. Concentrating hard, he saw that all three had the bigger forty-round magazines that probably were designed to feed the gun in its light machine-gun role. These three leaned on the balcony, smoking, joking, joshing, goosing, goofing around. They'd been put there obviously because their vantage post was so much higher, their angle better, and in the event of an assault, they could bring fire not through the crowd but on the crowd. They were on the Marine sniper's level, but not across from him, rather to his right one corridor. He was Colorado, they were Rio Grande. He couldn't engage them from where he was, but if he rotated another corridor in the opposite direction, over to Hudson, he'd have a good shot at them. If he were above them, he'd have an even better angle.

McElroy took out the phone, punched the button. "Yeah?"

"Okay, three of them have come up to your level. They are immediately—that is a quarter rotation around the atrium—to your right. It seems to me that you might be able to get an angle onto them if you rotated to the left. Then you'd be directly across from them. Or if you got up a level, you'd have an even better angle on all three."

"I can't fire multiple shots with my technology," said the Marine.

"Well, maybe they'll separate. Maybe one will be left alone and you can take him."

"Good call. It'll take me a while, but I'll try and get around and up. You don't have any engineering diagrams, there's not some kind of passage by which I can find a short cut?"

"They just dumped us up here without any guidance. It was a big rush. There wasn't any chance to bring that stuff into play. Now, I can contact Command and see if—"

"No, no, that's just more time being eaten up, more people offering opinions, more people wanting to be heard. Today, action is king, action and only action. You get?"

"I get."

"Okay, I'll get into position. If you see movement in my direction, you alert me."

"Got it, roger," said the spotter.

McElroy settled down to stay connected to the targets.

Finally. He swaggered to the phone. This was his moment. His whole life he'd been able to synthesize arguments, turn them around instantly, and reiterate them in cajoling tones, until his opponent had agreed with him. It was his strength. He knew he could do it now, brilliant synopsizer, genius of empathy, purveyor of mega-earnestness. Colonel Obobo looked around, saw Renfro standing close by, giving him encouragement through sympathetic, even moist, eyes.

"It's your line three, sir."

Obobo peeled off his earphones, snatched up the phone, punched 3.

"This is Colonel Douglas Obobo, superintendent of the Minnesota State Police. To whom am I talking, please?"

"You know who I am," came the voice, calm and collected, untainted by accent, perhaps younger than might have been expected. "I'm the guy in the mall with a thousand hostages and ten thousand rounds of ammo. You do the math. I have demands."

"Sir, I'm sure we can work something out. Your demands will be given fair hearing. But I want to be clear, I must also advise you to immediately cease your activity, release all hostages, lay your weapons down, and turn yourself over to police authorities. No one else needs to get hurt."

"I really don't care if anyone else gets hurt," said the voice. "I have no objection to other people getting hurt. I have the hostages, ergo I have the power. You sit there and shut up and I will tell you what must be done, at what timetable, and what you can expect from us. Any more proffers of 'advice,' and I shoot a child. If you ever call me 'son' or 'young man,' I'll shoot another child. If you say, 'I want to be clear' again, I will kill ten. Now, if you want to save lives, you have to do exactly what I'm telling you very quickly. You don't have a lot of time. Do you understand?"

"I don't think anything is accomplished by belligerence. We must have a calm, clear, measured—"

"Shoot the little girl, holy man," the voice said.

"*No! No!* Please, you can't—"

"Actually, I can. I've seen you on TV, I know you're an ambitious political asshole who thinks he can talk himself into anything. Put it on the shelf or people die, do you get me loud and clear? I am not rational, I am not clear, I am not bartering. I will kill a lot of people. Do what I say and shut the fuck up, *Time* magazine cover boy."

Obobo swallowed.

"Please proceed," he said tightly.

"Excellent. Hmm, it's almost six. At six, I shoot six more. Unless you pay attention and I see action."

"You can't—"

"I can. Anything I want. Let me say this whole plan is predicated on speed. You will have to work like hell to make my demands happen in the short time frame I specify. But it can be done. I will enforce my demands with hostage executions if I don't see alacrity. I want you to have no time to counterplot, to plan reversals or assaults, to get cute, to hold meetings. You won't have time to discuss or consider or make counteroffers. This whole thing will be done in four hours or everybody dies and you go into the history books as the biggest fool in America. You do what I say, you do it at high speed, low drag, and most of these assholes will make it out alive. You care about them; frankly, I don't. They're the herd, and any herd can be thinned, that's the law of nature."

Get to it, the colonel thought.

"Go ahead," he said.

"There are three young men doing ten to fifteen in the Minnesota State Penitentiary for bank robbery. You remember the case, it was famous. Yusuf, Jaheel, and Khalid Kaafi. They got far more for their crimes because of the black-guy penalty, which nobody will admit to but which everybody acknowledges. Anyway, their crime was political, to raise money for the brigades back home. My friends here are very upset that you treated them like common criminals. It seems so unfair. Do you not understand that no infidel law can be applied to those of the Faith? This is the lesson they must teach you. The Kaafi boys, heroes and geniuses all, are to be *immediately* released and ferried to Minneapolis International, where they are to be flown to Yemen by an Air Saudi Super 747-8 ready to take that flight at seven fifty-five p.m. You should have just enough time. If the flight is full, kick three people off. Moreover, if I do not see visual confirmation on CNN of the prisoners boarding buses by seven p.m., I will execute seven more hostages. If they are not on that plane at seven fifty-five, I will order the massacre that you fear so much. Say, wouldn't that be a career black eye. You might not even make Eagle Scout or get into Princeton. As for the next batch I shoot, the six at six, I will begin with Jews. Then, if I am not pleased, I may break my own rules, though I hate to do that, and shoot seven and a half children at seven thirty. At a certain point, I will allow each of my men to rape any woman they choose, and if you know the Muslim mind, you know the women will be preteens. If there is any assault, I will order all my gunners to open fire on hostages. You *must* comply. Hostages will be released when I see the plane has safely taken off for Yemen and has crossed into Canadian airspace a few minutes later. When the hostages have been released, we will not surrender. We will take cover. You may assault. We will have a nice gun battle. We do not fear death. The narrative demands a climax, and we will give it one. America will enjoy it mightily. I would say to your assault troops that though you might ultimately prevail, bring many, many body bags. I know in those circumstances, the thing to do would be to destroy us with a smart bomb. But you won't do that. You'd destroy too many shoe stores. *Allahu akbar,* motherfucker."

He broke the contact.

Ray decided not to try to find a stairwell for the down-angle shot, which would cost him time as well as the effort to somehow get through the locked door. Instead he low-crawled as fast as he could along the shadows where the floor and walls joined, sliding under the retail windows. Good thing he was a gym rat still and did hard cardiovascular every day. Stamina is the essence of victory, he knew, and he was able to move at a high rate of speed, not really in the classical low crawl, with that squirming, swimming wiggle that pulls you along, but on all fours, like some kind of sniper rat, scurrying along. He thought, When they make the movie, they'll cut this bullshit out.

It was a long transit, and he fought the fatigue and particularly the neck strain, for he had to keep his neck pried back so that he could use his eyes to scan ahead for threat. Whoever was monitoring the hall cameras was not paying much attention; no call came from McElroy indicating a reaction from the gunmen, and ahead of him, he saw nothing, though as he passed each store, he could hear scurrying, breathing, shifting, as people sought security deep inside. It took six minutes, down the length of Colorado to the outer ring, down the outer ring, then back down Rio Grande, until he came to rest at the balcony overlooking the atrium, though one quarter of a turn to the left.

He set up not at but a little behind the railing.

Peering between its steel struts, he saw his targets. Now there were two, as one had departed for destinations unknown. Ray uncorked his iPhone.

"Okay, I'm here. Where'd the third guy go?"

"He kind of casually left a few minutes ago and took the elevator down. I guess that one central elevator is working. I've seen him; he's rejoined the downstairs bunch."

"Okay, two. This'll take some tricky work."

"What are you doing?"

"My secret weapon: the deadly potato."

Ray had a shirtful of the starchy tubers with him. He'd dipped into the Boardwalk Fries outlet near the Frederick's of Hollywood, picked seven or eight of the biggest, gnarliest, grossest spuds.

"A potato!" said McElroy.

"Potatoes make excellent field-expedient suppressors. You watch, bud."

He selected the biggest, unslung the AK, and wedged the vegetable over the muzzle, feeling the flash hider and sight blade cut into the crunchy fiber of the thing as he slid it over, until a good two inches of potato embraced the weapon. The potato was stoutly mounted.

He set himself up in prone, brought rifle to shoulder, slipped the big prong safety off by pressing it down on the right side of the receiver. Ancient memories came back, associated with the weapon. Some firefight in the sand—Afghanistan, Iraq? who could remember?—he and a mixed force of Marine infantry and Army rangers in a house in some godawful ville. He'd gone to a captured AK and fired and fired and fired, the whole night through. He must have killed thirty men that night, and in the morning, when the Bradleys got to them, nobody in the house was dead, though several were badly hit. That gun was crude, rattly, unclean, but baby, it had done its work hard and well over the long night's ordeal.

"But won't the first one blow the potato? Are you going to have time to get a second one on the muzzle?"

"Good question," said Ray. He rolled slightly to the left and extracted another potato. He pushed it up, close to the muzzle.

"When the first guy goes down, the second guy won't believe it. He'll freeze. I'll get potato two aboard and whack him."

"I don't know," said the spotter. "He's been in war before. He just might empty in your direction and start screaming. Oh wait—oh wait. One of them just left. He's going, I lost him, I can't tell where he's going."

"I saw him. He went into the bathroom. It's four or five stores back down the corridor. I'll do him when he comes out. The other guy won't hear a thing and I'll do him next."

"Jesus, you have balls of steel," said the spotter.

"I'm a professional," said Ray. "This is what I do."

Ray found his prone and built it from the bones outward. Legs splayed, feet cranked outward for muscular pressure within the hold, rifle tight to shoulder, supported on bone not muscle, breathing cranked down to a slow seepage of air, ball of finger against the curve of the trigger. It's all in the pull. That is, after everything else, it's all about the pull. He'd made the pull a million times. He had a sweet stroke, firm, soft, untwisted by torque, a steady, ounce-by-ounce escalation of pressure until the break and something inevitably ended up with a hole exactly where he'd intended.

The jihadi emerged from the restroom a hundred yards away, at this distance a small man wiping his hands on a paper towel, well pleased and well relieved with his bathroom work, probably one of the few times he had relieved himself indoors, and it's good he enjoyed it so, for the next second he stepped smack into the bullet.

It hit him above the right eye and his head jerked as no head in full health could jerk, and he went down with what was presumably a thud, though Ray couldn't hear it at his range. What he had heard was a kind of wet pop as the potato, accepting the injection of supersonic gases from the muzzle behind the exiting bullet, detonated in a muted spatter, like a potato balloon, becoming atomized pulp in a nanosecond. Potato mist hung in the air.

Ray cranked the rifle back, crunched on another potato, and rebuilt himself the position in replica. This time he cranked over on the jihadi at the balcony, who leaned vacantly upon the rail. That a bullet had just passed by his shoulder and destroyed his partner's face was a fact he missed entirely, and he only recognized that it was his turn next when his own bullet took his existence from him, without him even knowing it.

"Find me another target," said Ray.

As it turned out, the Japanese were much less fearsome than the obstreperous Herr Doktor Ingenieur Jochim, and that transaction went well. And so it was that in a very few minutes, Special Agent Neal found himself with a landline receiver, punching in nothing more exotic than an 800 number. Neal had downloaded a modem app to his iPhone and connected that via Wi-Fi to his computer. Thus his phone was sending and receiving the modem tones via the Wi-Fi connection and then via the landline circuitry to the mall. He quickly engaged the Wi-Fi application on the phone and linked it to his desktop PC using a Wi-Fi USB stick.

Meanwhile, the drama around him had attracted quite an audience to his little chamber. Dr. Benson was there, a couple of interns who could be bullied into getting coffee, Holly Burbridge, whom no one had the heart to get rid of, she was that good-looking, and a few other ITs, Computer Service geeks, and special agents.

The phone rang, as it would in any pizza shop in America, and after a few seconds signified an answer by a series of clicks. He had the log-on code from the Japanese, punched in the numbers, and a robot voice informed him that he was "in contact."

He quickly disconnected the line from the phone and clicked it into the computer, and again in seconds, after some blinking and clinking, a busy menu in Japanese came up.

"Oh shit," he said. "Anybody read Japanese?"

"Aren't you an expert on Japanese porn, Neal?" someone asked.

"Yeah, but only the office lady variety, goddammit. No help here."

But then his iPhone rang.

He picked it up and answered. It was Juko Yamata, the Japanese engineer.

"Special Agent Neal, apologies, I forgot to tell you, our menu styles are very complex on Japanese software."

"It looks like a map of the universe," said Neal.

"Go to the third blank box on the right-hand column. That is external links. Punch anything in there, then hit enter, which you can see lower right, red box with just two emblems on it, looking like a flower and a broken ski jump."

Neal did as he was told and was instantly informed he had accessed MEMTAC 6.2 English language version.

The colonel talked immediately by phone to the governor, then called Renfro and asked him to make an announcement to the press that demands had been issued by the gunmen and that they were being considered at the highest level of state government.

No hostages were shot at six.

"Well, that's something," the colonel said. He said it to nobody. The only person near him was Kemp, who had come up with an urgent look on his face to make the expected assault. Renfro had steeled Colonel Obobo for this and so he was ready for it.

"I see your point," he said, after Kemp had finished his rather overlong argument, "and Special Agent, rest assured I will consider it very carefully. And perhaps, in the fullness of time, that's the route I'll choose to go. But it's important to make these decisions carefully."

"Goddammit," said Kemp, "the demand for the freedom of these Somalis proves these bastards *are* international terrorists. This is an FBI operation and local law enforcement will assist in any way possible. But it's not up to you to make these decisions anymore."

"Agent Kemp, possibly you're jumping to conclusions. Your investigators and mine have come up with no connection of this group to organized terror cells. I heard no evidence of connection to overseas entities. I heard an accent-free young white man. And these prisoners are hardly international terrorists. They're local bank robbers, petty criminals."

Kemp was somewhat limited in his argument, because he knew that in a certain way the colonel was right. Behavioral Sciences had done a scan of the colonel's conversation with the terrorist. Their conclusion was that he was an American-born male, early to mid twenties, with a high IQ and verbal facility. His vocabulary alone—"alacrity" for "speediness" for one, "the narrative demands a climax" for another— would put him in the 790 area of the standard SAT verbal test. They pointed out other things too, such as a penchant for correct parallelism in speech, very rare except among the highly cultured, and a use of sophisticated irony. He used the well-known terrorist cliché *Allahu akbar* in conjunction with *motherfucker,* from urban argot, the two chosen for ironic shock value in that they are the last thing one would expect from diction such as his. Whatever Islamic terrorists were known for, it wasn't irony.

But that wasn't the real issue. The real issue was strategy.

"Colonel, I am not trying to seize command. I say again, and I speak for the Bureau, I am bothered that you have made no contingency plans to assault and seem inclined not to do so. These guys could start shooting at any second, people could start dying, and we are not ready to do a thing. We have to do *something.*"

"And just as easily, he could read our contingency

preparations for assault as provocation and start shooting. We save more lives by adjudicating than by assaulting." Another excellent gambit Renfro had come up with.

"We don't have enough men," he continued. "We don't have the equipment to blow the doors simultaneously until the National Guard engineers get here. Any assault will create a bloodbath. It's much better to cooperate and get this thing over. I cannot in good conscience go any other way."

"Sir, we have got to be in some kind of posture where we can operate quickly if—"

"I don't know what is taking them so long to make up their minds, but I am now officially recommending that the terrorists' terms be met, that those Somali prisoners be removed to the airport and sent to Yemen. Let's get this thing over, let's get those hostages out. It's the only way I can morally proceed. It's important to keep our moral guidelines intact."

"Yes sir," said Kemp.

"Now please, return to your investigation. That's very important and I'm trusting you implicitly on it." He tried to sound utterly calm and serene.

Kemp muttered and ran off.

"You handled that well," whispered Renfro.

"Thanks," said Obobo, slightly more upset than he cared to reveal. These macho people always wanted to shoot. That was the problem with law enforcement— too many shooters, too many bigots, too many old John Waynes who reveled, even if they weren't honest enough to articulate it, in the license for violence, had some sort of pornographic obsession with the guns. The last thing he needed was gunslingers screwing things up. Kemp, Jefferson, the same kind of—

But then he had a moment of mortal fear.

Where was Jefferson?

"Where is Major Jefferson?" he barked beyond the hovering Renfro to Major Carmody.

"I haven't seen him in—"

He was getting himself gunned up, the colonel just *knew* it.

"Get me Jefferson," he said to his commo guy.

Again, no one noticed Mr. and Mrs. Girardi. The people at the press tent lounged around, separated by an impregnable line of yellow tape from the state police Command van a hundred feet or so back, and next to it, the smaller FBI van.

But parked here, at the jerry-built tent where soft drinks and coffee urns had been placed, men and women simply stood and talked, or talked over cell phones. The cameramen, who had to lug the heavy equipment with them, took advantage of the lull to park themselves on the many folding chairs that had been set up for a canteen before the site had been turned into a chaotic press tent by the reporters.

Finally, a man in a suit came over to them. He seemed not to be a reporter, for he didn't have that sort of scruffy look that most of the reporters affected, and he didn't have a notebook or a cell phone in his hand.

"May I help you?" he said. "I'm David Jasper, corporal, Minnesota State Police. I'm Mr. Renfro's assistant. I'm in charge of this facility. Do you have press credentials? You have to have press credentials to be admitted to this area."

"We're the Girardis," said Mr. Girardi. "I don't know anything about credentials. Nobody asked us for credentials."

"Well, the officer must have been otherwise occupied. It's a very tense situation."

"We're here about Jimmy."

"I'm sorry?" he said, as he tried to gently herd them away from the reporters.

"Our son Jimmy. He's fourteen but small for his age. Today was the first time I let him go to the mall by himself."

"He hasn't called?"

"No, sir."

"Folks, you have to know, it's a mess in there. It's total chaos, and nobody's quite sure what's happening."

"We thought you might have a list or something. Of casualties. Maybe he was hurt, maybe he was sent to a hospital."

"Have you tried the Red Cross?"

"They were the ones who said come over here."

"Oh, I see, the runaround. Well, I'm sympathetic, but lots of people are in your situation. It's going to be days before all this is sorted out. Best advice is simply go home and wait for notification. Maybe Jimmy will—"

Suddenly there was a spontaneous whoop from a group of reporters, and at that moment, several broke and rushed to the young corporal, pushing the Girardis aside.

"WUFF is on air saying there's an agreement, why the hell don't we have that?"

"Where's Obobo? We need a confirmation!"

"Okay, okay," said Corporal Jasper, "let me check." He turned from the Girardis to grab his own cell phone, and the two watched as the circus moved elsewhere.

The phone rang in Nikki's hand three thousand feet above the mall in the WUSScopter, and she saw that it was Mrs. Birkowsky, the hiding clerk's mother.

She punched answer immediately.

"Mrs. Birkowsky?"

"Ms. Swagger, I just got what I think is good news from my daughter."

Nikki did a little jump in her copilot's seat, and the sparkly horizon on the plains above Indian Falls seemed to leap with her. Was this thing going to end happily? Could it?

"Please, share with me," she asked.

"Amanda says the gunmen are all jumping happily and some have shot their guns off in jubilation, she thinks."

"What could that mean?" asked Nikki.

"Whatever their demands are, I'd guess, the government has just agreed to them. It means that the hostages will be released soon."

"Yes, ma'am," Nikki said. "Is that all Amanda said?"

"Well, she said there was also a kind of roar from the crowd, she called it a happy roar, a roar of excitement. I'm going to see my little girl again soon. I just had to share it."

"Mrs. Birkowsky, I'm very happy for you. But please tell Amanda not to come out of hiding until after the police authorities have taken over. With people like this, you never know."

"Yes, yes, of course, but isn't it wonderful?"

"It's fabulous," said Nikki.

She switched to Marty at the station.

"Okay, is anything going on?"

"What do you mean?" he asked.

"I mean from our ground people. Has there been a newsbreak? Is there a new presser scheduled? Are there any signs, say, of buses moving up or ambulances getting into position or even the armed men drawing back?"

"Not a thing. It's still a holding situation."

"What about gunfire from within the mall?"

"No reports. Nothing, all quiet on the western front. What is this all about?"

"I have a report from inside the mall that the gunmen are celebrating, shooting off their guns in jubilation, and that the hostages are suddenly, I don't know, happy, or relieved."

"Is it enough to go live?"

"It sure sounds like the state has met their demands."

"I don't know, Nik."

"Well—wait, wait, I'm seeing buses beginning to feed in."

"Okay, that's it, let's go with it now, on air."

"You got it."

Jim the cameraman leaned in, supporting himself in the bulwark, turning his camera light on. She heard her vocal wired into the main feed, heard the ridiculous dit-dot-dash bullshit intro music, and heard Phil Reston's syrupy, staff-announcer voice say, "Breaking news from WUFFnews, the WUFFcopter, over America, the Mall, where terrorists are holding a thousand hostages as the Crisis at America, the Mall, goes into its fourth terrifying hour. Here is Nikki Swagger, WUFFnews."

"WUFFnews has just learned that inside the mall, gunmen have fired weapons skyward in jubilation and that hostages themselves are relieved and excited. Some believe these factors indicate that the state government has agreed to terrorist demands, as yet unspecified, and that the terrible crisis might reach a peaceful conclusion, and that freedom for the hostages might be imminent."

Though she couldn't see him, she knew that the shot had cut to the anchorman, who now said in his best Ted Baxter profundo, "Nikki, can you confirm a timetable for this terrific news?"

"Reports here are still preliminary," she said, "and we will be following developments as they occur and—"

"Nikki, Nikki, I'm getting word that the state police superintendent and incident commander Colonel Douglas Obobo is about to make a statement, we're going live to Incident Command headquarters."

She stared off into space, and, no monitor being available on board the WUSScopter, simply listened to the audio feed.

The colonel's voice was calm and reassuring. "Less than an hour ago a man calling himself the commanding general of Brigade Mumbai communicated with us from within the mall where he and his colleagues hold approximately a thousand hostages at gunpoint, many of them hurt and in need of medical attention. He demanded immediate transfer of three brothers, Yusuf, Jaheel, and Khalid Kaafi from the state penitentiary, where they are imprisoned for bank robbery, to the airport, where they are to be put aboard an Air Saudi airliner bound for Yemen. He gave us an hour to begin compliance or he would begin to execute hostages. I have just received word that his demands will be implemented, that indeed the prisoners are en route to the airport."

One of the cameramen poked Nikki, then held up one finger, signifying that she had it first, that she was number one, goddammit, and this was the scoop of all scoops. Didn't matter that she was only ninety-odd seconds ahead of the announcement: she broke a worldwide story!

"When they have cleared American airspace, the hostage taker says, all hostages will be released unharmed. That is all I have for you at this time."

Nikki heard a thousand questions launched and not a one of them answered, and imagined the pompous goat turning and exiting smartly stage left.

"Great work, Nikki. Baby, you own this story. You will be in New York before the week is over, I swear."

"I just got lucky," she said, "and in the long run it doesn't mean—whoa!"

The chopper suddenly dipped sideways, falling about ten weightless feet, until Cap'n Tom got his two rotor blades back in synchronicity. At that same second, a black shape slid by, uncomfortably close, before it too leveled off.

"Bastard," said Cap'n Tom. "Man, learn to fly before you come up here into crowded airspace."

"WUSScopter almost got clipped!" said one of the cameramen, unsettled.

"You ought to report him, Tom," said the other cameraman.

"Ah," said Tom, "he's just a traffic amateur, he's not used to being in formation or a jammed area. Still, what a jerk."

But Nikki had watched the craft slide by, so close, and her insides were still roiling. It occurred to her, Yes, you could die up here.

"Tom, really, someone's going to get hurt. Call it in."

"I'll make a formal complaint tomorrow," said Tom, meaning, of course, he wouldn't.

But something else nipped at Nikki.

"I saw his emblem. He was from that all-traffic crowd, POP."

"Like I said, an amateur. His idea of flying is holding stable over a highway."

"But I thought they had run into hard times. I don't know who told me, can't remember, but I heard they were grounding their chopper and buying their traffic from a big outside vendor."

"I heard that too," said one of the cameramen.

"Maybe so," said Tom. "Whatever, he's gone now."

And he was. Whoever POP was, he'd shot up high and she couldn't pick him out in the dimly lit skies above.

The message came to Major Mike Jefferson, huddled with his surreptitiously collected shooters, in a parking lot near the entrance to the system of heating ducts that would eventually lead to the chamber beneath the amusement area concession stand. He had put this little operation together on the QT. Hanging around Command was only going to get him demoted. So he thought, I'll just get some people and move into the area.

"Mike," another major told him on the secure tactical radio channel, "the colonel wants you back here. He's also pulling all the SWAT guys back and bringing in a fleet of buses."

"*What?*" said Jefferson. "Are you nuts? What the fuck?"

"Hey, Mike," said his colleague, "don't blow at me. It's the colonel's decision. We're going to let this thing play out. You heard, they've made demands, we're acceding to those demands, and they're going to let the hostages go, maybe within the hour. Any sign of offensive action against them and they could open up and take out dozens, maybe hundreds, of hostages. You're to stand down, return to Incident Command, and return your shooters to their original units."

"And what happens if after it's all done, and the Kaafi assholes are on their way to freedom and glory, this motherfucker still opens up on the hostages? Only this time, we have no way to get to them in minutes and they just kill and kill and kill while we're blowing doors?"

"It's not our decision, Mike. It's the colonel's call and the consensus up and down the line is that it's a good one. Media's gone nuts about him. He's their guy, he's the hero, he's the winner. That's the narrative. Suppose you go in, set up underneath just in case, and one of your people drops a forty-five and it goes off, and the bad guys panic and start blasting."

"These are trained men. Nobody is going to drop a forty-five. Plus, forty-fives don't work like that. Plus, we all carry Glocks or Sigs."

"Mike, just bring it back, okay? We'll make a note of your objections, that's the best I can do."

Jefferson announced the decision to his all-star SWAT group and got from them what he had given to the other major: disbelief, anger, a sense of something important slipping away.

"If you let these guys get away with this," somebody said, "it's open season on America all over the world. We have to fight them now and kill them now. That's our responsibility."

"Are you suggesting a revolution?" said Mike. "You want us to go rogue? You realize what that means? End of all careers, for a start. Possible legal action because without formal authorization, we're just vigilantes. I'm talking prosecution, fines, maybe prison time. You want to do hard time after all the skells you've busted? You wouldn't last three nights in the showers and your ass would get royally fucked before your throat was cut."

So that was it.

Walk back to their units, join the pullback, make way for the buses, hope that the colonel and all the heads on suits had made the right call, and if they hadn't, go in afterward and supervise the forensics and the janitorial.

"Tell you what," said Jefferson. "Let's go real slow. Now obviously we're not going in underground, but some of you guys have door-breaching rounds for your shotguns, right?"

There were a few yeses from the assembled crew of helmeted guys with MP5s, ARs, and Rem 870s.

"Okay, I'll play for time. Meanwhile, I want you guys to chamber your breaching rounds. If it goes down, we're only fifty yards from that set of doors"—he gestured to an entryway boasting the name NORTHEAST, where one township's SWAT people were withdrawing—"and we can get to the doors, breach them fast, and get into the fight maybe not in five seconds but maybe in one minute."

"Mike, I have a better idea."

"Yeah?"

The man explained. Then he said, "And it's not quite a revolution. More of a coup d'état."

"No," said Mike, smiling, "it's a coup de SWAT."

McElroy had found him another target. Still on the second floor, Ray was rotating another corridor to the left, moving down the outer ring toward Hudson, when he heard the sound of the shots.

He recoiled, thought someone had seen him, was shooting at him, and rolled backward, slipping the rifle off his back, knowing he was behind the curve and would take one in the head soon. But the shots were ragged, not a volley, more spontaneous, and he realized that they were echoing down the hallways from the wide-open amusement park where the hostages were being held. Then he heard this other thing, this animal thing, he wasn't sure what it was, some kind of crowd noise, a hubbub, a roar, a vibration. It communicated . . . joy. Well, excitement, maybe relief. It was, of course, the sound of a thousand people letting out their breaths involuntarily, as if they'd just gotten the good news. It was somehow the opposite of mass dread; it was mass undread.

Ray waited for it to die down. He was puzzled but alert. He settled back into his scuttling position, ready to proceed, waiting for some kind of cue to suggest a path, a course, a possibility and, seeing none, decided to continue on plan.

He moved ahead, slowly, his eyes scanning for motion. Nothing. It was quiet. Ray rounded the corner under the window into a bright, still-lit retail space called DSW Shoe Warehouse and peered down Hudson to the atrium space. This angle afforded him a close-up view of the log flume ride, and the smell of chlorine, from the heavily disinfected waterway, reached his nostrils, recalling the pool on the Subic Bay Naval Base of his childhood and the many summer days he'd spent there. He wondered absently what had happened to the installation since the Navy closed it down. Then he got his war brain back, excoriated himself for taking a little mental vacation in the middle of a combat zone, and started to scoot ahead, hoping he'd reach the railing before whatever gunman was lounging there had gotten bored with his cigarette break and taken off.

But then—the vibration of his phone.

Always at the wrong time! Jesus Christ, *don't* call me, goddammit, Molly.

But it wasn't Molly.

"Sergeant, this is McElroy. We just got the news. We're to stand down. They reached some kind of agreement, we're going to pull back, the hostages will be released as soon as the plane takes off—"

"What the hell are you talking about?"

"A deal, a deal. We're sending some supposedly 'political' Somali prisoners back, they'll let the hostages go."

Fuck, Ray thought. It went against everything he believed in. If you don't stand up to them, you embolden them. You teach them that we'll quit and it only makes them hungrier and crazier and the killing goes on and on. You fought wars to win or you didn't fight them at all.

"Do you hear me, Sergeant? Please acknowledge."

"Fuck," said Ray.

"It means you too. They're very worried at

Incident Command that some kind of accident or some guy not getting the word could queer the whole deal. So you have to cease operating. You'd best pull into a store, take the rest of the day off, and we'll let this play out. Then we'll come and get you."

"Ray," came a new voice, "Memphis here, listening in. Obobo thinks he's got it done, you have to do what Five is telling you. Let it cool."

"Suppose these guys don't play fair," said Ray. "I've had five tours fighting these guys and I know they can look you in the eye and give you total sincerity from the bottom of their hearts and be lying like a son of a bitch, and to them, lying to an infidel isn't a lie, it's a gesture of love for Allah."

"We have our order," said McElroy.

"Ray, yours not to reason why, et cetera, et cetera. It doesn't sit right with me either, but—"

"Are they choppering you guys out?" Ray asked McElroy.

"Nobody's said anything yet."

"You have any demolition there?"

"Of course not."

"Okay, listen to me. You have to have a contingency. That's all I'm saying."

"Listen to him, Five," said Nick.

"You have to be able to blow a hole in that window."

"That's fine to say but—"

"You have to be able to blow a hole in that window. You squad with the other snipers, you figure out something, just in case, to get through that fucking window fast and start taking people down. You may have just seconds to engage. Solve it yourself, solve it now."

"You're basically asking me to disobey orders."

"Sniper Five," said Memphis, in Washington Crisis, "you do what Cruz tells you, and if it comes to flak, you give them my name and I will swing for it, got that?"

"Got it, yes sir," said McElroy.

"And you don't know anything about this, Webley, if you're listening."

"I never heard a thing, sir," said Webley, who had been listening. "Now McElroy, get busy, you have work to do."

Ray put the phone away and tried to search out a retail outlet near the balcony where he could get into action if something happened, but he sensed a presence. Turning, his eyes met those of a jihadi gunman not three feet away. The man stared at him quizzically, and in the split second of stillness, Ray saw him trying to solve certain problems. Why, he had to be wondering, is this fellow here, in our uniform? Why is he not Somali? Who was he talking to?

And then he and Ray leaped at each other.

Dead Santa, atop his throne, gazed with sightless eyes upon the mortal anguish his passing signified. A woman on the other side of the crowd had also died, of a heart attack. There was a man near the Tilt-a-Whirl who was very, very close to death; he needed blood badly. One of the babies had started to cry and would not shut up. Everywhere, people were giving up or surrendering to bitterness and despair, trying to sneak last phone calls to tell relatives how much they loved them. Worst of all, the odors of colonic release filled the air. Generally it felt like the end of the world in the mass of hostages packed on the byways of the amusement park, dwarfed by the skeletal struts of various thrill rides, mocked by flappity-flapping banners and signs for refreshments and insane Christmas muzak from unstoppable speakers. "Silent night, holy night, all is calm, all is bright," yadda yadda.

But Mom had seen worlds end before and gotten through, so she was not upset. She held Sally close to her. She did not want Sally looking around, with her bright face and bright eyes. She knew the child's charisma was like a beacon and that it attracted attention, the wrong kind.

In her native language she prayed to Buddha for deliverance, but she also prayed for death to come to the filth that had engineered this thing. Everywhere she looked, she saw bleakness and turmoil. She continued to steal a handful of dirt into her bag every few minutes or so, as yet unnoticed, uncaught. It was just about time for another load.

But then—

Simultaneously two or three of the gun boys began to leap with what looked like joy and clap each other on the back. Then one pointed his rifle upward and jerked off a batch of shots while others pounded him raucously. A whisper ran through the crowd and it came to and blew over Mom and Sally.

"There must be an agreement! We'll be getting out of here soon! We just have to hold on a little longer!"

Mom didn't buy it, not for a second. She'd seen boys like these before: they loved their guns, their power, their uniforms too much. They had too little wisdom or imagination; they'd never felt responsibility. They were just children, really, and even if someone was directing them—no evidence, except in the earphones that suggested a leader somewhere addressing them and giving orders and instructions— they would behave like children, pointlessly, foolishly violent and cruel.

Then a confirmation came. Someone with an iPhone had managed to call up CNN, which was reporting an agreement in the Minnesota standoff! This news flew through the crowd and was confirmed by other iPhoners faster than the first news. Now the optimism was palpable, the sense of relief. Oh, it was so good. Mom allowed herself to half believe, but her hard experience in the world still left her worried.

Sally peeked up.

"Mom, what is it?" she asked in Hmong.

"Good news. They say we'll be out of here in a bit, some kind of deal has been made."

"Thank God," said Sally.

"Sally, do not let yourself believe until it is true. Guard against feelings of gratitude and relief. It may still be a long, tragic day and you might still have to use all your skills to survive it."

Suddenly a shadow crossed them. Both looked up.

The black man who'd shot the hostages and who'd bought Sally as his bride stood there, all insolence, pride, glee, his weapon resting casually on his shoulder. He smiled, white teeth showing brightly. Then he knelt down.

"I will have my wedding night," he said, "when the time is right. You will come to love me, and possibly when you give yourself to Maahir, Maahir will save you. The martyrs are cheering because they know that the killing is near."

———————

The young man turned to the imam.

"So can you watch the shop for a while?"

"I'm sorry, what do you—"

"Oh, nothing's going to happen for a while. They'll be driving the Kaafi boys to the airport, you'll see, and then there'll be the TV drama of the boarding and takeoff and all the talking heads will check in, and then we'll move up to another game level on them. But meanwhile, I've got a little something to check. You can hang here. I'll be back in a second."

"Yes, of course."

He reached under his console and took out a plastic bag that could only contain a gas mask. Or another head. But it was a gas mask. He pulled it on carefully, making adjustments. Then he went to the console, armed himself with the mouse, dragged the cursor to SECURITY OFFICE, and clicked. The icon told him it was still remotely locked. He ordered UNLOCK.

Then he rose, snatched up an AK, and left through the front door. It was only a quarter rotation around and there was no pedestrian traffic. A few windows had been broken, a few carriages abandoned, a few shoes lost. It had an after-the-zombie-apocalypse feeling he kind of liked, thank you, George Romero and all your clones. He passed the big, bright, deserted RealDeal that sold more TV sets than any other retail outlet in America, saw more zombie ruin inside but still utter stillness as all the trapped shoppers would presume him a killer and quake in their hiding places, and beyond that he came to the unmarked door that was the security office.

Unlocked by computer fiat, it yielded to his push, admitting him to a tunnel that led to more heavy doors, and they too opened cheerfully.

Inside: not pleasant.

Six dead guys. Wrong place, wrong time, fellows, the way of the universe. He felt not a morsel of pity for them and—this was his gift or something—could not imagine them as men of families, with lives, relatives, kids, histories, contributions. They were just sort of repulsive in their twisted grotesqueness.

He walked to a device of some mystery mounted on a wall. A small green bulb gleamed brightly. Oh, they think they're so smart. Oh, they think they've got it figured. Some boy genius of the FBI or the NSA or the CIA, working away, he'd managed to connect with the system, thinking that Satan had forgotten something. Too bad for him. So it goes with the weak and virtuous.

He smashed the green-lit modem two times with his rifle butt, the second driving the shattered plastic mechanism, its guts of circuits and wires and smashed plastic hanging out, to the floor.

He was doing what he had always dreamed of. He was smashing the machine. In its tangled, ripped wiring, in its shattered plastic, in its broken solenoids, he saw the future.

Ain't it cool?

TWO MONTHS EARLIER

Mr. Reilly was baffled. The owner—actually, the FFL was still in his wife's name, though she'd died three months earlier—of Reilly's Sporting Goods and Surplus, in far suburban, nearly rural Twin Falls, Minnesota, stared at the two crates, one quite large, one quite small, that rested on the UPS man's freight dolly. He bent, saw the return address on the shipping label as WTI, Laredo, Texas, which he knew to be West Texas Imports, his supplier for low-end Eastbloc surplus military weapons, which he sold to working-class hunters and gun folks who couldn't afford a big-ticket American deer rifle.

About a hundred mounted animals witnessed the somewhat confused transaction between the old fellow and the man in brown, and most of them had horns, though of course a few were badgers, ducks, even, whimsically, a groundhog noted for its sagacity and insight. Also on the cozy, wood-paneled walls: rifles, rifles, rifles, most bolt guns, a few ARs, a few shotguns. In the fluorescent-lit cabinets lay the handguns, gleaming, laid out neatly by someone who took the responsibility for display of merchandise and price, the bedrock of retail, seriously.

"I just don't see why it's such a big crate," he said to Wally, the UPS man.

"Mr. Reilly, do you want to refuse it? No big deal, I'll just dolly it back to the truck and we'll return it."

"Well," said Mr. Reilly, still a little foggy, "let's ask Andrew." He turned and called, "Andrew. *Andrew!*"

Andrew stepped from the stockroom. He was a tall, thin young man in his early twenties, and he was the best thing that had come into Mr. Reilly's life since Flora died. He was punctual, hardworking, entirely trustworthy, good with customers, reliable, and honest. He had a shock of blond hair and a fair complexion. He could have been any neighbor's son, and it was his compulsion toward tidiness that had turned the store into such a masterpiece of organization.

"He doesn't understand why the WTI crate is so big," said Wally.

"Mr. Reilly, I'll check it. Maybe it's two or three orders in one."

"You don't want to refuse it?" said Wally.

"No, I guess not," said Mr. Reilly. "Okay, Andrew?"

"Yes sir. I'll run it down through the computer records. They do make mistakes, but I think we did have an outstanding order on Chinese SKSes, and maybe this is them. Or maybe it's them plus a duplicate order. Wouldn't be the first time. I'll straighten it out, and if it's wrong, you can pick it up tomorrow, Wally."

"Sure."

Carefully, Wally ran his digital reader over the bar codes on each package label, thus recording accurately and in perpetuity the fact that both packages had been delivered to their destination.

Andrew hefted the handles of the dolly, got it unmoored from the floor upon which it rested, and wheeled it back into the stockroom. He returned with the empty dolly and slid it over to Wally, who took control of it from him, turned as Mr. Reilly unlocked the door, as it was well after closing time, and returned to his brown van. Reilly waved goodbye, then looked around his store, part of a decaying strip mall that had been on the downhill since big boys like Cabela's and Midway USA put everything one click away.

"You'll get it straightened out, Andrew?" he asked.

"Absolutely. It may take a while, I've got to go through the records. I may have to call them. And I haven't even begun to put the handguns in the safe."

"Oh, I'll do that."

"No, no," said Andrew. "I know you're tired. I'll take care of everything."

That pleased the old man. There were over seventy handguns on display in the store and, though it had never been robbed, the old man wanted it never to be robbed, which committed him or Andrew to a half hour's hard labor every night, picking up the guns and carefully stowing them in the two big safes behind the counter, then locking them tight. The rifles he could leave on display; the thieves were mostly black people from the city and they only wanted handguns.

"Okay, Andrew. I think we're due for an ATF walk-through anytime now and I don't want any trouble. There was never any trouble with Flora, she kept the records so neatly. It's not my skill, you know. Not my kind of mind. I'd rather talk hunting with customers. I don't know what I'd do without you."

"It's not a problem. I'll get to the bottom of this and by the time you get in tomorrow, we'll be ship-shape."

"Make sure to—"

"I know, I know," said Andrew, "log the shipment into the ATF bound book, no worries."

Andrew knew the ATF regs forward and backward, maybe better than Flora. If any gun spent twenty-four hours in a retail outlet, it had to be accounted for in the big log book ATF required, which would show its arrival and ultimately its dispersal, either via retail sale or, rarely, shipment back to wholesaler.

"Mr. Reilly, you go on home. I'll run this through, and if it's a mistake, I'll relabel and ready for shipment back and Wally can pick them up tomorrow."

"Thanks, Andrew. Don't know what I'd do without you."

It took the old man more than a few minutes to get himself together enough to leave. Since Flora's death, he'd become a ditherer. He'd start one thing, get halfway through, then move on to another. In the end, he had accomplished nothing except to half start a bunch of things that poor Andrew would have to follow through on. Mr. Reilly knew he had this tendency and he was too reliant on Andrew, but he'd never really come out of the fog that his wife's death had caused. Anyway, in time, he was set to leave, and he yelled good night to Andrew, unlocked then relocked the door, and got into his car and drove away, wondering if he could still make the early bird rate at the Walloon Lake Sizzler.

As soon as the old man left, Andrew used an X-acto knife to slice the shipping pouch on the big crate and slid out the bill of lading. He knew that it contained sixteen Bulgarian AK-74s from WTI. They'd arrived in the United States as surplus kit purchased by Century Arms, of Vermont. Century's not particularly subtle armorers had replaced the full auto parts with American-made semiauto parts, which by regulation qualified them for US retail sale, and somewhat haphazardly reassembled them. Usually they worked; sometimes they didn't. Those guns were wholesaled to WTI, who overstamped them with their own emblem, then repackaged them for entry in the great American gun ocean, 300 million and growing. The smaller package contained two hundred of the orange Chinese magazines held to be the best on the market. Nobody cared much about them and they went uncovered in ATF regs.

Andrew recorded each gun by serial number off the bill of lading as well as all other pertinent data. Then, using the blade again, he sliced the box end open skillfully, careful not to make any jagged cuts or rip anything in haste. He slid out the guns, each of which arrived packed in a Styrofoam box, then sliced the tape on the boxes. The guns lay inside, along with a moldy leather strap, a ten-round after-market magazine, a bayonet, a brass oiler, and a poorly translated manual. The 74s were real cool. He'd seen them initially in the first edition of *Modern Combat,* where Merc Force Blue used them to take down a Soviet missile silo in Uzbek that had been commandeered by Muslim terrorists. In that game, they'd worked well, though of course the 74s fired a smaller round than the 47s, an Eastbloc variant on our own 5.56 NATO. The cool thing about the *Modern Combat* series, as opposed to *Medal of Honor* or *Black Merx* or *Commando Ops,* was that the game took into account the muzzle energy of its weapons, so when you smoked a muji on the 74, it took more center of mass hits to put him down. You had to make that adjustment, just like in real life, or he was the one that got the kill.

In any event the guns bore no surprises: standard Red design, utilitarian, untroubled by aesthetics, uninterested in making a statement other than "This machine exists to kill people," with rough triggers and painted or baked enamel finishes. It was a gun for small, brown people, with a smallish pistol grip and a shortish buttstock, just the thing for little men trying to upset a big, US-supported government, the rifle's purpose the world over. The metal was pressed—that is, stamped out crudely—or industrially bent to form by some huge, clanky device in a hellish, dismal, steam-punk factory next to a river of sludge in some perpetually smog-shrouded Eastbloc or ChiCom city. Its makers were all government workers, paid in pennies by the national defense industry; they went home to nothingness and squalor, while the guns, in the millions, were shipped to hot spots, under license to their original artisans in the then Soviet Union. That's why the pieces were so crappy; no gunmakers' craft here, as was evident in the older Winchesters and Remingtons in the old man's rifle racks.

Next, Andrew filled each of the Styrofoam boxes with scrap metal from decommissioned shopping carts he'd bought with cash and smuggled into Mr. Reilly's store. About six pounds in each box, just an array of coaster wheels, tubes, gratings, screws, washers, and bolts. When the lids were retaped over the trays to form a whole, the whole reinserted in the crate, the crate carefully sealed by packing tape, the result was a package equally the size and weight of the one that had arrived, with the same shifty, noisy density. Short of an X-ray exam, no one could tell the difference between the first package and this one.

Now he went to the store computer and printed out a West Texas Imports address label to patch over the Reilly's Sporting Goods label. Except that it contained carefully engineered errors: the return zip code for Reilly's Sporting Goods and for West Texas Imports were both a number off, the 4 from West Texas being where the 3 from Reilly's should be, and vice versa. Computer error, obviously.

Then, the pièce de résistance. It was a UPS Next Day Air bar code, self-adhesive, and the key to the UPS system. It was fake, carefully hand manufactured by the clever Andrew in his lair in a Minneapolis suburb. No human eyes could read it, but the computers would send the package to New Mexico, to a store that didn't exist on a street that didn't exist. At that point, the confused driver would use his optical reader on the bar code for the return address and send it on its way. But its way was not back to Mr. Reilly; it went instead to another store that didn't exist on a street that didn't exist. Then it would go to the UPS undeliverable warehouse in Schenectady, New York, with thousands of other items, a facility bound to become overloaded with misaddressed packages during the upcoming Christmas shipping season as clerks struggled to keep up with and track each package either to its proper destination or back to its point of origin.

Tomorrow he would log them out and record the transaction in the bound book for ATF and in the notebook of shipping records that UPS issued to all commercial customers. The missing guns, thought delivered to their destination by the sender and thought returned to their sender by Mr. Reilly, would go unnoticed for months. No money was missing to alert any bean counters either, as Andrew stole about five thousand dollars a month from his wealthy father by equally intricate computer strategies and had financed the transaction out of that fund.

No need for ceremony or delicacy, not with guns like this. Grabbing them five or six at a time like pieces of firewood, Andrew hauled them to the truck bed of his vehicle and dumped them in. The magazines got the same rough treatment. These babies were all designed for rough treatment, that's what made them so perfect for what he had half-facetiously named Operation Mumbai after the Pakistani murder mission in that Hindu city that killed 160 people.

Andrew had a momentary lapse in his otherwise tightly focused attention. He had nostalgia for Mumbai, almost as if he had been there with the kill team, had stridden boldly down the great hotel's corridors, down the city's backstreets, through its bazaars, with his own AK-74 and a satchelful of grenades. Everything that moved or breathed was a target. It was a night of pure anarchy slouching to Mumbai to be born in the hot spill of the empty brass from the hyperactive bolt of the gun in full auto mode, from the pop of pressure when the Sov grenades detonated, from the scurrying figures in the darkness, stilled forever when lanced by a fleet of 5.45 hurtling into them. Andrew was a collector of apocalypses; he loved those final moments of the fall, when Troy went up in flames, when the Red T-34s rolled through Berlin at the head of an army of rapists and looters, when the sepoys went crazed and put all the British women and children, screaming, helpless, down the well at Cawnpore.

Why was this? Andrew could not tell you, nor could his many expensive medical and psychological advisors. Perhaps it was some excess brain chemical, perhaps he'd walked in on his mother giving his father a blow job, perhaps one of the bigger boys at school had smacked him in the mouth, turning him forever into a hater, or perhaps he was simply evil in the Old Testament sense. After all, as he had noted many times, evil is fun. It truly is.

He came back into the world as we know it and reacquired the self that he showed the world most of the time—steady, handsome, thorough, creative, obsequious. He went back into Reilly's, carefully put the seventy handguns into the safe, swept the place out for the tenth time—some habits die hard—made sure everything was secure, then armed the alarm, stepped out the back door, and pulled it shut and locked behind him.

He drove about thirty miles through the early-fall Minnesota night and at last turned off the highway to follow the signs to his destination, a freakishly large building in the center of a vast plain of now-empty parking lots. The sign read, WELCOME TO AMERICA, THE MALL.

Ray got off the X first, leaping, driving his crown into the man's nose, feeling it crush flat and spew blood. But where that would put most men out of the fight in an instant, this tough little skinny simply took it, took the pounding thrust of Ray's full body weight and went to the floor under him, but upon hitting it hard, he became a squirming dervish, his small but leanly powerful muscles twisting desperately for leverage. He was faster than Ray, who was faster than most; he was clearly a guy who'd done a lot of close-quarter combat, and somehow he found enough leverage to slip from underneath Ray so that the bigger man couldn't use his weight as an advantage, and the two knitted limbs and tried to break each other's backs, faces about an inch apart.

Ray saw insane strength in the wide black pupils, ignored the bloody snot and saliva that flew from the flattened nose and the rancid breath contained in the gaseous, propulsive exhalations through the mouth, and tried to get enough floor contact under him to move the guy back down to the submissive position, but the bastard was too active. Ray had one of his arms by the wrist, which also meant that the enemy had one of Ray's hands by the arm, and the other arms were tangled like fighting snakes as each tried to find a path to the throat. Ray head-butted again, hard, but didn't have enough neck to get the torque to deliver a disabling strike, and all he did was knock stars into both men's eyes.

Then the guy got a leg free and kneed Ray hard in the balls, and as his breath was driven from his body sharply, Ray's grip loosened and the guy snatched his arm free and got it to his bayonet and got that blade out before Ray caught up and snatched the wrist again. But now the blade was in play, and both men, in wrestling stalemate of enmeshed body on body, put all their focus and strength into controlling the blade, with the ultimate hope of driving it deep into the other's body and piercing a blood-bearing organ. But then Ray, formally trained in hand-to-hand and the owner of six black belts in six disciplines, yielded suddenly, knowing that the man's strength would overextend him, and when that happened, he re-asserted control; now the Somali's arm was straight and lacked space to set up for a plunge, and Ray bent it back, back, and back, and that's when the guy managed to bite him hard in the ear. The pain wasn't so bad as the surprise and the intimacy of it, and Ray lost concentration; the man, who'd lost the knife-hand battle, came quickly to victory on the nonknife side, snaking his arm through a brief hole in Ray's defense and getting his wrist crossways across Ray's throat. He just had to press the windpipe closed and hold it so for three minutes and he'd get the kill.

The fight sounded like six pigs in a pen built for three, all grunting and yelping and gulping. Their lungs pumped in-out; the breath came and went like waves on a beach; oxygen, fuel of battle, was as precious as gold, and they sucked for it whenever possible, in a medium lubricated by copious sweat outflow that slimed their pushing, sliding musculature like some kind of battle grease. Not a conscious thought formed in either mind; it was just instinct for the geometry of bodies, strength, will, and survival.

Ray risked his leverage contact with the floor, and with one leg pried loose, he got an ankle-wrap around his enemy's leg and began to torque it hard, perhaps to loosen the body from the clamp it had on Ray. It seemed to be working too, but then the guy did an incredibly creative thing. He dropped the knife and Ray took the bait, releasing the arm to grope for the knife, and the tough Somali shot his hand through the opening and clenched Ray's throat with his thumb driving into Ray's larynx. Ray blinked, some bloody snot rained into his face, and suddenly the guy, quick as a snake, regripped his left wrist, pulling it from the neck, then plunging back in supertime to wrap that wrist around Ray's windpipe, rising enough for enough play to get his arm strength factored into the equation, and then had both thumbs on Ray's Adam's apple and was driving in. Ray could only force him to an upward posture so that he couldn't get the fullness of his power into the dynamic, but now, really, it was a matter of time, for he'd cut Ray's oxygen intake by a good 70 percent.

Ray tried to get his arm inside the vise closing down on his throat, but his opponent half collapsed and there was no space to penetrate, even if it meant the Somali had to reset his hand just slightly, pulling it to the right so that one pressing thumb moved on top of the other one. Ray knuckle-struck him in the ear, hard, feeling tissue rip and more blood spurt, but the little man was too close to victory to let the strike throw him off, and his eyes mad with the killing lust, he drove his thumbs—

Ray had just the most fleeting impression of something flying horizontally through the air, and whatever it was, it hit his would-be killer in the temple with the force of a heavyweight's punch, sending a resonant cracking, breaking sound into the atmosphere, and the Somali went semi-limp for a second, relinquishing his control, his hands flying involuntarily to protect his head as fear fought the unconsciousness that threatened to overwhelm him from the power of the blow. Somehow Ray found the bayonet, and at the same time did a power roll, and in a moment achieved position on top of the squirming man. His other hand suffocated any screams in the throat and he fingered the bayonet into a grip strong enough for thrusting, then brought it back and shoved it forward. He felt it penetrate and open the softer flesh between the ribs, slide off of deep, interior objects, then sink point-first in something fibrous. Ray withdrew, placing more strength on the man through the wrist clamp, getting more leverage as he rose to his knees, and drove again and again. The guy bucked through spasms, fighting it, his eyes cue-balling, his tongue writhing like a dying snake, until at last, supersoaked in blood, he went limp.

Ray rolled off him, feeling close enough to death himself. He lay flat on his back, sucking for oxygen at the effort he'd spent, and it seemed he'd drained the mall of all of it, but then it flooded into his lungs, bringing coolness and clarity. He sucked hard through three or four strong breaths, felt his limbs tremble with salvation at having survived the ordeal, noticed how much blood he now wore on his jeans, and looked up into the eyes of his savior.

It was the black girl La-something, he couldn't remember, Lamelba, Lavioletta, Laviva, *Lavelva*.

"Jesus Christ, you got here just in time."

"I clonked his ass with a eight iron," she said, holding up the now-bent club. "I hope they ain't mad I busted it."

"When this is over, I will buy you a bagful of clubs, sweetie," he said. "Now let's get out of here."

Renfro called a press conference, fast, and still had to wait a few minutes for the network cams to set up. Colonel Obobo, flanked by the governor and all his majors except for Jefferson, took to the podium, nodded to a few friendly reporters, pivoting this way and that to accommodate the flash cameras of the print guys, then turned on the microphone. Renfro hoped he wouldn't overdo the I-did-this, I-did-that shit, but then he always did.

"I am happy to report that I have achieved success," he said. "I am happy to announce an end to the killing and the dying. I have been in discussion with a man calling himself the commanding general of Brigade Mumbai—a reference to the terrorist attack on Mumbai, India, in 2008—and I have negotiated an end to the standoff. He has made certain policy demands to which the state has acceded. When those demands have been met, he will release his over one thousand hostages, and we will retake possession of the mall."

He left out any information about the man's threat to have a nice little gunfight after the civilians were out of there. He didn't want some orgy of recriminations and doubts exploding before his assault teams had even fired a shot.

The press reacted to this news with muted glee. Yes it was satisfactory, yes it was wonderful, yes this and yes that. But of course a narrative had been set up and a primal tradition evoked. Evil had attacked from nowhere and spilled blood; it must be punished in blood. Too many movies demanded a big climax. Without any man admitting it, the press as well as the millions worldwide who watched were subtly disappointed; they wanted a gun battle at America, the Mall.

Not Obobo. He saw this as another triumph of his theories of progressive law enforcement, evidence that if you treated even the most jaded of perps with respect and a view toward their common humanity, then great things could be achieved.

"What concessions were made?" shouted a dozen voices.

"For the time being that information is classified. You will be informed when the time is right. Meanwhile, I want to say that the first responders of Minnesota handled this unprecedented crisis with—"

"Suppose they're lying. Suppose they just want to kill people but first extracted massive concessions out of—"

"I, personally," the colonel said, "handled these negotiations. I listened carefully to this man's voice and I believe I made human contact with him, and despite the gulf in our cultural systems and political beliefs, we both understood that the killing had to stop. I am extremely proud of the progress that was made here today. Thank you, ladies and gentlemen."

As he stepped away, Renfro collared individual reporters with unattributed stories.

"Actually," the line went, "you should report that the old-line cops wanted to go in guns blazing, but Colonel Obobo had the guts to stand up to them. He himself worked the phone with this guy and he himself got us out of this jam. That should be your angle."

Finally, a payoff. The Bureau tasked ATF to start checking wholesalers for unusually large shipments of surplus Russian or Eastbloc AK-74 rifles or 5.45×39 ammunition, preferably the 56-grain Russian 5S7 bullet, to the Minneapolis–Saint Paul area, and ATF operators got on the phone to wholesalers the nation over. In less than an hour Reilly's Sporting Goods, Twin Falls, Minnesota, came up, which, according to West Texas Imports, had been steadily receiving a two-case crate—two thousand rounds— a month for six months. Moreover, WTI had shipped them sixteen of the rifles, rebuilt from kits by Century Arms, just a few months ago. ATF agents from Minneapolis got out to Reilly's house fast, under siren, and rousted the old man from his afternoon nap. It was another ten minutes before the team brought him to the store and he opened the building, which was alarmed to UL-3 level protection.

He checked his records. No, no, he had no AK-74 kit guns on hand, though he did remember an accidental shipment weeks earlier that was never opened and returned, which is why it had been logged out of the big book beneath the line in which it had been logged in. Possibly it contained AK-74s? You see, the 5.45mm bullet isn't big enough for a deer, which is why he had no interest in it. Now, the SKS, an earlier-generation Eastbloc assault rifle with a ten-round magazine, it fired a .30-caliber bullet about the same power range as a .30-30 so that—

Agents backchecked with WTI and discovered that they had never received the return and still held the wholesale money; they had assumed Mr. Reilly had taken the shipment. Moreover, the guns were AK-74s, they confirmed. UPS was alerted, and yes, they had a record of a pickup that particular day but none of a delivery. That meant it was probably in their undeliverable warehouse, which would mean some heavy record-searching—

One agent got the idea to track the ammo. Mr. Reilly opened the storeroom and discovered that he only had one tin of the surplus stuff left. Going to his computerized records, he went through his wholesale expenses and saw that the store had a steady order for a double crate—21,016 rounds—of 5.45 Russian combat ammo for six months. Only one tin of it was in the storeroom, which meant that eleven tins were not there, and he couldn't believe that he'd sold that much of it in six months. He himself had never sold a box of it, just as he'd never sold anyone an AK-74, because he specialized in hunting rifles, not guerrilla raid and assault weapons. He was baffled, a little hurt, and in the dumps to begin with because his superb clerk Andrew had left a week ago, sadly, and he knew he didn't have the focus anymore to run a retail business, especially now that the ATF rules had gotten so complicated and—

What was the name of the clerk? someone wanted to know.

His name was Andrew Nicks. College boy, very decent, hard worker. He was a fine boy. Mr. Reilly went to look for Andrew's address. Could Andrew be in trouble?

Ray dragged the dead terrorist to the nearest store, the Mocha Spectrum chocolate shop, and stuffed him inside. A blood trail led to his body, but that couldn't be helped now. He stripped him of combat gear and handed the rifle and the magazine bandolier to his new partner. Then he gestured and she followed, and they made their way down the corridor and dipped into a place called Pandora Jewelry, and both collapsed.

"Thanks," Ray finally said.

"It's okay," said Lavelva, still wearing her name tag. "I couldn't just sit up there during all this with all them ladies, yakyakyakyak. Lord, how they talk. I had to get out of there, like to give me a headache. Who are these guys? What do they want?"

"It seems to be some Islamic paramilitary unit, possibly connected to Somalia by the looks of these guys. There's a lot of Somalis in the Twin Cities, right?"

"You got that right. Too many, you ask me."

"I don't know who's controlling them. Somebody smart, who's taken over the mall security system from the inside. They've got a thousand hostages down in the amusement park area. They've already executed five and they're threatening to kill more. They've made demands and, as I understand it, we've acceded to them. My last order was to stay still and wait for it to be over."

"Nobody told the boy fixing to choke you."

"No, he didn't get the bulletin. Okay, let's just cool it here and see what happens. I've got a phone link to an FBI sniper on the roof. If they need anything, they'll call us."

"You know what?" she said. "This was my first day. I can't lose this job. I ripped up a notebook, you know, to get a piece of metal that I used on that first guy. Am I going to get in trouble?"

"So far," Ray said, "I think you're doing swell."

Fuck!

That's the way it goes. It's there, then it's not.

Special Agent Neal had navigated the SCADA diagram and was dragging toward the security functions block, to call it up and open the doors and—

Nothing. Zip, nothing, nada, zero. The dead blank of unviolated cyberspace.

"What happened?" yelled Benson.

The crammed-in audience ignited. Hoots, squeals of anguish, a chorus of profanity. Even luscious Holly Burbridge winced.

"Goddamn, he knew," said Neal.

"What?"

"Well, that's a very frail way in. It's not permanently hardwired. It's not wireless. It's old tech, like science fiction rocket ships with clusters of cords everywhere. It's not in space, cyber or otherwise, it's there in a gadget, a magic box, something that looks like a climate control gizmo on a wall; it's not covert. So, whack. He sees it lit up, he smashes it to bits, and we're totally fucked."

Nobody said a thing.

Finally Neal said, "Dr. Benson, you're the boss. Can't you say anything inspiring?"

"No," said Dr. Benson.

"So since this went nowhere," said Neal, "do you kids want to put on a musical?"

"Jeff, how can you be so good at pulling perverts out of the woodwork and so goddamned bad at this?"

"Because perverts are idiots and this sonovabitch is super smart."

"Or lucky."

"Smart makes luck. Dumb makes bad luck. Too bad he's not taking pictures of four-year-olds in— *Okay, okay, okay.*"

The okays tumbled out of his subconscious like a fluid from a broken bottle, but they did not signify breakage so much as connectivity. He thought he had, he maybe had, there was something, it was so vague, it was just beyond knowing, he had it, it skittered away, he—

"What?"

"Just a minute. Let me think something through."

ONE MONTH EARLIER

The imam watched his two daughters play in the twilight of an early-fall Minnesota night. It was sixty degrees and clear, the air tranquil, the stars beginning to show in the glow under the elms, which had begun to go red/orange/brown as they dried. The girls, Sari and Ami, were bright, lively, beautiful children, full of gaiety and mischief. They were easy laughers, as if much in the world merited delight, and now they rode the swings in the Twenty-Third Street Park, first Sari pushing Ami, and then Ami pushing Sari.

"Don't push too hard," the imam called to Sari. He was afraid that the older child's energy and enthusiasm would catapult the younger from the seat and off she would sail, into space. It was an image that came to him in dreams sometimes: his children, falling. He would waken in the dark, drenched in sweat, then go check. No, the girls were all right.

He saw a figure slide onto the bench beside him but didn't turn to look. Through his peripheral vision, he saw this fellow—young man—take out a paperback of a huge novel called *Crime and Punishment,* open the dog-eared copy to a certain page, and pretend to read.

"You are late," the imam said.

"Not really," said the young man, not looking up. "The FBI was on you on the way here. It was only one agent and he didn't have listening gear and he didn't stay long. I think it was just a random checkup. Now he's gone. I followed him to the expressway to make certain, then doubled back."

"Ah," said the imam. "So we are secure?"

"Unless you're a double agent, then yes, we are secure. How was your trip?"

"It went well. I connected with General Aweys. He selected twelve of his youngest fighters. As you requested, they are unsophisticated in Western ways, uncontaminated by the Internet. They barely know how to operate cell phones."

"Good."

"One of them, Maahir, is a bit older, more jaded. He is what you might call a sergeant. He is the commander, such as it is."

"Good. He can kill Santa Claus. He'll obey me, right? I don't want attitude. He's not going to give me shit when I give the orders?"

"I have spoken to him. He is the instrument of your will, as you are the instrument of Allah's will."

"We will have to have a theological debate in hell as to whose will I'm obeying."

"It is a tragedy that you have no belief, not in the Faith or any faith, or any system that seeks to impose order. You love only death and you live only to destroy, a fine young man like you, and Allah has selected you for this task and brought you to me, and together, atheist and holy man, we will strike such a blow, avenge the great, tragically fallen Osama. Then

I will go to paradise, brother, and I will be the first to greet you, as I'm certain Allah will grant you provisional entrance."

"It's actually not true that I have no faith," said the young man. "I worship at the church of Saint Joan Jett. I love rock and roll. It's *my* deity. Now give me the details."

"Through a brother who runs a Somali Relief charity in Toronto, I have brought the men—the jihadis—in by groups of three and four. They have been granted temporary Canadian visas and are staying in the relief organization's dormitory in the suburbs of Toronto. They have their instructions. Do not mingle with the others, do not talk to anybody, do not talk to infidels, obey all rules of the facility, be a humble leaf, floating with the current. But on the day of days they will be ready; all have seen battle. All have fought with Hizbul Islam, in battles and operations in Wabra and Mogadishu, in—"

"Please. I tried to understand the Somali civil war from Wikipedia. It was like reading Herodotus in Chinese."

"Always the comedy, even if I don't understand it. All have lost brothers, sisters, parents. All are hard and bitter and can do the necessary without flinching."

"My kind of folks," said the young man.

"When the week arrives, all will be driven to the busy border crossing at Niagara Falls and cross over secretly, hidden in a truck which makes regular passage over the border, owned by another believer who owns a carpet company. I myself will drive them from Albany across America to the safe house here, where they will rest for a few days. Are you sure you don't want to bring them to the mall one or two at a time and let them get a feel for what they are doing?"

"Sorry, no. One of them would fall in love with a Somali girl selling videos or waitressing in a coffee shop or collecting parking fees, and his mind wouldn't be on his work and he'd fuck it up. Somehow, he'd find a way to fuck it up. They have been promised jihad, the slaughter of infidels, and a ride to paradise. I will make good on those promises but they must obey operation discipline until the fun begins. That's the basic rule—no comedy here, or we will be penetrated and destroyed. I shouldn't have to tell you again. Do you need more money?"

The imam was a little guilty about the money. He had used some of it to purchase the services of a prostitute twice in Somalia and to buy some extremely profane pornographic DVDs and to take his girls to Chuck E. Cheese's, which they loved. He still had over six hundred dollars left. But he couldn't turn it down.

"Well," he said, "one can always use cash."

"No feasts, no Last Suppers with the little lambs. Anything, *anything* you do out of the ordinary might alert the feds. So far, they don't seem to be onto anything, but we're so close now, I'd hate to see this thing fall apart and spend the rest of my life getting reamed three times a day in prison for nothing."

"I understand, I obey, I am thankful."

"Good, then that's it."

"There is one other thing."

"Okay, what?"

"Death."

"My favorite thing, in any color. Whose are we talking about?"

"Yours and mine."

"It will come when it will come. It is nothing in exchange for larger goals. I'm not particularly afraid."

"Yes, but . . . have you no one you'd like to see again?"

"Only to laugh in their faces."

"But consider the possibility of escape."

"There is no possibility."

"But . . . if there was."

"Hmm," said the boy.

"It so happens that I have a follower who has a brother. This brother was a helicopter pilot in the Moroccan Air Force. He got involved in radical politics, he was arrested, tortured, imprisoned. He escaped, he managed to end up in Canada."

"Interesting."

"He's quite a good pilot. He now works for an agricultural dusting firm. He sprays poisons on weeds. He kills things."

"What a great job."

"Now, I am thinking, on that day, the air will be full of helicopters, police and military but mostly from the news organizations."

"It'll be a chopper hullabaloo, no doubt about it."

"Suppose it were arranged . . . ," and he continued with his plan.

It surprised no one that the house was so nice. It was set back from the road by a driveway, possibly one hundred feet in length, and stood shaded by trees, with all kinds of flourishes like porches and gables and a three-car garage. It was in one of those posh million-dollar developments to the north of Minneapolis, among houses of equal or more value, the whole gated neighborhood itself protected from the rigors of actuality by a 24/7 uniformed patrol.

Three cars of agents pulled up, and Bill Simon, acting on behalf of SAIC Kemp, took the lead. He had the warrant number, though no actual paper representation, as the warrant had been arranged on the fly on the drive from downtown headquarters.

He knocked, and a man in his late fifties, with an ample head of gray hair teased attractively about his head and a scotch glass in his hand, answered. Simon noted emblems of upper-boho gentility: running shoes, tight-fitting jeans, a lush Scottish heather turtleneck over a health-club disciplined body, wire-rim glasses. Over the man's left shoulder lurked his wife, maybe the trophy edition, for she looked a decade younger, a handsome woman with an adorable mess of tawny blond hair, also in jeans—great, tight bod—and an oxford button-down shirt. She held a glass of wine.

"Mr. Nicks? Jason Nicks?"

"Yes sir," said Nicks, who thought he knew exactly what was going on. "You're FBI, right? Here about Andrew? You have some news. We haven't heard from him and I've tried the store a hundred times. I'm so worried."

"Yes sir," said Simon. "Actually, yes, we are FBI, and yes, this is about your son, and yes, we know he manages one of your stores in the mall, but we're here to serve a search warrant."

"What?" said Jason Nicks.

"Sir, there's some suspicion that your son is involved with the gunmen who've taken over the mall. He was definitely involved in procuring the arms and ammunition they're using. I have a number for a federal warrant that's been issued by the Fourth Circuit US, Judge Raphael, to search his house. You can check if you want by looking up the warrant number on the Internet."

"Oh, Christ," said Jason Nicks, stepping back to admit them.

Simon himself ran the interrogation, while the forensics and evidence collection team went downstairs, where Andrew lived. As Simon addressed the parents, they all could hear the cracks as the agents used tactical entry battering rams to knock down the locked door.

"Does Andrew need a lawyer?" asked Nicks.

"Possibly, sir. Do you want to make a call? We are in a hurry, as you might imagine, but at the same time, I want your son to have the full protection of the law."

"No, no, go ahead."

In the background, NBC was reporting that the van had arrived from the penitentiary and that the prisoners would file aboard the airplanes within a few minutes.

"I'm looking at his record now," said Simon. "Andrew has had some difficulties, I see."

"He's been a hard kid to have around, yes," said the father. "So bright, so angry. I've spent a lot of money on lawyers, just trying to keep him out of jail. He's my only child, what could I do?"

"Yes sir. Just scanning here, I see some drug busts, I see that he has been kicked out of three private schools and just barely managed to graduate from the fourth—"

"He's got a genius-level IQ."

"Somehow he got into Harvard."

"I made a very large donation to the school, and that may have had something to do with it. But he was certainly smart enough. He just wasn't mature enough."

"He didn't stay long?"

"Less than a year. A very unfortunate year, I'm afraid. He let himself get angry, he sent some unwise e-mails to people, he didn't invent Facebook because someone else had already, he got lost in writing code, hacking, designing games, stopped going to class, ultimately returned to his drugs and his music and his trendy nihilism. You know the profile: love of destruction, heavy metal, a fantasy life full of violence. I don't know what's wrong with that kid. We gave him everything, we supported him through it all. He's been in psychotherapy since he was twelve. He's been in every program you could imagine, taken every antidepressant, every ADD drug, Ritalin by the long ton. It works, sometimes, for a while. But he always regresses: rock and roll, computers, violent nihilistic fantasies, anger at . . . I suppose at me. I made a lot of money. Big mistake."

"You're an entrepreneur?"

"I have a gift for retail," Jason said. "I just surf the zeitgeist looking for opportunities. I'm not Steve Jobs or Bill Gates, believe me, just a storefront guy. I had hippie clothing stores in the seventies, running shoes in the eighties, computers in the nineties, now computer games. That's the cool stuff. There's some other stuff too, not so cool. I own several fast-food franchises, the better part of three local strip malls, a complete mall in Kansas, a restaurant and three motels in the Wisconsin Dells, three Sheetzes along I-ninety-two. I own the First Person Shooter shops, do you know what they are?"

"I'm afraid I don't."

"Shooting games in cyberspace. Andrew grew up with them. He's probably one of the best in the world when it comes to fighting with your thumbs on a PlayStation. My flagship store is at the mall. Two years ago, I asked Andrew to manage it, and for the first time in his life, he applied himself. He's run it very well."

"And that's where he is now?"

"Yes. And every day."

"Are you aware that for six months he had a job in a sporting goods store in Twin Rivers?"

"What? That's not Andrew."

"He used the store's FFL to acquire sixteen assault rifles, sixteen surplus German pistols, and over ten thousand rounds of ammunition."

An agent entered the room.

"Bill," he said, "you ought to come see this."

"Everybody's so happy," said Mr. Girardi.

"They say it's almost over."

They stood essentially nowhere. They'd been exiled from the press area, and there seemed to be little point in going back to the Red Cross area, especially as it would be buckling down to receive the seriously wounded. They were more or less in between those two stations, about three hundred yards from the bulk of America, the Mall, which was a hub of activity, still surrounded by cops with their lights flashing. A few minutes ago, buses had begun to assemble not at the mall, per se, but a few hundred yards off to the right, so that when given the signal, they could progress to the entrances and load up on freed hostages, who would then be taken to triage stations and then to other destinations. The whole thing was immensely complicated, and it seemed everywhere they looked, they saw vehicles and scurrying men.

It was cold now, near forty degrees, and the woman shivered.

"I don't think we should get any closer. They'll try and stop us," she said.

"We'll just stay here. It'll only be a little while longer, I'm sure."

"You see," said Colonel Obobo to his friend David Banjax of the *New York Times,* as they sat on folding chairs outside America, the Mall, with Mr. Renfro hovering over Obobo's shoulder. Behind them the buses to transport the freed hostages pulled into position. "I'm of the belief that we in law enforcement shouldn't be bullies or tough guys or sucker punchers. I've believed that since I walked a beat in Boston all those years ago."

Banjax knew the colonel had walked the beat in Boston for less than three weeks before being snatched up to more glamorous duty, as befit his spectacular personage, but he wrote it down anyhow, while his tape recorder purred away, even though Obobo had used the same line when he'd interviewed him before, for the magazine.

"I've always thought of force as the least and last part of law enforcement's job. Rather, guidance, advice, steady presence, absolute fealty to the letter of the law, but also patience and compassion and discipline, all of it driven forward by a commitment to diversity. No one should look at a policeman and feel fear. That's the law enforcement I hope I embody and I hope I represent."

"Sir," said Banjax, "I'm hearing that there were elements in your command who wanted to go in guns blazing. Is that right?"

"We discussed many ideas, David, many possibilities. But sometimes courage comes in doing nothing. Sometimes it comes in not applying pressure and in letting the alleged perpetrators understand the absurdity of the situation they've engineered and letting them see that the sensible solution saves lives rather than takes them. Most people aren't killers. Most people are simply trying to make themselves heard, to have a selfhood, an identity, whatever you want to call it. And once that is permitted, it defuses the situation. I'm sure these folks consider their cause right and just, and who's to say, really, that it isn't? There's room here on earth for different ideas; that's why we treasure diversity as a value and I've tried to increase it wherever I've been and wherever I may go."

"Well said, sir, if I may. But speaking of 'wherever you may go,' is it true that you're in consideration to become director of the Federal Bureau of Investigation? The successful closure of this emergency certainly can't hurt that."

"Well, we'll let the future take care of itself, David. It will be what it will be. Yes, it would be a great challenge to be in charge of the FBI and to see my ideas applied on a national scale, but—"

Mr. Renfro leaned in. "I hate to break this up, but we're receiving word the Kaafi brothers have arrived at the airport and been trucked to the plane. Doug, we have to make you available to TV now."

The colonel and Banjax turned. A monitor had been set up, and indeed the screen showed the three prisoners, still in their orange jumpsuits, all twitchy and excited, climbing up the steps to the giant airliner one by one.

"You should be proud to see that," said Banjax.

"I am. Off the record, I had people who wanted to explode bombs underneath the floor and go in shooting. Jesus Christ, can you imagine the carnage? For what, to save three measly bank robbers who'd be out in a few years anyway?"

"We'd never be at this moment."

"No, and we'd have to send out for more body bags. I don't think there are enough in Minnesota for something like that."

Simon walked through the shattered door into Andrew Nicks's large, paneled bedroom on the bottom floor of his father's mansion. The first thing he saw were posters from a group calling itself Megakill on the walls, jagged images of rockers made up as the angels of Armageddon, with crazed screwball makeup, long black nails, coils of hair to the shoulders, lips red as blood, electric instruments like weapons, faces contorted into the pagan killing mask, like Conan on a good day outside the walls of some doomed Hyborian city-state. Other pix: smiling shots of Dylan and Eric of Columbine fame, a solemn loner named Seung-Hui Cho of Virginia Tech, the great Charles Manson, Charles Whitman, a strange guy with haunted eyes and a bushy '40s haircut, even two little squirts in period outfits he recognized finally as Bonnie and Clyde. All screwball shooters, little men with big guns, artists of destruction and mayhem. Then the guy in the haircut clarified for him as he realized it was Howard Unruh, who'd taken a Luger for a walk in 1948, murdering thirteen, first of the big-kill maniacs.

Then he saw the elaborate computer setup, and an agent had called up MEMTAC 6.2, which Simon knew to be the software package that controlled America, the Mall's, security system. An immensely detailed and possibly impenetrable flowchart seemed to be on display. On a table across from the unmade bed were stacks of blueprints, all of them from Oakland Engineering and Architectural, one of the firms that had constructed the mall in 1992. On many of them, red pencil lines tracked pathways, corridors, stairways, choke points, areas in square footage.

The bookshelf held a variety of texts—classic revolutionary strategy by Mao, Debray, Guevara, and Trotsky, to say nothing of Sun Tzu and Machiavelli, Dave Cullen's *Columbine,* a variety of US Army and

Marine Corps insurgency and counterinsurgency manuals, sniper guides, improvised explosive handbooks, psywar op pamphlets, ambush tactics and man-tracking guides from various survivalist or radical publishers.

"Mentally, he was getting ready for war," said someone.

"Mentally, he was nuts," someone else said.

"Oh God," somebody said, "look at this."

He held up a batch of newspaper clippings on a Reverend Reed Hobart, of a Church of the Redeemer in some outlying community, who had been famously demonstrating at downtown mosques with a group of his followers but then had suddenly vanished without a trace.

"Maybe Andrew made the Reverend Mr. Reed go bye-bye," said someone.

"Okay," said Simon, "I think that pretty much tears it. I'll call Kemp, and meanwhile let's get this stuff photoed, tagged, and removed. It'll all have to be looked at."

"What's in the closet, I wonder," another agent said, and opened the door.

The detonation represented itself even before it was a blade of light as a wall of immense energy that stopped time for a split second, and in the next everybody in the room had been blown back until they hit something that stopped them. The noise was stupendous, and shards of wood flying viciously through the air opened a hundred or so wounds in the men and women so blasted.

Simon, who had been deeper in the room at the time of the blast and thus missed its killing force, found himself the new owner of three broken ribs. He fought the terrible, suppurating lassitude that leadened his limbs and tried to shut down his brain. He blinked, exhaled a plume of acrid air, looked about, and through the smoke that hung everywhere in the room, noted a young agent against another wall so still he had to be dead, and grew angry at himself that he could not remember the young man's name just now. He tried to pull himself up, get himself together, take charge, make a report, get medical and ATF bomb people out here, all at once.

Then he saw, through the fog, the boy's father standing in the doorway.

"Oh God, Andrew," he was screaming, "what have you done!"

Tick tock, tick tock, Jeff Neal thought. He looked around, saw the eyes of all the leaners-in boring in at him. But he was trying to put pieces together. Somehow "perverts" and "mall" and . . . and what? He thought he had an idea, an inspiration, a possibility, a—

"Sorry. I thought I had something. I didn't."

"Well," said Dr. Benson, "I guess you ought to just run penetration programs on it again, and just maybe—"

"Okay, okay, okay," said Neal suddenly, again very fast. "Stay with me on this. We track pervs, right?"

"That seems to be the consensus," someone said.

"Now, I do have a California guy in my crosshairs. His name is Bruce Wyatt, thirty-four. I've been all over his hard drive. Kids dressed as cowboys, you don't want to know more. Okay. Okay, he works, I think, at a RealDeal in Sacramento. So I'm going to get on his drive, search for links. He's computer-savvy, sort of, so he's got a link to RealDeal Corporate. So from him I can get into RealDeal Corporate. I get into that, their main setup, not the bullshit public website, I get into their guts, where all their maintenance and security and financial programs are, and maybe there's a link to each branch, even if it's only e-mail. So maybe I somehow figure out which of the fifty or so branches—"

"Jeff, there's probably over five hundred of them."

"So I get into their operating system and from there I get to the system here at this mall, at their big fourth-floor store and maybe, depending on who built it and how much money they spent, maybe, maybe maybe there's some kind of undocumented portal from it into the bigger SCADA thing and I can get in through that. And I can take it down that way."

"Go for it," said Dr. Benson.

"So we wait till it's all clear," asked Lavelva Oates, "then we come out, is that what they're saying?"

"That's what they're saying. It's over, the bad guys won. Hostages for prisoners. The prisoners go, then the hostages go."

"What happens then?"

"I don't know," Ray said. "We'll let the geniuses figure it out."

"It ain't right," said Lavelva. "It ain't right all those people dead and messed up, and they git what they want."

"But do you kill a thousand innocent to punish fifteen or so bad? I don't know the answer but I thought the point of all these special police units was to set it up so you could kill the fifteen without the thousand. But it didn't seem to work out here today, did it?"

"No, it didn't."

"The one that was choking on me, you punished him but good. So there's a little justice here today, and you're the one who brought it, and you should be proud of yourself for the rest of your life for that one."

"It still ain't right," she said, disturbed.

They sat behind the rear counter of a store called Perfumaria, amid odors so sweet they had a gaggy quality to them. Cruz felt like throwing up. But he had his orders, and he would sit tight and make explanations later. There was no percentage in any other line of action.

The vibrator on his phone buzzed.

He fished it out of his pocket, slid the bar to answer.

It was all of them: McElroy but also Webley and, from far away, Nick Memphis.

Memphis did the talking.

"Where are you, Cruz?"

"In a perfume store still on the second floor. We killed one more bad guy, but I don't think anybody's caught on to that."

"Okay, we have an ID on the big man, a kid actually, twenty-two. He manages a store in the mall called First Person Shooter. He ordered the weapons through a dodge, he's got the computer chops, and maybe he's trying to do Columbine on steroids."

"So it's just some little fuck?"

"He would have access to the mall, he'd know all security arrangements, all the corridors and tunnels, and he has a record of disturbing behavior, from drug arrests to Internet harassment to arson, always quashed by Dad's money. He's been under a psychiatrist's care for years and it was thought he was 'getting better.'"

"Guess not," said Ray.

"You're the only asset we have in the mall. What we need you to do, Ray, is find a way to the fourth floor and to the Rio Grande corridor. This First Person Shooter is there, Rio Grande 4-312. It's where his headquarters would have to be, we think, where he's got this thing wired. When you get there, you set up outside. If everything goes well, we may not need you. If it goes bad, you may have to bust in there and cap him and whoever else is there fast. Sorry I can't get you body armor or anything. I suppose you don't even have to go if you don't want, but on the other hand, if any man in America would go on this one, it would be you."

Yeah me, he thought. I, warrior. I, hero. I, Marine. I, sniper.

"Cruz, are you okay?" asked Memphis.

"I'm on my way," said Ray.

"Look," said Memphis, "I get it. You thought you were out of it, and it followed you home and it's still trying to kill you. You have a beautiful fiancée and a thousand job opportunities and it's all looking swell, and then these guys come along with their little thing. I'm sorry, but that's the way it is."

Stay away from the W-word, Cruz told himself. There is no *why* in this world. There is only *is*, that is, what has to be done next, and this has to be done next. His father would do it without a second thought, and if he got killed in the very last seconds, he would not die tainted by bitterness. There is no *why*, there is only *is*.

"Cruz, are you okay on this one?"

"It's past my nap time," he said, "but I think I have one more day without a nap in me."

"Cruz, when this is over, I'll buy you a mattress store and you can nap all day long."

"I'll take you up on that," Cruz said.

Wearily, he rose.

"Don't know where you're going," said Lavelva, "but I'm going too."

Some things hadn't worked out. For one, the gun cameras. Now and then, as in the execution footage, they yielded something very interesting. But mostly they just tracked the random imagery that the muzzles covered as the gunmen haphazardly wielded them, at a speed that increased the abstraction to near totality and the information to almost nothing. Rather quickly, Andrew had ceased paying attention to them. They were like lava lamps mounted on the wall, nice if you're high and feeling kinda groovy, otherwise useless.

He sat in his command chair in the back room of First Person Shooter before a wall of such imagery. On the other wall, more important to monitor, were all the image feeds from the security cameras. They at least communicated security responses to his event. He could see in the exterior exit cameras, for example, that the murky black-clad ninjas known as SWAT teams had pulled back, or at least out of the picture, and that at each entrance a line of buses had pulled up. According to Andrew's instructions, each bus driver had opened his doors and left his bus and now stood in front of it, arms held upward and without jacket to display his unarmed status.

Ho-hum, another day at the office. It was all going swell.

The big board, which had the hacked SCADA pictorial of the MEMTAC 6.2 security program, showed nothing. Everything that was supposed to be locked down was still locked down; everything that wasn't, wasn't.

"What is going on with number six?" asked the imam.

"I don't—"

"He is still, He is on the ground. What is wrong with him?"

Andrew looked back to number six on the gun camera wall. It took him a while to make any sense of it, but then he realized it was an inverted image, and twisting his head to find the proper orientation, he saw that it was a floor-level observation of nothing, that is to say, not ceiling, not hallway, nothing containing data, but rather what, upon concentration, appeared to be the lower foot or so of wall beneath the window of a retail outlet, on a level with the floor.

"The gun is on the floor," Andrew said. "Like the kid just dumped it and went and got himself some ice cream. Or maybe the camera fell off in some roughhouse and it landed on the floor sideways. He wouldn't notice it. He didn't even know it was there."

"Or someone killed him, left the gun on the floor, and it's just lying there, showing nothing."

"Call him," said Andrew.

The imam spoke in Somali. "Number six, Hanad, are you there? Hanad? Has anybody seen Hanad?"

The imam listened to the return messages and

then reported, "Hanad went up on the second floor with Feysal."

"Which one was he?"

"Number eight."

He looked at number eight. Hmm, it seemed okay, just more blur and dazzle as the muzzle bounced about, pulling the camera with it.

"Asad? Where is Asad?" asked the imam. "I sent him to get the babies an hour or so ago. Where is Asad?"

Asad was number three. They both looked at that image and for a second it seemed to show nothing much, just the same blur and dazzle. But then it stabilized. It seemed to show a door. Then it went up to the ceiling and a man's hand reached around from the left and both the imam and Andrew watched as something large and irregularly shaped was crushed over the muzzle until it was held secure.

Andrew almost laughed. It looked like a potato.

Then the muzzle was lowered and it reacquired the door, settling just over the computer-controlled lock. The muzzle leaped, the irregular object—it *was* a potato!—dissolved in a blast of mist, and the doorjamb was blown out of the door frame, freeing the lock bolt. Hmm, interesting. The shooter had known not to fire into the lock itself—unbudgeable—but into the door frame, which was wooden and vulnerable to high-velocity energy. This fellow—was he a professional? It was like the moment when Dirty Harry leaps onto the school bus roof from the rail trestle, driving Scorpio nuts!

On the monitor, the muzzle dropped to the floor, displaying a pair of New Balance cross-trainers, and Andrew was aware that the owner had just moved through the door he had shot open and begun to climb some steps.

It suddenly made sense. Somebody in the mall was hunting his people. Some vigilante had killed Asad silently, gotten the rifle, and then improvised a suppressor from the potato—that was straight out of Marine Field Manual MC-118-341, "field-expedient suppression techniques." Now that person had shot his way into one of the locked stairwells and was headed upstairs, that is, upstairs toward him, Andrew. Was it Bronson, the young Eastwood, Bruce Willis? Or was it some clumping cheese eater who had disobeyed the mall's privately imposed law and brought a carry piece inside and now waged war?

No. He knew how to blow the lock; he was a professional. Maybe Delta, maybe SEAL, maybe some real good FBI HRT guy.

He hadn't counted on that, but at the same time, instead of being scared, he was exhilarated. This is *really* interesting. Oh, this will be so cool in the final document. Every story needs a tragic hero; this guy would be it. This would also give the story another narrative strand to twist in and out. It revved him way up.

He realized he must have, in his voluminous recording stick, the actual moment when the mystery man took out Asad and Feysal and Hanad and whoever else he'd taken out. He also realized that the hunter was now carrying the rifle, not having yet figured out that it was camera-equipped.

He went to his software screen, found the elevator on switch on the menu, and turned the elevators back on.

"Tell Maahir to send two guys up to the fourth

floor by elevator and set up in a storefront across from us. They'll be getting visitors soon. Oh," he continued, "this is going to look so cool in the game!"

"There it is," said Renfro. "That's it, that's the ball game."

He and the colonel stood in the Command trailer, watching the network feed from NBC. It showed the three Kaafi boys bounding up the stairs into the Air Saudi plane. Joy pulsed through their limbs and loins, three young men who two hours ago faced ten years of incarceration in an antiseptic, dreary Western prison, now able to dream and plan and feel freedom and anticipate the softness of a woman's flesh, the awareness of Allah's approval, the congratulations of imams and mullahs, and, eventually, another chance to strike and bring death to the infidel beast and vengeance for the murder of the Holy Warrior.

"You did it," said Mr. Renfro.

"You did it," said the colonel.

"We both did it," said Mr. Renfro. "And now, look out, world, here we come."

"It'll only be another half hour before they clear airspace and they're home free. Our people would never shoot them down and the Saudi pilots would never obey orders to turn back. The hostages will be freed, the Kaafi brothers will be in Yemen and shortly Mogadishu, and I think I'll let the mopping up devolve to my good friend Mike Jefferson, who likes the bang-bang stuff so much, he can go in and have his little gun battle with the bad guys. They'll all be punished that way, my hands are clean, and as you say, look out, world, here we come."

"Colonel, you have a one-on-one now with

ABC. It's the only major you haven't hit yet. Oh, and Fox—"

"My good friends at Fox," said the colonel.

"Even they will kowtow to the colonel on this day."

"Okay, let's—"

But like a bad dream, someone stood between him and the doorway, beyond which lay the ABC team, with its lights and camera and love.

It was the FBI hotshot, Will Kemp.

"I thought he was off running the investigation," the colonel muttered to Mr. Renfro, but as Kemp drew within hearing distance, he blossomed into his wise, cool public personality and said, "Will, your people were unbelievably fast and proficient on the Andrew Nicks ID, really, and that's such a help once we get those citizens out of there and go in and take the little bastard down."

"Thank you, sir," said Kemp.

"I'll be sure to tell the director how well you and your team operated and under what great pressure. I'm sure he'll be pleased, and I'm sure you'll be pleased."

"Yes sir," said Kemp, "but if you'll forgive, I want to discuss something else."

"Will, I'm on my way to a media thing, unpleasant but, unfortunately, it goes with the territory."

"Yes sir, but just let me express myself quickly, if I may."

"Sure, Will, shoot. But please make it snappy."

"Sir, I'm wondering if it was wise to pull the SWAT people so far back. Equally, I'm worried that it was unwise to give these people in the mall so much operational freedom. I mean they start shooting hostages, we're a good five to six minutes away from confronting them with force, and they could do a great deal of killing in that time. Our intelligence says they have at least ten thousand rounds of ammunition in there and sixteen fast-firing assault weapons."

"Will, you know, that troubles me too. Troubles me *immensely,* in fact. But the truth is, you have to take some risks in operations. I decided to take this one. I think the Muslims will be content with their propaganda victory, hollow though it is. I mean, these are basically thirteenth-century minds we're dealing with, and they're easily distracted. The glory that awaits them in this life, the chance to be heroes to their coreligionists, that's too much for them to give up on."

"Sir, it's not them I'm worried about. It's this goddamned white kid, with his crazy nihilism and bloodlust, his love for Eric Harris and Seung-Hui Cho, he could do anything, anything. I'd feel so much better if we had a sniper put a bullet in his head."

"Will, your concern is well placed and admirable. But by now, if we move SWAT back into place and authorize the rooftop snipers to get through the glass, I'm worried that we'll set him off. So my judgment is to stay passive, just a little longer. Then we'll let the SWAT boys off the leash and teach this kid a thing or two."

He turned, smiling, and went out to face the ABC cameras.

Up they climbed, up the steel steps in the unlit shaft of the stairwell, slowly, Cruz in the lead, tough little Lavelva behind, from the second floor to the third.

"Sir?" she said.

"Call me Ray. Not sir."

"Is this a machine gun? I haven't fired no machine gun before."

She was gripping the AK-74 that Ray had snatched up from the jihadi Lavelva had conked with her eight iron and he had finished with a bayonet. It made him realize: she knows nothing about that gun except what she's seen in the movies, but she's going on anyhow.

"It's not a machine gun, no. Here, I better show you how to use it."

They knelt, and he talked to her in whispers.

"Okay, this one fires as fast as you pull the trigger. No machine gun. Thirty times. But it's got to be loaded, the safety has to be off, it has to be cocked, and it's much better if you're aiming it."

He pushed the magazine release and snapped out the magazine.

"This orange banana-shaped thing is full of the cartridges. You know what a cartridge is?"

"The bullets."

"Yeah, close enough. You can see them held by the lips of the magazine, showing."

"Little things."

"They are small. But they move fast, they hit hard, they do real bad damage. So to load it, you have to lock in the magazine, the bullet part up, the bullets facing down the barrel. Look how I do it. Think of it as a kind of hinge. You sort of wedge the front part of the magazine into the front part of the magazine well, until it catches. See?"

He showed it to her two or three times. Then she took the mag and the small-framed, tinny, even toylike weapon, and mimicked him, ending up with the mag forward lip lodged into the mag well until it lightly clicked.

"Good. Now that it's set, you pivot the magazine back, or up, all the way into the well. There, that's right, pivot it in, see how it fits? And sort of force it or shove until—"

It locked.

"Okay, turn the gun over."

She did so.

"See that lever, that piece of rotating metal on the right side of the receiver, see how it goes up and hooks over this open slot in the gun?"

"I do."

"That's the safety. In that condition, up, the gun can't be fired or cocked. It blocks the bolt. See that?" and he pulled the bolt back about an inch until it hit the safety obstruction and would go no farther. "Bet you can figure out what to do."

"You push it down."

"You got it."

With her thumb, she rotated the long safety lever downward, so that it no longer blocked the bolt raceway.

"Now you have to cock it, set the bolt back, allow a cartridge to come up into the chamber."

"Okay," she said. She rearranged the gun so that she controlled it more efficiently, its stock against her hip, secured by her tightened elbow.

"Now see that latch or prong thing?" he asked, pointing to the bolt handle.

"Yes."

"Pull that back and let it go."

She pulled it back without trouble and then let

the bolt fly forward and seat itself after having moved a 5.45mm cartridge into the chamber.

"Okay, now you're ready to rock. It'll fire each time you pull the trigger. You know how to shoot it, like the movies. Just don't hold it sideways. Look over the top, line up the rear sight with the front sight, put it on target, watch the front sight, and press, don't yank, the trigger."

It reminded him of a time he'd taken Molly to a civilian rifle range. Molly tried gamely. She pretended she cared. She pretended the gun was interesting.

"Will it hurt?" Molly had asked him.

"No, not if you do it right. I'll show you how to do it."

He'd seated her behind a bench, fiddled with wrist and arm and upper body, aligning the barrel, her head, focusing the scope for her, tidying the sandbags.

"Okay, what are you thinking of?"

"What we're going to have for dinner."

He laughed. "You're hopeless."

"I'm not hopeless at all. I'm full of hope. I'm hoping this will be over soon."

And it was. And they went out and had a nice dinner and laughed their way through it, and now he wondered if he'd ever get back to that simple peacetime ritual of just hanging out with a woman you loved. Was it that big a deal? It seemed the whole world had managed it.

They made it to the top of the stairs.

"Okay," he said, "beyond there is enemy territory. I'm going to shoot open the door just like I did before and jump into the hallway. I'll be low. We'll check left, we'll check right. Then I'll dash across the hallway and cover for you. Then we'll move into the store, it's just seventy-five or so feet down to the left on that side."

Lavelva suddenly said, "No. Don't do it."

"What?"

"You'll be killed."

"What're you talking about?"

"They waiting for you."

"They don't even know I'm here."

"Yes, he do. That boy, he knows."

"Lavelva, what're you talking about?"

"Don't you see? It's in the game."

"I don't—"

"It's a game. This boy, he turned this whole place into his own giant-size game. You said he run First Person Shooter? I been there. All these geeky little E.T.-lookin' motherfuckers, black, white, yellow, it don't matter, they all be trippin' on killing and blowing shit up. It's so real to them, they don't remember they sittin' in a mall surrounded by gal underpants stores. And he's the king of all that. And what do a king do? He spread his empire, right?"

"Yeah, he's nuts, but why do you—"

"I play the game too," she said.

"We're wasting time."

"You get killed, you won't waste no time anymore. You listen to me. I play the games a lot. I like to leave my thing too. I don't want to be no girl in the projects with a brother dead and another nailing carpet and no prospects for nothing. I want to be Alex in *Wizards of Waverly Place,* and I'm all the time trying to get through the maze, you know. I like that story. I don't like the boy shit, which is all blowing up, but I like the girl shit, the Wizard Alex shit. And so I know the rule of the game. It's *you never go in the first way*."

"What?"

"That's the way the game work. Some people get it, some never do. But there is *always* another way into it. *Always*. That's the way you win. You look and look and look and find that other way in, 'cause if you go in the first way you find, you get whacked."

He looked hard at her.

"Ray, please," she said. "I'm telling you straight: through that door, death, sure enough."

That is it, my brother," said the imam. He was weeping. He had been so moved by the three young fighters in their orange suits leaping up the stairway into the plane, and now, all were aboard, and the hatch door was secured. The plane had to taxi to position at the head of the runway and then roar airborne. It was a triumph beyond his imagining.

He looked at Andrew. The young man, handsome enough in the Western way with his blond, short hair, his little ski jump of a nose, his sweatshirt and blue jeans and hiking boots, his baseball cap on backward, was lit by the glow of the news feed. His face showed nothing. He was not weeping at all. He showed no trace of joy or liberation, no sense of the meaning of the great thing he had accomplished, a thing no jihadi, not even the Holy Warrior himself, the martyred Osama, had come close to achieving.

He had actually freed prisoners from the American prison system. The Kaafi brothers, innocents, naifs, idiots, who had bumbled into an American bank on the day after Osama's death and, in a fit of Islamic passion, attempted to rob it with airsoft pistols with the idea of contributing to the cause. It was perhaps the stupidest robbery in the history of crime, more farce than threat, as the idiots had not even bothered to cover the orange rings appended to the gun muzzles to signify nonlethality. They were arrested by a smiling sixty-three-year-old security guard.

But some prosecutor decided to ride the prank as far as he could, and the three emerged six months later with massive sentences and were quickly shipped to the pen, where their frailness, their gentleness, their Somali beauty and grace got them fucked savagely every night by the depraved of America. The imam could not stand it. It hurt him so much. And now the boys were free, thanks to this American of dubious faith and principle named Andrew.

"We are so badass," Andrew finally said flatly.

"Andrew," the imam asked, "I have to know. Why? No virgins await you, only nothingness by your own beliefs. If there is no afterlife, this life is meaningless, so it must be so for you. But I cannot abide that. Please, now, on the cusp of your greatness, tell me your reasons."

Andrew didn't bother to repay the earnestness with eye contact. Clearly the W-word—*why*—wasn't of much interest to him. He'd been asked it a thousand times, by teachers, deans, cops, shrinks, counselors, parents, short-term girlfriends, everybody, anybody. He preferred not to hassle with it. It was psychobabble Muzak to his ears. He shrugged his shoulders.

"One reason I did it for you is because everybody hates you. That is so cool. I love the way you guys feed on that hate and it makes you bigger and stronger and more intent on your cause, which otherwise makes no fucking sense at all to me."

In fact, he really didn't give a shit about the dumb-bunny Kaafis. Anyone that stupid was doomed, and the rational functioning of natural selection had worked within design specifications to cull them from the herd, and what the Crips and Bloods did to their asses in the dark of a jungle penitentiary night was of little concern to him. Empathy was not one of his gifts; he actually thought the idea of the thin and beautiful and young and tender Somalis being gangbanged was pretty funny. The point of the prisoner release had really been just to stall things out for three hours or so, in order to let the networks set up so that the final act would play out in prime time before a world audience.

He thought a bit—meanwhile, the majestic jet had made it to the end of the airstrip and was rotating on its tires to orient itself for the long surge to liftoff—and finally applied himself at last to the conundrum that was Andrew Nicks.

Ideas, abstractions, conceits, causes—all were more or less hazy to him. He had no sense of nation or state, none whatsoever of "American interest," and to him the government was simply the entity that prevented the Osama kill shot from making it to Fox.

The game was everything. It superseded all. It provided framework, a set of rules, a rising litany of satisfied expectations, level by level, until the ultimate moment, and that moment was the point. Didn't they get that? Come on, assholes, I want to see the ultimate moment, the kill shot, when the SEAL operator double-taps pieces of flying steel at three thousand feet per into the famous mug of the Tall Guy, and he spasms backward amid a sudden atomized mist of Cuisinarted plasma and brain cells.

I want to see his eyes go all cue ball as the pupils rotate upward in the split second before his knees give and he notices his brains now decorate the wall and the ceiling. But no. We're so delicate all of a sudden. You have violated the rules of the game. You have set up the greatest narrative since World War II and demanded our attention, and when the climax arrives, you demurely avert your eyes, you assholes. You unbelievable pansy jerkoffs. You have violated the rules of the game.

How could he say to this guy, Hey, dude, I just transformed America, the Mall, into the greatest massively multiplayer online game. It will support thousands of players simultaneously, and players can be on the same side or play against each other in large-scale combat simulations set in a real place. They can be me or the SWAT hero who takes me down, and I bet a surprising number choose to play me. I am creating the scenes for a new game. Rather than using computer-generated images and sounds, I will be the first to use actual pictures and sounds from actual slaughter and carnage, in a real place, in a real time, with real characters, real life, real death. The stories! The miraculous mistakes, the brave moms, the gay waiters who give up their lives to protect their customers, the teenaged killers, the dedicated if hopelessly fucked-up imam, Maahir the killer of Santa Claus, it just don't git no better!

I believe that this will provide the realism lacking in the other games and in my world, which is the only one I care about, the only one I succeeded in, the only one where I found respect and loyalty and love and my ideal self, that is, immortality. No, it's more: it's godhood. And they will understand, the generations of players who are absorbed into the culture of my creation and become its heroes and villains. So—am I crazy or what? And it's all on disc. The finest first person shooter in history. Get the disc to WikiLeaks and it'll astound the world. It is first person shooter as art, as *The Odyssey* or *War and Peace*. Not only did I have the imagination to conceive it, I had the will to engineer it. All before the age of twenty-five.

But the imam would have not even begun to grasp the conceit that if art was creation, then it also had to be destruction. Instead Andrew settled on a trope that seemed to satisfy most people, and in which he himself even slightly believed.

"I have always liked to wreck things," he said, more to end the conversation than to explain anything. "It may be a drive as human as sex or greed or fear. Think about it. A certain tiny portion of the population has since time immemorial had a hunger to destroy so deep, so consistent, it has to be chromosomal. A gene for destruction. The DNA theory of anarchism. Maybe Allah or possibly the Wonderful Wizard of Oz, whichever one is really behind the curtain, he seeds each generation with a few of us natural-born blowers-up-of-shit because he knows someone's got to wreck all the crap so that someone else can start over and rebuild and have something to do on Monday. Else what would we do all day, year after year? Make cuckoo clocks?"

The imam, of course, didn't catch the refs to *Wizard* or to Welles's chilly speech in *The Third Man*, but he caught the gist of it.

"I think," he said, "Allah has touched you. He just forgot to whisper his name into your ear."

"See," Andrew said, "*everyone* makes mistakes."

EARLIER THAT DAY

The truck pulled into the sublevel loading dock for the Rio Grande corridor at 11:30 a.m. and Andrew was there to greet it. As usual the place was deserted, as the deliveries that kept America, the Mall, running came in late afternoon, between morning and evening crowds, even on Black Friday.

Andrew watched them unlimber from the truck interior, twelve Somali youths, ragged-looking and bewildered, in poor men's clothes, Pakistani copies of designer jeans, Malaysian Men's Club clone jackets, and Chinese-made athletic shoes; the boys were clearly overwhelmed by what they saw, which was nothing more than a large warehouse space in the mall's dark underground, far removed from the consumerist glories of the place itself. The imam barked orders and got them quickly herded into a freight elevator, where all fourteen men, crowded together, rode to the fourth floor and found themselves in another dark tunnel that ran behind the retail outlets on the Rio Grande corridor. Andrew led the way, and a hundred or so feet later, he popped the computer lock on his store, opened the door, and admitted them to his stockroom. He had industriously cleared it out for them, so there'd be plenty of room.

Moreover, six ten-piece buckets of Popeye's fried chicken and a cooler full of Cokes awaited the jihad warriors, who—even the oldest, called Maahir—at this point seemed in a kind of sloppy daze, unsure where they were, what their mission would be, what fate lay ahead. They had been told that this was a martyr operation, about which they had no doubts, that this day would end in paradise, that even before paradise they would serve the Faith more spectacularly than Mohamed Atta and the holy nineteen of 9-11, that they would enjoy every single second of what lay ahead, and that their job was to obey Allah as represented by the will of the imam. Who the white boy was held no interest at all to them compared to the chicken, which they found delicious, as they did the Coca-Cola, though one wondered aloud, in Somali, if there was Diet Coke available and seemed disappointed when he found it was not.

The imam bade them rest. He knew the travel had been overlong and uncomfortable, and he himself was quite agitated as, unblooded, martyrdom was not something a certain part of him welcomed, the part that had turned him into a chronic masturbator (three times last night!), secret imbiber, and occasional whoremonger.

What sustained him was not his faith in Allah or his love of fallen Osama but his belief in Andrew. Andrew knew everything, had foreseen everything, was calm, decisive, kind, just, decent, and sensitive to the iron mandates of Islamic culture, particularly as regarding infidels, though he himself was an infidel. That fact could be overlooked: such a gifted boy, such a committed warrior. He loved Andrew in a way that was almost unhealthy, though of course he was not a deviant—the holy text is quite explicit on the fate of men who love men—but he saw now how such a thing was at least possible. He loved him, then, as the Arab leaders had loved Lawrence in the Great War decades ago and could give themselves to the care of an infidel, knowing that in his heart, this white man rode with the Bedu.

Andrew's theory was to keep the boys occupied in these last few hours and far away from bigger questions of fate and duty and faith. Too much thinking was inappropriate now, so late, so close. Thus, through the stern guidance of the imam, he had three of them drag out the eleven crates of Soviet 5.45×39 ammunition, knife open the tins, rip the ammo out of the cheesy Russian military cardboard boxes, and all gather about to load the orange magazines. This was no easy task, and the boys didn't enjoy it, but Maahir, the oldest, was rough on the loafers and commanded them to their task, even though fingers soon grew sore forcing the cartridges into the narrow slots in the magazines, through the sharp lips that abraded or even cut their skin and stiffened in resistance as the boys loaded more and thereby increased the spring pressure against which they worked. All, of course, had loaded Kalash mags before, but never in such abundance. They usually carried but two or three with them and, barring conflict, they could have those tucked into pouches for days, sometimes weeks. Now, suddenly, they were loading twenty magazines apiece, and it was not enjoyable duty, even if it portended a big killing and much glory ahead. Then, to break the misery, Saalim told a funny story about the time his goat had been hit by a lorry and he had defrauded the driver out of three times the animal's worth. Punchline: it wasn't even Saalim's goat!

Through all this, not a word was said about plans. The actualities of what lay ahead were as mysterious as ever. And time was passing. Finally, at around two o'clock, when the last of the mags had been topped off, each boy had made sure his shoes were tied tight and had visited the pail in the little room to the left and made an ablative contribution, when prayers had been said again, finally, it was time.

The imam asked the boys to separate into self-selected twosomes, and there was some unanticipated difficulty here, as Ashkir was irritated because Saalim had already teamed with Asad. For Urgaas, the idea of spending the last hours of his life on earth with Ashkir was especially annoying, but finally Maahir grabbed Ashkir as his partner, which left Urgaas to buddy up with Madino, whom, though he had nothing in common with him, Urgaas at least did not actively despise.

That done, the imam walked among them, handing out tribal scarves, which he demanded they wrap about their necks but stuff low, inside the collars of their shirts, the idea being to pull them out at the moment of action, making each boy easy to identify by the others. He also gave them radio headsets with little throat microphones, through which, during the operation, he would address them.

He bade them sit. He nodded to Andrew, who slid a blackboard in front of them and spun it on pivots to reveal a map. The smartest among them recognized it instantly as a cross section of the very structure in which they were present, as viewed from the top down. It revealed a somewhat lopsided pentagon, with the two bottom sides slightly concave. The center of this odd structure appeared to be open, though it was latticed with walkways and at each corner, a larger box bore an odd name, in English, which some could sound out as Nordstrom, Sears, Macy's, and Bloomingdale's. Four corridors—strangely marked Colorado, Rio Grande, Mississippi, and Hudson— led from the outermost ring to the center area.

He spoke in Somali.

"Today, my brother pilgrims, is the day we strike the beast of the West in his lair. In a few short minutes, I will release you. You will be fully armed with your guns, your knives, warriors of the Faith, here to slay and ravage and rampage as is commanded by the holy text. You will rest tonight in paradise, my pilgrims, attended by a fleet of winsome virgins, who will bring you wine and dates and carnal pleasure and glory unto eternity. Let me show you the path to glory.

"But first let me warn you. We have shielded you thus far from the seductions of the West. You were chosen for your purity, your innocence, your devotion to faith. As you move along, you will see wondrous things that only a decadent civilization can conjure, clothes and toys and foods and other trivial but colorful delights. You must be strong. You must resist. This is a day of jihad, not vacation! Moreover, you must not be tempted by the shameless flesh of the West. You will see it everywhere, and in its beguiling licentiousness, it has brought many a true believer to ruin. I have chosen you because you are strong in the mind and in the heart. You can look upon such filth and spit in disgust. You will not be tempted, swayed, weakened, or in any way turned from duty.

"And that is as follows: You will smartly progress to the elevators as marked. Your rifles, hidden under your coats, will not be visible. Your earphones are common in America and the infidels will take them for the cell phones that dominate their lives. Each team of two will take the elevator to the first level. There, each team will progress to the corridors marked by the names of rivers, Colorado, Mississippi, Hudson, and Rio Grande"—he pointed them out—"and at the given hour, as I signal, Maahir will shoot the king of the infidels atop his throne, here, and you will hear the shot, pull your scarves up over your heads, shout *'Allahu akbar'* so that the infidels will know who has come to slay them in their sanctuary, and you will open fire, moving down the corridors toward this."

He pointed to the intricate pattern of roadways in the center.

"This is a Western playland, full of absurd contrivances that give them the safe joy of speed. You will drive them into this area by gunfire, killing as you see fit, drive them forward into the playland, where all will commingle and halt in progress. Maahir and his three will receive them. There you will command them to sit and you will commence to guard them.

"An hour, perhaps two, will pass, while I and my friend here make demands upon the infidels to help our cause. We mean to order them to free our three brothers unjustly imprisoned, so that they too will return to glory and the West will know our unquenchable will and that no bars can ever truly imprison a jihadi warrior prince."

At last it was time for the guns.

Andrew had checked each for functionality and distributed them with confidence. For the young men, new guns were like an aphrodisiac to the sex of violence. They crowded in, hungrily, to touch, to hold, to caress, to possess a new weapon. The usual orgy of rifle love took place, as each newly equipped and wide-eyed gunman tested bolt and trigger pull and sight alignment and heft and feel and point-ability. Some of the more immature aimed, issued copious, phlegmy machine-gun sounds, and mimed the shaking of the instrument on full automatic, as deployed in fantasy genocide against Jews or, if Jews weren't available, mere infidels, equally worthy of death but somehow lacking in the pizzazz of a Jewish kill.

"Yes," said the imam, "it is play now, but soon, my young, fearless jihadis, it will be real, as will the blood that you spill, including, in martyrdom, your own as you make the trip to be loved by Allah."

"Allahu akbar!" someone shouted, and the others took it up, until it grew alarmingly loud, and Andrew elbowed the enthusiastic imam, and that gentleman came to his senses and ordered silence.

The young men drew a single orange banana clip from the pouch they wore on their chest and now pivoted it into the well of the AK-74, almost in perfect syncopation, as if on drill, so that the sound of twelve clicks snapped through the space. To some ears, it was music.

Finally, each of the young men was handed a large overgarment, cheap blue gabardine overcoats formerly issued to Czech draftees that had been picked up by Andrew, XXXL, at a local surplus joint.

They were easily big enough to swallow the young men and the rifles they held cradled tight across their chests or down along their sides, hands nesting on pistol grips. To look at them in this condition was to see little that suggested lethal intent: young Somali men, each handsome in that Somali way of which Somalis were so justly proud, with high, fine cheekbones, chocolate skin, a fine pelt of frizzed hair, and bright and vivid eyes, each wrapped in some garment indistinguishable from the garments worn by others of the age and cohort, Somali or whatever, pretty much the world over.

"When the Kaafi brothers are released," the imam concluded, "then you will have your killing. No one will interrupt you, as the infidels are cowards. If they cannot bomb from afar or fire missiles, they lack the will to fight. They do not like the sight of blood or the damage a bullet may do. But you, my young lions, are hardened in battle. The destruction to flesh which you bring to them, the lakes of blood you spill until it is thick upon the floor, all of that is your contribution to the Faith and the vessel of your glory. You will avenge Osama!"

Asad thought, Who was Osama?

Any reports from the mall?" asked Colonel Obobo, himself bathed in the glow of the TV monitor in the dark of the Incident Command trailer, as the same imagery of loading, sealing, and then taxiing was playing out.

"All quiet, sir."

"Great," said the colonel.

Then he felt a presence; it was Mr. Renfro leaning in quietly.

"I haven't seen Jefferson lately," whispered Mr. Renfro. "I don't trust him. Maybe he's up to something crazy. Better check on him."

"Tell me, where's Major Jefferson?" the colonel asked loudly.

"Sir, I haven't seen him."

"Commo, get me Major Jefferson."

"Yes sir."

The colonel put on his earphones and throat mike, just in time to hear the channel one request, "All personnel, this is Command, where is Major Jefferson? Major Jefferson, please report in, ten-four."

The silence was ominous.

As the colonel watched, the jet began the pirouette that would place it on the proper vector for takeoff.

"Ah, Command, sorry, Jefferson here, checking in."

"Major, where are you, please?" asked the colonel.

"Sir, I'm with the Mendota Heights SWAT commander, trying to adjudicate an argument he is having with Roseville in regards to the coffee situation. Nothing I'd thought to trouble you with, though if you want, I can return ASAP when I get it settled and brief you."

"No, no, you handle it, Mike, I trust your judgment, you know that. If you can, get yourself to a TV and watch these bastards fly away home. Then get ready to receive the hostages."

"Yes sir," said Jefferson. "I'll do that."

"Okay," said Cruz, "you are the wizard of America, the Mall. You know games, I don't. You get to be the intelligence officer; I'm just the grunt. I'll find another way."

"Thank you, Ray," she said.

He thought quickly.

"You got a cell?"

Of her age and generation and culture, who didn't have a cell?

"Sure." She took out her Nokia.

"Write the number down on my wrist."

She did, with a Bic she had in her jeans pocket.

"I'm going back. I'll get up there by some other way. I'll figure it, don't know how yet."

But she knew how. There was only one way. He had to get back to the atrium overlooking the amusement park and risk climbing from the third-floor balcony to the fourth. Somehow, some superhero USMC goddamned way.

"When I'm ready, you go to the door and fire five or six rounds into the door jamb next to the lock, like we did before, push it open. If Geniusboy has his gunners out there waiting, they'll run to the door to pop you coming out. Only you won't be coming out. I will be, from some other place. I will do the popping. Then we move on to the store where he's running this game and we get ready to deal with him. Got it?"

"I won't let you down, Ray."

"That's the one thing I know for a fact."

"So, the plane is at the runway," Marty told Nikki over the radio. "It'll be off in a few seconds, a minute or so at the most."

"Got it. I don't like it. To me, we're trusting these guys to keep their word like, I don't know, they're bridge club ladies or something."

"The Frabjous Obobo has decided. Anyhow, I have a great shot in mind. Oh, you'll like this. This'll get me to New York too, Mary Tyler Moore."

"Mary Tyler Moore doesn't have room for moochers or slackers in her organization, Marty," said Nikki. "What's this shot you want?"

"Well, it'll get me a local Emmy, that's for sure."

"You want an Emmy, Marty? Buy some more tables at the banquet."

"So young, so cynical."

"Go ahead with your *Gone with the Wind* shot."

"When the planes take off, I want you to have Cap'n Tom, assuming he's still sober—"

"Hey, Marty," cut in Tom, "I haven't had a drink in at least three minutes."

"Tom drops down and hovers over the big entrance there on the east side."

"Got it."

"You should get dramatic shots of hostages pouring out and heading toward the buses and climbing aboard. Some'll be limping, some'll be being helped, there'll be crowding, but also joy and thankfulness."

"Got it."

"Get me faces, I want faces."

"Faces."

"Then the camera op pulls back, comes in tight as he cranks focus way in, and sitting in the doorwell of the WUFFchopper is new star Nikki Swagger. Ms. Scoops-R-Us herself, reporting on the hostage release. In one continuous shot. It'll be terrific, and maybe it'll go national."

It was a good idea.

"Gee, you're wonderful, Mr. Grant," she said.

Cruz made it out the doorway and slid down the Rio Grande hallway toward the balcony over the atrium. He went prone, slithered to the metalwork, and saw, two stories down and through the screening of possibly artificial trees, the spread of hostages on the walkways of the amusement park, and the gunmen standing all around. He got a good look, through a hole in the trees, of Santa. Still dead.

He picked up his phone.

"Sniper Five, go ahead, Cruz."

"They've set an ambush at the stairwell, we think. I'm going to go around it, but there's no easy way. No nearby escalators, all the stairwells are locked. So I have to climb in plain sight from this level to the next. Can you see me?"

A pause, as McElroy worked his binoculars, and

then found the Marine lying on his back just off the balcony.

"Got you."

"I need a recon. See any bad guys?"

"No, they're all downstairs, I have no movement on any of the upper levels. Are you sure this is a good idea?"

"Do you have a better one?"

"Man, I don't have *any*. But that's a long exposure and, if they see you, an easy shot, and if the bullet doesn't kill you, you land on your back or head and break something important and permanent. And maybe that queers the hostage deal."

"You forget the best part. I'm scared to death of heights."

"All right, I'd relocate about fifty feet to your left. There's a support beam between the balconies. Looks like it's decorated with some kind of phony turn-of-the-century-according-to-Disney shit. Maybe it has enough hand- and footholds."

"Good work."

"Do you have buds for your phone?"

"Yeah. In the box at home."

"Okay, I can't talk you up. I'll watch and—"

And what? There was nothing McElroy could do but watch.

"Good luck, Marine. Semper Fi, all that."

Ray put the phone away and low-crawled the fifty. He knew he didn't have much time. He knew he couldn't make any noise. He knew he couldn't sweat, grunt, breathe heavy, swallow, anything. This was just pure acrobatics against a lethal height in front of an audience of killers, who, he hoped, weren't in the habit of looking up. Fortunately, since the happy architects of Silli-Land had planted the grounds with those interfering trees, direct vision across or up was always impeded by the fluffy weaving of artificial leaves. One word: *plastics.* That might help.

He pulled himself up, made a last check.

None of the Somali guards was in a particularly alert status. They lounged, gathering in little groups—probably against their general orders—and seemed somehow quite happy. If any wondered where pals A through D had gone to, they weren't showing it.

Okay, he told himself, *go.*

I don't want to go, his self answered.

What was it Molly always said with a smile on her face? *Too bad for you.*

First he pulled himself up to the balcony railing, securing himself by hand to the pillar, which was itself about six inches wide, the same sage green as everything else in this green metal universe. Then he planted his foot on a nub of scrollwork, a filigree to the conceit of New Orleans balcony wrought iron overlooking Bourbon Street, and indeed, it held, and he hoisted himself up, aware at the same time that his entire weight was supported by just a stub of fake wrought iron. He rose by pulling, felt secure enough to free his off arm, and reached up. Once a tremor came to his foot; he slipped but somehow managed to check himself before he went by getting ahead of the slippage and jamming the foot in hard. He stabilized, holding tight, then brought his other leg up, searching for a foothold with his toe.

Where the fuck was it? God, there wasn't one. Meanwhile, his twisted fingers, all that were between him and the serious intentions of gravity, began to cramp in pain. They slipped too, costing him a little purchase, so that if he wasn't on by fingertips quite, it was only the last joints of one hand that secured him.

Don't look down. Don't look down.

Ray stabbed again with his free leg, like a show horse stomping out its age in the dirt, one-two-three, higher each time, until almost at full extension, it lit on something just big enough to hold him, and he hoisted again.

Very quickly this turned into a bad career move; he was supported in his two-hundred-pound entirety by the leverage of about a toe and a half, wedged against the meekest of protrusions, and with a hand he reached high, searching for a grab-on, aware that his purchase was slipping, slipping, slipping, and in the second before he knew he'd go, swing inward, and torque his support hand free and send himself into outer space, his fingers closed on some kind of steel tube, clamped hard upon it, and this stretched him a little further into extension and his foot also found a mooring point, and up he shot.

He rested, still, feeling the tracks of sweat running from hairline to eyes and nose, down from his armpits, the breath coming in hard gusts, even as his primal fears of falling expressed themselves vividly and he saw himself as in a '60s movie's crummy special effect, spinning laterally, getting farther from the lens as he descended until at last he plunked hard to earth, broken, like a doll or a toy. And then he heard a scream.

That's it, he thought. I'm dead. He tensed against the shot that would hit him and bring him down.

It cannot be discovered who first saw him. But it is known that Esther Greenberg, sixty-nine, stockbroker, mother of none, mentor of many, supporter of dozens, was the only one who figured out what had to be done and had the stone guts to do it.

Someone poked her and leaned close.

"They're here," came the whisper. "Commandos. Cops. Somebody."

She nodded, frozen, suddenly overwhelmed by this new reality.

"Up above," came the whisper.

Slowly, as if she were merely stretching, she elevated her head, and she saw him. At first she thought, It's one of them. But then she thought, No, it can't be. He's trying to move slowly, he's not black, he's one of us.

She looked over and saw two of the gunmen jabbering, until they grew uninterested in each other. The tall one was the dangerous one. He disengaged from his buddy and began to look around innocently, the way a young guy will let his eyes roam out of boredom. He looked left, right, and then began to look up and—

"Noooooooo!" she screamed. She stood up. "I can't take it anymore," she yelled as if there were one thing on earth that frightened her. "Please, please, let me go."

She ran at the tall boy with the gun, who watched her come with lightless eyes, even as other hostages tried to grab her to stop her from suicide. But she made it to him, and he smashed her in the head with his AK-74 between puffs of his cigarette.

Crazy American bitch, he thought. What was that all about?

No shot came. He heard turmoil and scuffling below but was in no position to check it out. Instead he waited a second, the panic passed, again he reminded himself to not look down, and he hoisted one foot up, up, up, found a toehold, God knew what, and again launched himself upward, feeling the pain of exhaustion sizzle through his arms and the yearning of his fingers to cease their death grip.

And then it occurred to him that he was there, he had made it. He was now resting on the solidity of the fourth floor, except on the wrong side of the balcony, and it just took an adroit but controlled roll and spin, and he was over and landed on the floor of the next story. He sucked at air, waited for his racing heartbeat to diminish, and finally, sliding next to a wall, stood, got himself up.

He looked up at the skylight, not nearly so far away now, and waved, and the figure that must have been McElroy waved back. Ray got out his phone, pressed the button.

"Jesus, I thought you were going there for a second," said McElroy.

"God looks after fools, I guess," Ray said. "Do you have an angle to the corridor?"

"Not enough of one. I can only see about fifteen feet down it."

"Okay, I'm going to move down there, set up. If something happens and they start shooting hostages, I'll step out and drop the ambushers and move into that First Person Shooter place."

"It's on the left, about halfway down."

He then called Lavelva.

"Okay," he said, "I made it up, somehow. I'm just

inside the balcony, to the right of the corridor. What have you got?"

"Nothing. I'm just waiting here."

"Good. If I give the signal, you shoot the door frame, not the lock. You have to blow away the lock-work, which is only buried in wood and plasterboard, then you kick in the door, then you drop back. That should draw them, and I'll put them down and go to the store. When you hear my shots, you're clear to follow. Sweetie, are you up for this? You don't have to go. You can just back on down the stairwell."

"I am so up for this."

"You are a true warrior princess, bravest of the brave. Okay, in just a few, it'll be our turn for some first person shooting."

The snipers huddled at, roughly, Racine.

"The only thing we have is flashbangs," one of them said.

"And they don't go boom, they go pop."

"Fuck," said McElroy, who'd just returned from scouting for Ray and hoped they'd solved their prob-lem but was disappointed to discover they had not.

"I have two red smokers," someone said.

"Forget the smokers."

"Maybe if in concert, all of us whacked a certain small area with our butts."

"A, probably doesn't work, B, throws the scopes out of zero. No go."

"I'm just thinking out loud."

"That's good, that's good," said McElroy, "think out loud, everybody, maybe we'll come up with something."

"Hey," said a state trooper sniper, "we have Kevlar

tactical helmets." He snapped his finger against the hard tactical shell. "Maybe smash with them, open the hole, and that way we don't throw the zeros out."

"You'll never get through that shit with plastic helmets," someone else said.

"Hey, this shit is hard," said the trooper.

"Any entrenching tools?"

"This isn't World War Two."

"What about with our knives we chip away at that groove FBI opened. All of us working hard, maybe we get it loosened, *then* smash it with our helmets."

"That seems about the best. I mean it's all we can do, right, FBI?"

"I guess," said McElroy, reaching for his knife. But as he did, his wrist passed over the smooth cylinder that was the flashbang grenade, more a pyrotechnic than anything else, meant to produce a loud percussion and a disorienting flash. But not enough junk in it to—

"Okay," he said. "How many flashbangs?"

A quick survey produced the answer: twelve.

"Twelve. I'm wondering, what happens if they all go off at once?"

"You'd have to contain it," said somebody. "Direct it. They can bring down a huge building with a few pointed charges."

"Use the helmets and—"

"But it has to go simo. You'd need wiring, dets, a whole tech kit that the Army has but we don't. I don't—"

McElroy saw it then.

"Here's what we're going to do. We take one of those helmets. We load it with flashbangs. Hmm, let's see, they work just like grenades, right?"

"Yes."

"Okay, we wrap, I don't know, gauze, bandages, duct tape, something soft and malleable around the levers on the flashbangs, got it? That secures the levers. Then we pull the pins but nothing happens because the levers are taped down. Then very carefully we run a wire or a piece of tape or something through the tape on the flashbang levers. Then very carefully, we put the flashbangs on the glass and we cover them with the helmet and maybe you put something heavy on the helmet."

"Is this a game you're playing? Are you Mac-Gyver or something?"

"Why not just run the tape through the rings on the flashers?" someone said. "Simpler."

"Simpler, yeah, but those pins take a lot of pull to free up, and I can see the tape or whatever breaking or getting hung up," McElroy said.

"He's right," said the trooper.

"So if this thing goes bad and the bastards downstairs start shooting, we pull the tape line, which pulls the tape loose, and all the flashbang levers go ping, and three seconds later all twelve of them go off more or less simo, and the helmet directs the considerable force of their detonation downward, I'm betting you blow a nice big hole in that glass. Then we go to war, and we shoot every gunman we see in the head. Do you get it?"

"Yes, I do."

"And if the hostages are released, all we have to do is replace the pins and give everybody their toys back. Okay. Have you got it?"

"It's a plan, Stan."

No, no, no, no, no.

He'd made the jumps from Bruce Wyatt to RealDeal Opsys to RealDeal Secsys to RealDeal Secsys Linkage to—

A wilderness.

Deployed in front of him on the screen were nearly four hundred—more than three screens' worth of scrolling—coded units, each representing some kind of RealDeal franchise or outlet. One of them had to be the RealDeal on the fourth floor at America, the Mall, in Indian Falls, Minnesota. But which?

The geniuses at RealDeal Opsys so knew their empire that they didn't bother to split the list by category as any sane outfit would do. It wasn't broken down by store profit levels, major markets, region, or state. No, just an endless column of bullshit listings like RD/OPSYS5509-3.4X. What? What the hell was that?

"Someone call RealDeal Corporate," said Dr. Benson. "We'll get an engineer on the phone and we'll—"

So close, thought Neal. So goddamned close.

The Air Saudi 747-8 seemed to take forever. The colonel watched it; a heat mirage rose from the engine structures, shimmering as it blurred the reality behind it, signifying the mounting temperature of jet engine exhaust. Then, finally, it lurched, picked up speed, and the camera stayed with it while behind it the farm plains and dreary suburbs of Minneapolis began to blur. At the end of a long, slow fifteen hundred yards, it rose, shivered, then shucked the ground, shivered again as its landing gear retracted and disappeared behind closing wheel wells, and then banked right against the black sky, heading north on the great circle route, to Yemen.

There was no cheering in the Command trailer, but the colonel felt a stir in his heart. He had done what he could do. He had given them what they wanted. He had bridled in his wild cowboys who wanted to go in with guns blazing. He felt at peace, secure in the knowledge that no one else could have negotiated the treacherous terrain and the many obstacles between what he had discovered upon arrival and this very moment.

Mr. Renfro whispered in his ear, "Congratulations, Doug. You brought it off. You did it."

"Thanks," he said, "I couldn't have—"

"Sir, it's him. Andrew Nicks."

The colonel took the phone, surprised to find himself drenched in sweat.

"You saw?" he said. "You have your prisoners. Good riddance to them. Now give us our hostages."

"Excellent. By the way, change of plans," said Andrew. "Please witness the firepower of the armed, fully operational Death Star." He paused, hoping the *Star Wars* ref gave his carefully considered statement more oomph.

"Imam," he said in a loud voice so that all could hear, "tell the jihadis to open fire. Kill the hostages. Kill them all. Colonel, I now restore the security television cameras so that you and all of America can watch the massacre and learn to cower in fear of Islam."

Nick, in the Pennsylvania Avenue crisis center, heard the kill order from Andrew Nicks, Eric and Cho wannabe, soldier of Islam, first person shooter champion, and all-around asshole, and almost before the sentence was finished, was screaming and body-Englishing into his mike, "McElroy, blow the window now, blow it now and engage targets. Ray, can you suppress from your position?"

But he was a second behind the action curve as McElroy, having heard the same declaration of purpose, had already yanked the master cord and felt the tape securing the levers of the twelve flashbangs under the Kevlar helmet on the thick glass of the skylight pull free, and in the next second or so, the det went loud and hard, made more pointed in its effectiveness by the cupping effect of the helmet—a batch of bulletproof vests lay atop it, pinning it—which blew all force downward into and through the skylight, shearing through the heavy Plexiglas, atomizing it into a spray of glitter, like droplets of water, yielding a jagged opening, almost like a hole in the ice.

It blew like a howitzer shell. The Kevlar helmet was sent into orbit, the noise of the purposefully loud flashbangs magnified by twelve seemed to put a needle into every nearby eardrum, and the pressure wave and subsequent vibration shivered the foundations of the planet.

Still, ears ringing, McElroy was on the gun almost within a second, finding a braced position on the window well and peering through the scope into the smoky interior. What he could see wasn't detailed; it was a seething blur, almost abstract, as beneath him, en masse, the hostages seemed to rise and scatter while at the same time, at the edges of the crowd, the flashes of gunfire, the percussion of reports, the shockwave of energy signified that the gunmen had opened fire. In another second, another agent, on binocs, screaming, "Two o'clock, I have a shooter, I see flash, Dave, two o'clock."

McElroy traced the imaginary clock hand out to the two o'clock orientation and found the flash, saw a thin black youth in black and green tribal scarf pumping rounds from his AK, the flash lighting the boy's face, displaying his excitement, his joy, his pleasure as he shot from the hip into the screaming herd before him, and McElroy put the X-marks-the-spot on the bridge of the nose—10 power blew it up big as a movie screen, HD no less—remembered he was shooting radically downhill and so brought point of aim down a minute of angle or so, and then felt the gun recoil—he had fired instinctively, without order, his trigger finger making all decisions for him—and took his first kill, as the bullet split the head, spewing a foam of black liquid, and the boy's limbs melted, as he went down hard and forever.

"Clean hit," screamed the spotter.

McElroy raced through the bolt ritual, up hard,

back hard, seeing the empty pop like a muffin in his mom's kitchen, forward hard, down soft.

"Go left to ten, I see more flash, two of them, take them, Dave, knock them down."

McElroy found the shooter at the end of blurred transit across space and frenzy, felt he was too low on the body to take time to find the head, and his oh-so-clever trigger finger put a 175-grain hollowtip through the top of the guy's chest, so that it would follow its downward angle, opening like an umbrella or some kind of steel rose with razor petals, find and explode the heart, which is what it did, the result being another instant splash and collapse.

"Next to him, next to him, next to him," screamed his spotter, and McElroy jacked the spent shell out, planted a new one in the chamber, and found his next target just as that young man was reacting to the death of his partner and looked up to see Dave one hundred or so feet straight up from him.

But he vanished in a split second, withdrawing under the canopy of the second-floor balcony and Dave felt a surge of groaning frustration.

"Find me targets," he screamed.

"Looking, looking, looking," the spotter said.

"Oh no," said Mr. Girardi.

A flash, followed by the crack of a detonation, seemed to blossom upon the roof of the great building.

Suddenly, activity burst out all over the compass.

The explosion seemed to galvanize every figure on the landscape, and in seconds, people were running by them, cars were mobilized, even the hovering helicopters seemed to descend from the sky.

They heard, though muted, the sounds that could only have been gunshots.

"I thought it was all fixed," said Mr. Girardi.

"Something must have gone wrong," said his wife.

"I thought it was all over," Mr. Girardi said. "And now this."

Each gunman heard, over his earphones, the scream of the imam.

"My pilgrims," the man raged, "it is time to avenge the sins of the Crusaders and the murder of the Holy Warrior. Kill the infidels. Kill them, my brave warriors, and purify the world of their filth and disease."

Faaid put down his box of Caramel Corn and winked at Hani, who was eating cold french fries out of a cardboard box, and Hani winked back merrily. Now for the fun part!

The remaining boys spread around the perimeter of the large, docile crowd of white sheep in the amusement park, lifted his rifle to hip, and pivoted, a candy-sticky finger going to the safety levers for those who had bothered to put their safeties on, and each opened fire.

Only Nadif and Khadar were reluctant. They had spent most of the time eating and never really made eye contact with any of the white people. They had more or less found each other over the long ordeal of travel and hiding, each reading the other's lack of killer zeal among the harder faces of the truly demented. By nature passive, they had done their duty with a minimum of aggression and frenzy. They had strolled down Mississippi at the beginning, shooting out ceiling lights and blowing holes in store windows and watching mannikin strumpets dissolve under the multiple impacts of 5.45mm bullets traveling at close to 3,000 feet per second, which they found very amusing. As for actually blowing large holes in human flesh, not so much. Then they had more or less strolled the perimeter of the mass of huddled hostages, making no eye contact with the victims, interacting reluctantly, taking frequent bathroom and food stand raid breaks.

They were not particularly into jihad. Nadif had dreamed of being a doctor and Khadar a poet. A poet! He had soft eyes and gentle ways, was almost girlish in his winsomeness. But when General Aweys's militia had wiped out his village, and his parents as well, he had been given a choice: carry a rifle or die.

He chose the rifle and, alone among the boys, had never killed a soul. Today was supposed to be his first, but the approach of it had left a queasy feeling in his stomach.

Khadar said, "It's time to do the work of Allah," though without much enthusiasm. Both knew punishment of all sorts awaited them if they did not perform as expected. Numbly they turned to do the necessary.

But at that moment, from above, the sky exploded. All looked up to see the aftermath of some sort of blast at the tip of the oddly shaped skylight, and besides the unpleasantness of the noise, it rained sparkles upon them, a kind of sudden dry wind of interfering debris, and each involuntarily blinked, closed eyes, averted face.

Only a second or two, but possibly it was tactically significant, in that its violence was so unexpected and overwhelming, it stirred the torpid crowd in unanticipated directions. Suddenly, many rose, saw the rescue had commenced just as shooting had commenced, and at last found the courage to run. They scattered outward like cinders fleeing a fire.

Faaid fired at one runner, bringing him down, turned, fired fast at the crowd that suddenly roared toward him, was astounded that none went down and realized that there's a lot of air in a crowd and at that time figured he was much better off aiming instead of crazily cracking off rounds from the hip, brought the rifle to his shoulder, and—

McElroy's first shot splattered his brains.

The others didn't notice. They too tried to master the crowd-massacre learning curve, and they too discovered that shooting blindly into the belly of the beast is likely to produce displeasing results, and in the time it took them to bring rifles to shoulders and brace knees tightly for supported shooting, several others, assisted by McElroy, Ray Cruz, and others, lost interest in the point of the operation as they were felled for keeps.

Ray got the news. Dropping the cell, he rose to the balcony railing, winced as above him McElroy's flashbang bouquet flashed and banged with stunning malevolence, blew a hole in the Lake Michigan skylight, and a blast-propelled spray of glass spewed downward, and leaned over the balcony looking for shots. He only had a P7, the German police trade-in the killers had somehow come up with on the surplus market, though he knew it by reputation to be an accurate pistol. Two hands locked onto the small thing, the lever that bisected the grip compressed

by the adrenaline-pumped psycho strength coursing down his wrists, Ray stepped out, oriented on
a flash—he couldn't see well enough to pick out an
actual shooter—guesstimated where the shooter had
to be relative to the flash, and squeezed off three fast
rounds. The gun popped in his hands at each shot,
spitting an empty, yet its jump wasn't radical and the
barrel axis was so low to his hand that it just ate up
recoil, so Ray got back on target fast. Three fired, the
flash disappeared, and whether he'd made a kill or
just scared the guy to cover, Ray didn't know.

But he knew Lavelva's theoretical ambushers
would have been alerted by the flashbangs as well as
his own shooting, and he wheeled, still in the two-
hand, low isosceles stance, and saw them—goddamn,
the girl was right!—as they both emerged from a
shop about sixty feet away, rifles flying to hips to take
the infidel down. The P7 lived up to its rep; a long
shot for a 9-mil, he still made it neatly and crisply,
put one into the lead shooter, rocking him to stagger
and sit-down. He rotated smoothly, telling himself
not to hurry, onto the second target, tracked it as the
man was moving, laid the front sight on the leading
edge of the mover. Then Ray saw flash—he heard
silence because his war brain had shut the world
down to nothing but target—and knew instantly that
his opponent, shooting fast without aiming, firing
from the hip, had missed, and Ray felt his trigger pull
break, the gun leaped in its little way, and the runner
slowed, staggered by a solid hit, stopped, straightened
up a little. At that moment from across the hallway,
a door flew open and Lavelva, with her AK-74, fired,
and although she shot more or less wildly, at least

three of her twenty or so rounds went home, and the second Somali himself slid into coma and death on the floor of the mall.

"Bring a gun!" he screamed, and she picked up one of the fallen AKs and ran to him.

He took it as if it were a baton in a relay race, pivoted, looked over the sights for targets in the chaos and scramble below, vectored in on one muzzle flash as yet unquelled, and put three or four rounds into that spot directly behind where instinct told him a shooter crouched. If a man was there, he either went down hard or scampered back, under the overhang of the balconies, so that no angle was available to Ray.

Then Ray's eyes were drawn to a melee in the center of the space below him, and he saw that some kind of fight had broken out, a pile-on, as hostages had trapped and were beating on one of their tormentors. But he had no shot.

The coup de SWAT consisted of some neatly tuned disobedience.

"That's my unit moving back," the officer had said twenty minutes back, as they crouched in the shadows of the parking lot across from the Rio Grande entrance. "They all have the black helmets from Bravo Company for that cool Delta look."

"It is cool," another guy had said. "We tried to get them, but the budget—"

"Go ahead," Jefferson had said.

"Okay, so why don't we go to them, trade helmets, and send *them* back to Incident Command. If they keep their helmets on, nobody's going to know it's them and not us. I know Nick Crewes, who commands over there. He'll go for it."

"And then we're real close if the fucking balloon goes up," said someone else. "And if it doesn't, who knows?"

So this meant Jefferson and his ad hoc team of all-star SWAT mutineers were still in strike distance to the Rio Grande entrance, and they didn't need an official order to go. When they heard Andrew's orders to his gunmen, they just went.

It was a quick dash to the entrance, and both shotgunners laid muzzles next to the same metal door lock and fired simultaneously. Metal hit metal with a clang of super energy that, combined with the percussion of the two shells firing, sounded nuclear in its decibel level. Nobody blinked, they were so full of adrenaline, so ready to close and shoot, after the hours of doing nothing. The door torqued under the double slam of two hard-metal missiles being sent into its innards at a thousand feet per second and warped, twisting, showing two blisters and two smears of superheated carbon where the breaching rounds had tunneled through. Jefferson gave a hard wrench and—the door didn't budge.

"Goddamn!" he screamed, and yanked and pulled, but it didn't move. Inside they could hear the shots.

"They're shooting, oh Christ, it's a war!" came a terrified voice.

Oh, Christ, thought Neal. Think. *Think!*

Thank God for television. Was it a World War II movie? Nazis hunting a clandestine radio in an apartment building. They have the signal, they just don't have the floor. One by one, they turn off the power on each floor, and when the radio broadcast is interrupted, they know their guy is on that floor.

Thank you, Nazis. Thank you, television.

Neal dragged the icon to POWER DOWN ALL and turned off every single RealDeal outlet in every single mall, strip mall, town, suburban shithole, whatever, in America. From Toledo to Tucson, from New York to Natchez, and along any other axis you cared to chart, they all went blank, all four hundred–odd of them.

For a second. Then one by one by ten by twenty, they came back on, as branch managers went to their boards, pressed RESTORE, and got their juice back on fast and the two hundred screen images back on. That is, all except one, where the branch manager was lying on the floor hoping not to get shot, surrounded by weepy clerks and sobbing customers, all clenched in prayer. Neal dragged to that one, clicked on it to bring it up, looked for LINKS, clicked on that, and found himself in a program called MEM-TAC 6.2, went to the pictorial, found LOCKDOWN ENGAGED, put the cursor on it, and clicked.

LOCKDOWN DISENGAGED came the message.

You're terminated, fucker, he thought.

With the clunky sound of large pieces of metal shifting, the doors shivered and popped amid the stench of burned powder.

"Go, go," shouted Jefferson, as his people raced in. "Semiauto, lasers on, look for targets."

But the order was largely meaningless, as all six of them knew that.

What they found was the corridor called Rio Grande overflooded with a torrent of escapees coursing down the hallway at them, as the outer margins of the hostage crowd had already begun its race to freedom and safety, overwhelming the gunner meant to stop them by sheer numbers. He got off a few shots and then was pierced from above by one of Dave McElroy's .308s and taken from the fight and from the planet, both forever.

So the SWAT team formed a flying wedge, waving MP5s, screaming, "Police, Police, make way!" and magically the torrent spread, admitting them. They could hear shooting up ahead, see more chaos, had no idea other shooters were already engaging the killers.

The team spread out, bent low, looking for targets as they moved to circle those who still stood and fired. Two spotted a gunman fleeing into a CD store and pursued him, saw his feet as shadows where he crouched in terror behind a free-standing shelf unit, popped their fire selection levers to full auto, and hosed the rack with thirty rounds apiece, blowing images of rap groups, CW stars, and gospel music groups to shreds as they destroyed all that stood between them and their target. The gunman himself took close to forty hits in the few seconds that he remained standing against the onslaught, and when they got to him, they found him as dead as ancient history.

Meanwhile, in the center of Silli-Land, amid a pile of squirming hostages, a man rose in majestic thunder with his AK-74, a Conan, a Shaka Zulu, an Attila, as if he'd just crushed his enemy, driven them to the sea and heard the lamentations of their women, and in character he shouted a medieval bellow of warriorhood, as if he dared anyone to shoot him.

They shot him anyway.

Could this really be happening? Possibly it wasn't really happening. You know, it was so unlikely that it almost certainly wasn't happening.

But it seemed to be happening.

Colonel Obobo closed his eyes, held them tight shut, and when he opened them . . . yes, dammit, it still seemed to be happening.

The monitors leaped to life as Andrew Nicks restored the mall's security cameras with the click of a mouse, and the imagery poured into the Command van. The assembled police officers watched as the young men of Brigade Mumbai opened fire on the crowd. The contrast between the muzzle flashes and the unlit darkness of the crowd was so marked that the imagery resolved itself quickly enough into abstraction, the piercing stab of the flash essentially blowing all detail out of the backdrop so that the screens only showed white-hot light and jumble, incomprehensible to the eye.

"Colonel, should I send in SWAT?" asked Major Carmody.

"Find Jefferson!" somebody else said. "Where the hell is that guy, why isn't he doing anything?"

"Colonel, it would probably be a good idea to tell SWAT to blow the doors, and meanwhile, I think we ought to alert the FBI and our own snipers on the roof to engage."

"Where the fuck is Jefferson?" came another cry. "He was bitching all day about standing around and now the party's started and he's out to lunch."

But Obobo said nothing. He seemed utterly baffled by the craziness on the screens above him. After all, who could make sense of that insanity?

Finally, he said, "I don't want undue risk vis-à-vis the hostages. Let's let the situation clarify before—"

"Sir, they're shooting the hostages, for God's sake," said Carmody. "We have to stop them."

"I don't want to judge hastily. Maybe they're bluffing, maybe this is another warning, maybe they'll stop shooting. I see no need to further agitate them."

"Sir, I—"

What was wrong with these people? When he spoke, with his calm deliberation, his firm, perfect eye contact, his empathy and compassion welling in his voice, he expected to be listened to. It had always been that way.

"That's all, gentlemen," he said. "That's my decision. Now, you all wait until it clarifies and then contact me. Mr. Renfro, call my car, will you please? I'll be outside."

With that he turned, grabbed his coat, and left the room.

For a moment the officers stared at each other stupefied. Then one by one, they went back to the monitors.

"I think," someone said, "we must have some people in there. I don't know where they came from, but that sounds more like a gun battle than a massacre."

All watched as fleet SWAT operators, black-clad and bent aggressively as if their posture alone could protect them, entered the screens from various angles, shooting as they moved, their laser beams also vivid slashes against the confusion, darting this way and that. The monitors captured two SWAT heroes blowing the hell out of a terrorist in a CD shop, and then on another screen, a man in the center of the crowd was brought down by multiple hits.

"Good fucking shooting," someone said.

"There was some kind of blast from up top," somebody said. "Somehow the snipers blew the skylight and I think they're firing too."

"Jesus Christ," said Carmody. He turned to Mr. Renfro. "I'm going to send SWAT in for backup," he said, almost tentatively.

"You'll be violating the colonel's orders," said Renfro, but without much conviction. His pasty white face, normally so flaccid, displayed strain through tightened jowls and harsh cords standing out on the neck. "But maybe you should," and a tide of phlegm rose in his throat, and he cleared it with a growl of breath, "*Urggghhhh*—I don't know. I—I just don't know."

"All units," Carmody said into his throat mike, "you are authorized to close and engage. As soon as SWAT deploys, I'm authorizing first responders to set up triage units at each entranceway and have stretcher teams and gurneys ready to deploy when and if the mall is secure. Alert all emergency medical sites to prepare for incoming under siren but we have no idea as to casualty figures yet. It could be considerable. They'd better get all their people in and suited up."

"Ambulances, Larry," someone said.

"And get ambulances to the entrances to ferry the wounded. Do that ASAP."

Then it was quiet for a second, until a major's voice arose from the darkness, as the battle on the screens played out, with the SWAT guys shooting from standing, from moving, from kneeling, pushing in, getting closer.

"Go, babies, go," he said.

Maahir had more or less forgotten about jihad, and martyrdom; he'd forgotten everything except for the sex part. He liked killing too, and taking money from the wallets of the dead, but the best part was the sex, and further, sex and rape, to him, were the same thing or, at least in his experience, always had been. When the order came from the imam, he alone among the gunmen did not unsling his weapon to open fire. Instead, with his strength, his majesty, his fearsome warrior's vitality, he strode through the crowd, as the kneeling mortals rolled away from him, screaming and begging for mercy. Scum! No warriors here this day! Hah!

Death did not frighten him, as he had faced it and dealt it many times, and not just for jihad. Secretly, he didn't give a fuck one way or the other for jihad. It was just that jihad offered the best opportunity for brigandage, which was his calling, for loot, which was his love, and for flesh, which was his obsession, particularly on the wren-like bones of a child virgin. He knew exactly where the child was. He smashed and pummeled his way to her. Now she was his.

And he had never seen one like this Chinese. So pale, so frightened, so delicate. He loved the tendrils of her tiny ears, the perfection of her mouth, a rosebud yet to open, the length and smoothness of her arms, the grace of her hands and fingers. He imagined her naked, in fear of him, obedient to his will, forced to this blasphemy or that, and the result was a tumescence as hard and gigantic as a mountain. He would have her.

He reached her, cowering in the arms of her ancient protector—mother, aunt, grandma, whatever—and he kicked that old biddy aside, freeing the child for his taking. He bent, reached her, clasped his strong hand on her frail biceps, and pulled her to him, and the lights went out big-time, except behind his eyes, where Soviet rockets detonated, filling the night sky with incandescence. He blinked his way back to reality.

The old bitch had hit him hard with her bag, swung full-crescent around her head, and it had landed with such force, he realized now she must have filled it with lead.

But just as his vision restored itself, she hit him again, flush to the head, and his mind filled with stars. It was as if the heavens had collapsed on his skull, and he experienced a moment of utter stupidity, and then a tide of other bitches swarmed on him. The audacity of them, the fury, the arrogance! None alone had the strength to prevent him from blowing snot from his nostrils, but taken together, their weight and squirmy, ripping rage kept him flat longer than he expected.

He bucked, he writhed, he shouted, finally he bit some limb that presented itself and was rewarded with the sound of a scream and the taste of hot blood, and he got a leg free to kick someone away, he shimmied to the right, and then he rose, screaming, the mob of women rolling off him. Hyenas! Vultures! Exiled old lionesses with dried-up ovaries! Scavengers of the plains! He would kill them all. He snatched his rifle up, eyes blazing with hatred, and screamed in Somali, "Whores and sluts, now I shall rip hearts from your bodies before I fuck them," and then noted the constellation of red dots upon his chest. Fireflies?

Actually they were laser dots, followed immediately by 9mm bullets that struck him so hard and fast, they felt like the coming of rain, and he had a last, sad sense of the long topple to earth.

Nikki was looking for the sniper she called Chicago, who seemed to be all over the place. She spotted him in a crowd of snipers roughly at Racine halfway up the western shore of Lake Michigan.

"Film on the snipers, film on the snipers," she screamed, and in another second or two he had fallen away, and in the second after that, a shear of light blew a hole in Lake Michigan, unleashing a sharp hit of percussion felt even by her.

"Jesus, I got it," screamed Larry the camera vet, who had just recorded the only image of the skylight demolition, which would be seen around the world for the next seventy-two hours.

"They're assaulting," Nikki yelled, even as she watched Chicago reassemble himself at the shattered hole in the glass lake and begin the hunt for targets.

"Go, go, goddammit," she commanded, and because she was so fast, the WUSScopter led the mad airborne charge of media helicopters, heretofore locked in obedient formation at three thousand feet, as it broke and scattered. Theirs not to reason why, theirs only to get really cool vid for a network feed.

Down, down, down through the faltering dark Cap'n Tom took the WUSScopter, so hard and fast that each of the three other occupants rose slightly from their seats, feeling the impression of weightlessness.

The two camera jocks held on for dear life, but Nikki, the warrior princess and Mary Tyler Moore from Hell, was screaming, "Go, go, go, get us to the exit, goddammit, Tom, go!"

Then she turned back in the craft to the two older men.

"Get out there, we need some fucking pictures."

Being yelled at by an enflamed and enraged Nikki was actually a lot more frightening than freefall under the guidance of a slightly drunk ex–Marine in his sixties, and so they squirmed forward and started shooting, and since they were first, they got the only good feed under the right lens and in sharp focus of Mike Jefferson's illegal SWAT team racing into the mall through entrance SE, guns hot and loaded. And in another thirty seconds, the doors, all of them at this entrance, sprang open, and a human tide of refugees poured out. Simultaneously, columns of ambulances, red lights flashing, began to course toward that entrance—all entrances, in fact—from different directions. Medics and docs disembarked, setting up triage stations, while gurney teams stood by, waiting for the doorway to clear, as the hostages continued to rush from the building.

"Nikki, what's going on?" asked an anchorman whose name she had momentarily forgotten.

"Well, it appears that even as the terrorist leader ordered his men to open fire, SWAT elements of some sort, some outside the building, led by snipers on the roof, assaulted the terrorist team. Possibly there's a gunfight going on in the amusement center right now, but the hostages have either been freed or have made some kind of escape. That crowd of people you see pouring out of the southeast entrance, those are fleeing hostages and you can see that medical personnel have moved into place to handle the wounded. I don't know if the news is good or bad, I don't have a casualty report, I don't know what's going on inside yet, but events here at America, the Mall, appear to have reached their crescendo."

She heard the anchorman say, "We have yet to receive acknowledgment of an assault from Command, we have no idea where those SWAT members came from, we don't know who's inside."

Nikki's phone buzzed.

"Nikki Swagger," she said, answering it.

"I'm out, I'm out," screamed the voice, and she recognized it as Amanda Birkowsky's, the clerk in Purses, Bags and Whatnot.

"Amanda, can I put you on air?"

"I don't care, I just wanted to thank you."

Nikki switched to Marty and said, "Put me on live, I have a witness," and Marty was fast for the first time in his life.

"Nikki Swagger, WUFF-TV. I am talking to a witness, Amanda Birkowsky, who hid in a store throughout the ordeal. Amanda, can you tell us what happened?"

"We heard shots and screams and then right away some kind of explosion—I don't know what happened, as if somebody blew something up—and then more shots. It was a gunfight, just like in the movies. Then the hostages went racing by, and I ran with them and the doors were all open, and people hiding in the stores all up and down the corridor came rushing along and we're out now."

"Did you see any casualties?"

"I saw people crying, I heard gunfire behind from

all directions. I don't know how many were hit or killed, but I just want to say thank you, thank you, thank you to those brave policemen who came in and fought for us, oh, they were so brave."

"Amanda, find a first aid station, make sure you're okay, call your mom, and please, please relax and rest. And thank you for your courage and help."

Of course that feed, over the images of chaos below, the images of the detonation and then of the SWAT team penetrating, went national in about thirty seconds and international in about thirty more.

Nadif and Khadar were almost certainly the most harmless of the Somali gunmen. Thus the universe awarded them the cruelest deaths in accordance with its policy of punishing the meek the most savagely.

Now that hell was breaking loose, they found the idea of shooting the innocent somewhat disturbing. It was one thing to be in combat, as both had been, where the targets were fleeting and shadowy, another to simply blast people in blue jeans and baseball caps, even if, as white devils, their faces were indistinct blurs and expressed no emotion whatsoever.

Yes, they fired, in a somewhat haphazard fashion, from the hip, passive-aggressive to the end, more or less sloppily pumping out a round a second as the white people rose and rushed in total panic by them. But neither could find it in their heart to kill, and so they angled their shots slightly upward, blasting the facade of the second-tier balcony, about one hundred yards across the Silli-Land Park from where they stood. A large explosion from above frightened them and drove them back, and then also from above someone shot Nadif in the leg, not a serious wound, but it drove the two of them back even farther.

In seconds it seemed that American frogmenninjas were among them—how on earth had they gotten there so fast?—with guns with long, piercing red beams that sought to supply death to whomsoever they touched. They watched as Maahir, emerging from a sea of angry women, was brought down by a host of red dots that had bullets attached magically. Both young men panicked, but in different ways. Nadif decided to climb to heaven, while Khadar awarded himself a boat trip.

It actually was a log. He'd been eyeing the log flume ride for some time, finding it unbearably interesting. The water was so blue and smelled so fresh. It had no alligators, algae, dead fish, or oil slick in it. He raced up the ramp to what he had concluded was its starting station and found himself in some sort of loading area where a lot of logs were lined up, bobbing in the blue-green liquid. It occurred to him to climb into one and hide and wait until he was arrested, but he somehow knew that wasn't what was called for. He wished he had figured out how to make the logs go along the track where at a certain point they were magically hoisted uphill—but water doesn't run uphill, does it?—pushed through a tunnel, then sent zooming down a whirlwind of twists and turns. *Wheeeee!* But he had no idea.

Instead, he leaped into the water, which was warm as piss, and tried to run toward the upward mechanism fifty or so feet away, figuring that stairs were somehow under the froth and that he could get up the ramp and out of harm's way. Alas, his splashing attracted ninjas, who rose to the platform he himself had just occupied, and they yelled at him, almost desperately, in a language he didn't understand.

Without hesitation, he unslung his baby Kalash

and made as if to fire, though he couldn't remember if the safety was on or not, and immediately the water around him broke up into a disturbance of geysers and spray as his hunters fired first and he was pulled down into the blue-green urine, amid bubbles and, from somewhere, a gushing red cloud.

As for Khadar, his choice of death ride was the Wild Mouse. He did not actually have time to get in a car and go for a ride, even if he'd known how to run it, but he made his way over fences and through an artificial garden easily enough to the structure of the device itself, a steel latticework that rose four stories toward the skylights. He began to climb. Clearly, for maintenance purposes, the supporting network of beams and buttresses had been engineered to allow a fairly athletic fellow access to any portion of the track, and so up he scooted, graceful and nimble, propelled by the power of lean, strong muscles and thin, long bones. Up, up he went, climbing to the hump of the highest hill, with the idea he supposed of getting up there unnoticed and lying flat on the track. He had a brief fantasy in which this strategic move allowed him to escape and he disappeared into Minneapolis's Somali community, acquired fake papers, married, had children and a long and happy life. But he had been noticed. Unfortunately, by a sniper.

It was McElroy's last kill and the one that would haunt him. The others were armed and had been dropped as a lifesaving necessity, as duty compelled. But this guy was wide open from the back, his rifle hung by sling over a shoulder, and for all the world he looked like nothing more menacing than some kind of haute-bourgie recreational climber, the guy who reads *Outside* magazine and shops at REI and tells everybody he wants to "do" Mount McKinley, then the Matterhorn, and as for the Hindu Kush, well, we'll see. There'd been a guy just like that in the Cleveland field office.

At the same time, the guy was armed and he was heading vigorously to an elevation from which he could do violence to SWAT guys and citizens. So McElroy's pause lasted less than a second and was shortened even further by his spotter saying, "Dave, target on roller coaster structure, about ten o'clock, looks to be over a hundred."

It wasn't so radical a downhill angle, so McElroy didn't hold low but rather let the crosshairs settle between the shoulder blades as he began his press, and maybe they'd passed a little beneath that ideal spot when the trigger broke.

The results were pathetic, of course. The gunman didn't fall immediately. He was too strong and limber. His feet went, one of his arms spasmed out, and he hung for maybe three seconds by one arm, and one of his legs twitched. Then his final four fingers yielded on the death grip, he slid off into gravity, the tip of his shoe hit a strut and flipped him backward, and he fell almost horizontally, striking the earth backside first so that his legs and arms splayed outward in the dust that rose from the flower bed whose buds he crushed.

"Great shot," said the spotter. "That's three, or is it four?"

"He was three, but it's like prairie dog shooting," said McElroy, "in that it gets thin fast."

Ray could see no one left to shoot. And by this time, from somewhere, SWAT operators had broken into the amusement park and were clearing. He'd watched them take down a big guy in a scrum of angry women, pursue another into a store, where a double burst of full auto suggested Game Over, and finally his vision was provoked by rapid movement on the periphery and he saw a gunman in midfall from the top of the roller coaster's biggest hill to hit and bounce and then go limp in a flower bed.

Yells reached him from the operators below.

"Clear left, tangos down."

"Clear right, tangos down."

"Clear in center, I think all tangos down."

"Check tangos, be careful, shoot if you see movement."

The SWAT team moved through the melancholy ritual of mop-up, never fun for anybody, and then Nick heard, "We are clear, we are clear, many civilians down, get medical in here fastest."

Someone from Command came over the net.

"This is Command. Clear for medical, clear for medical. Get those medics in there and begin to assist the wounded. All aid stations, wounded incoming."

"Okay," Ray said to Lavelva as he reloaded a fresh mag in his Kalash. "Now I'm going into the place where I think this kid is hiding. You stay here, you stay down. Do not move fast, do not go down on your own. This is a tricky time, you could get shot by some hot dog real easily, do you hear?"

"Ray, you don't have to do this thing."

"Well, I'm closest."

"Ray, it's over. Let them police take that boy.

That's their job, let 'em do it for once. You just sit here by me and rest. We get some french fries."

He smiled.

"I hear you, yes I do. But that's not how it works. I have to finish this thing, I'm closest. Maybe he knows secret ways out or places to hide, maybe he means to set up and kill a lot of people one last time— whatever, the sooner he is put down, the better. And as it has worked out, I represent sooner."

"I'm going with you," said Lavelva.

"Sweetie, this is tactical entry, close-quarters battle; you need to know what you're doing and I can't be thinking on you. I'm giving you a Marine Corps order: you sit down over there and wait till the good guys arrive."

He turned, went back to his iPhone.

"McElroy and anyone else, I'm now going into First Person Shooter after this kid and whoever."

"Cruz, this is Memphis. Take off your scarf and whatever you're wearing on the outside. You have a white T-shirt on?"

"It's Marine OD."

"Webley, you direct all first responders not, *not*, I say again, to engage an armed figure in an OD T-shirt."

"There's a young African American woman here too," said Ray. "Lavelva, she is tops, she was with me the whole way. She should not be engaged either. She will be sitting outside unarmed with her hands in plain sight."

"Get that, Webley?"

"I'm putting it out now," said Webley. "They should be up there soon. Ray, go get 'em."

"I'm off."

"Good luck, Marine," said McElroy. "I'm on you with backup far as I can go."

Ray clambered up, but Lavelva tried one last time.

"Ray, why are you such a goddamned hero? Heroes die young and hard and leave their girlfriends all swole up with weepy snot on their faces."

"Maybe so, but I have ancestors to answer to."

"From China?"

"No, much worse: from Arkansas."

The shooting had stopped. Andrew turned to face the grave demeanor of the imam, who also realized that it was almost time. Andrew felt a little like another one of his heroes, Hitler, in the Führerbunker with the Russian peasant army up above.

He rose, went to the game console, pushed a button, and a memory stick popped out, which he in turn dropped into a buffered envelope, already addressed and stamped. He sealed it and handed it over to the imam.

"You will be all right. I will take you to the doorway, you will go up, your pilot will land, and you will be gone. In the mess no one will even notice. It's going to get way crazy around here. Then you drop that in a Canadian mailbox and it goes to a Canadian letter drop for WikiLeaks. They'll know what to do with it. A little editing, a little tightening, add a time-line and some production values, and you have the greatest FPS game ever made. You have the greatest story ever told. It will live for a million years, do you understand?"

"I do, my brother. But it is not too late. You can come with me."

"Nah, never in the cards. I always knew and I'm

prepared: narrative rules. It needs a climax. We've got a hero, I'm the villain of the piece. We need a duel: he and I must fight to the death. Whichever one of us goes down, it'll make the narrative complete. WikiLeaks will patch that stuff in from CNN and from all the cell phone vid, don't worry."

"So be it, then, my friend."

"If I see Allah, I'll say hello to him for you and hope there are some virgins left."

"I will see you in paradise."

"Or hell. Whatever."

The two men hugged, yet there was nothing left to say, and time was short. The imam turned with his treasure, exited the back door.

Andrew picked up his iPad, checked to see that it was receiving wireless feeds from all the gun cameras, selected number four, and brought it up. He saw what the gun muzzle of the man stalking him saw, which was the steady progress down Rio Grande toward the FPS store, where he, Andrew, awaited.

Andrew picked up his own AK-74, the one without the gun camera, and slung it. He turned and slipped into the interior corridor, raced past doorways, and finally pushed one in and stepped into the back of a Payless shoe store. A group of women crouched in horror nearby.

"Are you the police?" one of them asked.

"Not exactly," he said.

Ray did a quick pass-by on the First Person Shooter doorway, saw that the store inside appeared to be empty. He ran a last check on the AK, making sure he was cocked and unlocked, then went in hard and low, CQB-style, gun at the shoulder, moving erratically, eyes dilated so wide in the scan for data you could have landed a plane in them. Posters of übermenschen with the latest in stylized assault rifles stood heroically on all the walls, like in some sort of Waffen-SS fantasyland, as well as a couple of bulletin boards that tracked I, Killer tournament progress, quotes from battle gurus like Napoleon, Bedford Forrest, Jeff Cooper, Sun Tzu, all very nerd technowar. The place, however, didn't have that Marine smell of sweat but the scent of something else: plastic wrapping.

Most of the free space—dark and shadowy without lights—was given to racks of games in the center of the room. He prowled around them, going in low, coming up in shooter-ready position, finger aching to fire at every shadow or hint of substance, but the only thing to behold were the games themselves, neatly racked cover out—not just FPSes, but every war game known to man, from every war known to man, for every style of computer known to man. No sign, no sound, no movement. He declared the place cleared.

The door to some interior chamber stood behind the cash register counter, and he went to that, kicked it hard, went in low-profile, and again was met by silence and stillness, perceiving a gloom penetrated by the glow of electron light.

It was the room of screens, the lair of the beast. It felt empty too, but Ray dashed from position to position to make sure. Yes, clear.

Now he freed his concentration up to assess. This had to be the HQ of the mission. On the wall, security feeds lit screens that showed mostly empty corridors, except for the first level, where frenzy was the mode of the day: medics hustled, the wounded were attended to, SWAT guys offered perimeter security, and everyone tried to help and get a hold on what exactly had transpired, who were good guys, who bad, the whole law enforcement crime scene drill.

But on the other wall, he saw an odd array of camera feeds displaying, well, nothing. All seemed still. The images were black or horizontal and meaningless, though occasionally there was the blur of boots and shoes hustling by or the nothingness of a wall a few inches away. What the fuck was this? One seemed more agile than all the others, number four, and he looked closely and saw a pair of shoes, New Balances, the same model he was wearing and—

Jesus Christ! Those were his shoes! This little fucker had clamped a wireless camera on the rifles!

He looked, and behind the muzzle of his Kalash he saw a neatly milled unit connected to the barrel by some kind of clamp, and the unit held a lens. Among all the tactical geegaws mounted on the AK—vertical foregrip, a receiver with a Picatinny rail, new iron backup sights—he hadn't even noticed it. He pointed it at the screen and got that infinity of mirrors thing—where the camera records itself recording itself over and over again and the image diminishes in size as it sinks toward nothingness—but kept it moving, so if Andrew was watching, he wouldn't tumble to the fact that Ray had tumbled to the fact.

The game! Lavelva was so right. In his sick mind, this strange genius boy had invented in real time and space the biggest first person shooter in the world and had recorded it with wireless video for some editor in some bunker to put together some giant

cyberdeath tournament based on imagery from today's adventure in slaughter.

But now he realized, For the first time, I know
something he doesn't. I know that he knows where
I am and what I'm doing at all times. That's how he
knew I was coming through that door. Even now, on
the move, he's receiving my feed. He's laughing at
me, waiting for me to come.

He set the rifle down, pointing to nothing, and
moved to a central chair in a mesh of Star Trek
consoles wired into everything by a jungle of cord
hanging behind them, and went and crouched at the
big screen of what appeared to be the mother computer. The image still seemed to hold the security
system main menu, and he quickly slid the mouse
around until he'd nested it on ELEVATOR AC-
CESS, punched enter, saw some flickers and heard
some clicks, and finally an icon lit up explaining
ELEVATORS ENABLED, then ESCALATORS
ENABLED. But, he noted, the doors had already
been opened. Huh?

The phone on the desk rang.

He paused, waited, finally picked it up.

"You're the hero," someone said.

"Is this Andrew?" Ray said. "You'd better give
yourself up. The place is full of cops. They'll shoot
you in a second. I'll take you alive."

"God, you *are* a hero. You are fucking John Wayne.
This is so cool. I could never have written this."

"Look, kid, you're going to ride the needle for
sure, no lie. But that'll take years and for all those
years you and I both know you'll be god to millions
of people as fucked up as you are but not nearly as

resourceful. You'll love every second of it and you'll love the hatred everyone else pours on you and you will have the time of your life. Don't pretend that's not what this is all about."

"You've got it wrong, Duke. It's not about that. I'm shallow but not *that* shallow. It's about the game. And the game needs a big bang finish. So you better come for me before all those Minneapolis ice fishermen get up to this floor and shoot me to Swiss cheese. It's so much cooler if you kill me or we kill each other and give the thing a gleam of mythic tragedy. By the way, if you want to find me, here's a subtle hint: I'm in the movie complex."

"Give yourself up!"

"I can't. We're at the hyper level of the game. I have to see who wins."

8:47 P.M.—9:35 P.M.

Andrew was disappointed in the popcorn. It had gone cool and stale and had toughened somewhat. Now, a good employee of the Regal Theater chain, a true professional, would have stayed on station, keeping the popcorn hot throughout the massacre, because you never could tell when somebody would want some fine, freshly popped popcorn. You just can't find good help these days.

He sat in one of the megaplex's fifteen auditoriums down the hall a quarter-mall rotation over to Mississippi from First Person Shooter, watching a flow of images above him. It was an old favorite, and he was happy to see that the robo-screening mechanism had kept the images on-screen even if the human part of the system seemed to have failed, though you wouldn't want to judge a whole program on just one example. In this movie, lots of gunfire, lots of dying, lots of smart, snarky talk, the hero in an undershirt with a Jersey accent. It was pretty good, maybe the best in the series, even if some of the conventions of audience appeal—the cute, rotund black cop, for example—were by now a tiresome trope. He would have fast-forwarded through them if it were possible.

Now and then he looked at his iPad, which still received the camera feed from number four, that is, the gun muzzle view of the hero who was now stalking him, giving Andrew the man's precise location. He doubted he would show up in an undershirt. No, no, Andrew imagined some SWAT captain in a black combat outfit, maybe with a wool watchcap and one of those mikes bent around his face. Probably a dad, never done this before, scared to death the whole way, yet in the obdurate squareness of mindset utterly committed to the Rules. "Give yourself up!" Yeah, right, you have the right to remain blah blah blah and blah.

The guy should have warrior-pure thoughts at this time. He should be thinking, Kill this little motherfucker. But no, not in modern America. He was probably thinking, Will I get in trouble because I snapped at Commander Jackson a few minutes ago, will this count as overtime, will I be so hung up in paperwork I'm not free to go on my Caribbean cruise with the unit next week, should I hire an agent for the movie version, or should I write a book first, and if so, where would I find an actual writer to put the words on paper? That kind of thinking could get you killed.

Andrew checked again. The guy was outside the movie theater, running his gun muzzle over the box office. Now the camera bounced hard as he made a dash to that structure, took cover behind it, and tracked the gun muzzle through the door, scanning the vast but abandoned refreshment stand, peering hard into the darker "lounge" areas where sofas and chairs had been set up in pathetic imitation of the typical American living room. Then another dash as he moved into a position to scan the corner closet where the maintenance people ran their operation, seeing a few tipped-over garbage cans on wheels, dumped sweeper brooms, stacks of toilet paper for the johns, and vats of soap for the sinks. No paper towels, though. This theater complex clearly had those awful blow-dry things.

Nothing there, our hero crept around the corner and at last confronted the long corridor off which each of the auditoriums was sited. The guy had to know that he, Andrew, was in one of them. Would he get it right? Would he go by trial and error? Would reinforcements arrive? Would he call for backup? Hmm, probably he'd go straight ahead, because he had to realize that Andrew knew the mall forward and backward, and might know all kinds of escape routes and could even yet, this late in the game, make a getaway. So he had to move fast and close the distance, make the arrest or the kill.

Andrew chuckled softly. This *was* really cool. It was working out so much better than he'd thought, even if the kill number looked as though it would be the one disappointment. He'd thought those kids would do a better job, but it seemed that so many of them had been secretly taken down that the remaining guys could never get any heavy fire going, and the few that were left sort of wimped out at the end and weren't willing to aim and kill systematically, as they had been instructed. No, you really couldn't get good help anymore.

His back to the wall, Ray slid down the corridor, under art deco golden-movie-age affectations, posters of improbably beautiful human beings, another abandoned garbage can on wheels, to the first door. In one of the auditoriums before him, the kid Andrew lurked, probably set up behind the seats, waiting for someone to pop in, silhouetted in the glare of the door, lit from the front by the glow of the screen. Andrew would blast him down, then maybe escape by some predetermined route only he knew. Yet if Ray didn't press, the boy might vanish just the same, and the little bastard was so smart and had all this stuff so wired, maybe he'd actually have figured out some way to beat the game.

Ray looked at the signs jutting into the hallway, each a mini-marquee bearing the name of the flick on display inside. Sure, Junior might play on that too. That was him: nihilistic but in a "funny" way, hip, ironic, thought everything was a joke, even saw himself as a comedian as he took down the system on its biggest day. It wouldn't be worth it if he had to do it as some little Arab commando type, cornily shrieking his allegiance to Allah; no, Andrew was too cool for that. He'd do it, but the trick was to do it insouciantly, with some kind of snarky comedy element, so that no matter how it turned out, his followers—there'd be millions, in the way these things worked—would get the joke, smile at it, and hold a special regard in their heart for the great Andrew Nicks, cool to the end, cooler than Dylan and Eric, cooler than Cho, cooler than Jared.

Ray heard movie music blaring from the theater he was closest to, looked up, saw it was some Disney family comedy. No way Andrew would be caught alive, much less dead, in such a travesty of happy-fam cliché.

Ray realized, It's become a pop quiz on movie irony. To have a chance at him, I have to know which theater he's in. To know that, I have to decipher the names and meanings of the movies and decide which one would best express his sensibility. Too bad Roger Ebert isn't here to advise me.

He read the titles.

And he knew.

Of course. Had to be. No other. That was it. That was the one.

It was fifth in line, on the left-hand side. Ray sidled up to it, trying to figure how to—

He knows I'm here.

He'll know exactly when I'm coming through because he's extrapolating from the imagery of my guncam, that's the gig, and that gives him a one-second start on the action curve, and that's the one second he uses to dust me. I pop in, blink, can't see. He lays the front sight and jerks off three fast ones from point-blank range and I'm down. He goes out the back or whatever. Maybe he kills himself. But that's what the "narrative" demands, he and I, together at last. Ray's back, and Andrew's got him. Laurel and Hardy, Martin and Lewis, Scorsese and De Niro, Andrew and Ray.

Ray had about two seconds or so to decide what to do, and he looked up and down the corridor for inspiration while loud, thriller music came out of the room just beyond the doors, singing the adrenal-goosing rhapsody of syncopated FX destruction, of shots and blasts and falls and deaths in 4-4 time, with a percussion line holding the back beat while the guitar chords moved forward relentlessly, on toward Armageddon or at least *The* and *End*.

Ray let his muzzle rise to the marquee above the entrance so that Andrew, so near, so ready for this, knew that he was here at last, ready for his close-up.

The imam made it to the stairwell leading to the roof. He climbed the metal stairs, hearing his steps echo into nothingness, and reached the door itself. He pulled his phone from his jacket, went to CONTACTS, and punched the number. No need for an answer. The pilot would feel the vibe of the phone in his pocket, drop down, and the imam would run twenty feet to the open door, lunge inside, and off they'd go, running low and without lights, next stop Canada. Then the long, secret trip home, then infinite glory, the love of the Faith, the thrill of being Mohamed Atta without the inconvenience of a fiery martyrdom. And then, finally, years and years of glory beyond, the loveliness of death, and the embrace and adoration of Allah himself.

He opened the door—it clicked easily from the inside, according to fire department regulations—and stepped onto the roof.

The sun had set, leaving an apocalyptic purple smear across low-hanging clouds, like a wound in the wall of the universe itself, signifier of end times. A cold breeze struck him, filled his lungs with hope, and yet the spectacle before him was so extraordinary, he could not but respond with utter fascination.

It was like a scene from a war of the last century, where airmen fought in planes with double wings, looping and swirling close at hand, missing each other by inches, skidding this way and that, birdlike and deft, a true flock of death machines. The craft, of course, were helicopters, not biplanes, and now, at the moment of climax, they'd lost all sense of propriety and were swooping and jockeying for position, hovering low, then darting away. The air was aswarm with them, not so much as objects of defined specificity but as presences, blurs of weight and motion lit by red and white lights against the material of their construction, while the beating of their rotors buffeted him powerfully, the sounds of the many petrol-driven engines throbbed loudly, contributing their own vibrations to what he felt as he entered the maelstrom.

He hunched down next to the door, itself contained in a tiny, shack-like structure on the edge of the vast roof, one of many such abutments, rises, and abstractions that made the roof its own kind of featureless wilderness in the mostly dark. He pulled out a flashlight, scrunched it on, and began to wave it, aware of how tiny a signal it was in the immense cauldron of airborne activity.

Yet the angel watched over him. One of the whirling birds immediately detached itself from the mass overhead, and though he couldn't identify it by type, he knew by the purposeful dive on his orientation that it was his ticket to Mecca.

First person shooter. Andrew crouched behind a row of seats that yielded a perfect angle on the doorway into the auditorium, gun in one hand, iPad delicately balanced on his left knee. He saw what his opponent's gun muzzle covered. The man looked up to the marquee again, rifle already mounted, so Andrew saw the name of the film playing behind him on the big screen, then he saw the muzzle come down, he saw the man point it at the door, steel himself a last time, and make ready for this most basic yet most dangerous of all FPS exercises, the tactical entry.

The camera closed on the door, losing detail in blur, and at that precise moment, Andrew rose, lifted rifle to shoulder, shifted his view from virtual to real. The gunsight before him was not electrons in cyberspace but cold Eastbloc killing technology at the apogee the genius Mikhail Kalashnikov had achieved, and exactly as the door flew open ten feet from where he crouched in the seats and the man came in low and hard and straight to Andrew, Andrew shot him three times, putting three pills at about three thousand per deep into his center mass. But exactly as Andrew's focus clarified, he saw that he had not shot a man moving low and fast but a garbage can on wheels with an AK-74 and gun barrel minicam secured at the plastic rim and at that moment the man revealed himself behind the door frame and Andrew, light being faster than sound or bullets, saw three huge flashes blossom from his cupped hands— classic isosceles, like all the books said—and then he found himself lurching backward, catching clumsily on an armrest, and twisting into the chair, very wet, three deep and throbbing wounds beginning to generate enormous pain. In seconds, a face loomed before him, the face of a kind of half-Chinese guy with a crew cut, knocking his gun away, and talking into a phone, saying, "McElroy, I got him, he's hit bad, get medics up here fast, I'm in theater five in the movie complex."

He looked down at the young man, who coughed and said, "I thought I'd get Bruce Willis, but I got Keanu fucking Reeves."

The turbulence pitched the WUSScopter to the right, badly, and only Cap'n Tom's skills, eroded or not, kept them airborne even as the man cursed, "Goddamn him!"

It was the KPOP Traffic 24/7 copter beelining by them and missing only by inches as it descended toward the vast roof beneath them.

Both camera jocks cursed too, the brush with death particularly bitter in their mouths and minds as the danger part was supposed to be over, but Nikki alone watched the traffic bird diminish as it descended.

"Tom," she said, "what kind of copter is that? I don't recognize the type."

"Moving so fast I could hardly tell. I think it's an Alouette, a French bird, they use 'em for agricultural spraying and—"

"Do they use 'em for media?" Nikki asked sharply.

"Well, now that you mention it, I can't recall—"

She saw the small, agile helicopter settle on the roof adjacent to what was barely recognizable as some kind of shack that housed a door.

"He's terrorist," she said suddenly. "He's fake. He's here to help somebody get away."

Moment of silence in the chopper, despite the crescendo of noise pouring in from all sides and the waves of turbulence flushing through the open doors. What to do, what to do?

Nikki knew. "Get over there on top of him. Don't let him take off. We've got to stop him. And call five-oh. Get cops here fast. And you guys, get those cameras running, goddammit."

Cap'n Tom veered hard right on rotor pitch, upped the rpms on his big Bell engine, and began a Vietnam-LZ-under-fire power dive toward his prey.

The helicopter settled twenty-five yards away, its rotors pushing the air out like swells of ocean, and the imam stepped into their full force, then stepped back, lowered, adjusted, and solidified his posture, and began the short run to the aircraft.

It looked like some kind of large mechanical insect, its vivid bulb cockpit somehow representing eyes, its delicate landing struts folded legs, its frail, pipe-like fuselage standing for thorax, and the whirling blades in their blur representing the flashing of wings. He saw Haji beckoning him forward and he got to the thing, used the landing strut as a footrest, and hoisted himself upward and into the empty seat.

"Praise be to Allah! He looks after us!" he screamed, and though the other man could not possibly hear him, he smiled back, squeezing him firmly on the wrists, then turned his attention back to the controls before him and the flight outward.

But at that second, another presence was suddenly upon them. In horror, the imam looked up and saw through the encompassing bubble another helicopter settle over them, sealing them in a little coffin of airspace, the strange craft, being larger and faster, able to impose its will on them.

"Go! Go!" he screamed. "You must go!"

But the pilot above was agile with his heavier machine, and when Haji meant to zoom forward, somehow the intruder beat him to the space and infringed upon his angle, preventing him, and so it went sideways and backward, and the imam watched in horror as Haji's face clenched into despair, yielding to the look of the hunted.

"Go up, he will not stand against you!" the imam screamed, unaware of the fundamental stupidity of ramming the enemy copter's skids with his own aircraft's whirling rotors, but that is indeed what happened, either by intention or imprecise maneuver, and the smaller Alouette shook spastically as its rotors broke apart on the struts beneath the WUFFcopter Huey and, unstabilized, began to chase its own tail as it spun, finding a last surge before it gave over to its death spiral.

The imam screamed as the jaws of hell on this earth opened wide, and the flames were so hot, so very hot.

"Stop talking," snapped Ray. "You're hit in both lungs and bleeding out, and I'm going to try and stop the bleeding. Relax, think about something nice, the medics will be here soon."

Andrew laughed. "Joke's on you," he explained. "I wasn't in it for the money or the chicks, but the glory. As of tomorrow, I'm the most famous man in the world, and nobody will ever remember your name. Memo for next time: Always play the supervillain. Heroes are so last week."

He laughed again, then winced as, intent, Ray peeled the *shemagh* off Andrew's neck and tried to stanch the welling blood from the three 9mm entry punctures, seeing that it was basically hopeless, feeling, despite the circumstances, the depression he usually felt when someone bleeds out helplessly, making ugly sounds, twitching, before going slack forever.

"You might think—"

"I'm telling you to shut up," Ray said. "Where are those goddamn guys? You need transfusion, surgical clamps, and clotting agent fast. Where the hell are they?"

He looked at the dying boy's eyes and saw

merriment. You had to give it to him: no contrition, no bullshit, Andrew 24/7 to the end.

"Keep fighting," Ray said. "You can stay around on willpower. Concentrate. Do not let yourself die. Fight, goddammit, the medics will be—"

"It doesn't matter," Andrew said. "Tomorrow my game goes up on iPads and Nintendo DS's and their clones all over the world. You can't stop it now."

Ray held the scarf wadded hard against the wound producing the most blood outflow, seemed to slow it for a bit, but so hydraulic is the human body and so critically injured was the boy that the blood simply found another exit point, and thus another wound increased its outflow in response.

Then—an appalling thunderclap split the air accompanied by an instant flash of megaheat and illumination. The flame sucked the air out of the auditorium, that vacuum effect, and then the flare-up subsided, and oxygen became again available. Ray breathed hard at the coolness even as he shielded Andrew with his own body, then turned to see that at the far end of the theater, the roof had caved in under the thrust of a flaming machine, a helicopter, its bulb canopy shattered into a constellation of spiderweb fracture, its struts bent, melted, or sheared, its two passengers mute as the fire ate their corpses.

"Damn," said Andrew. "I hate it when that happens."

Suddenly, FBI people were all around Ray, and someone had grabbed him and pulled him out of the theater as medics squadded on Andrew to perform services too late to matter.

"How did you know? How did you know?" someone in a helmet and goggles was yelling into his ear, incomprehensibly.

"I don't—"

"Which theater?" the fed demanded. "He could have been in any of them."

Ray gestured upward, as more emergency personnel and other SWAT people ran by him.

The marquee on Theater 5 read:

The Minneapolis Film Society presents
One night only
Hits of the Eighties
Die Hard
Yippie-ki-yay, M*****-F******!

Finally, someone threw a sheet over dead Santa.

Mr. Renfro understood: aggression is the key.

"All right," he said, "I am speaking for the colonel. No officer is allowed to speak directly to media. All media contacts will be cleared through this office. I say again, no media contact except through the superintendent's office. Now get me this Major Jefferson, fast."

"Excuse me, sir, who are you?" asked Kemp. "I think I will control press access to FBI personnel in this instance."

"No, Special Agent. This is a Minnesota State Police initiative. I speak for the colonel on media relations, and if need be, I will get on the phone and get a court gag order on you in three minutes' time, and if you don't believe me, you just watch it happen."

Thus in time, the official hero of the event, Mike

Jefferson, was brought into Renfro's corner of the Incident Command trailer. Renfro cleared the room out before speaking to him.

"Congratulations," he said. "Now, let's get to it. Here's the bargain. You and I know that the colonel didn't exactly distinguish himself today. So I am going to give you what you want. I am going to get him the hell out of here. That was always the plan anyhow; this just accelerates it."

"Sir, I—"

"Shut up, Major. I don't have time to argue. I speak with the full authority of the colonel's office. Here is the reality. The media love him. You know why as well as I do. They yearn to credit him with a brilliant operation. Thus we will give them what they want. He came up with the idea of these secret assaults, and you followed it. His plan worked out brilliantly. He outthought and outfought this nutcase kid and all the Somali gunmen. That's the narrative, get it?"

"He froze like a popsicle," said Jefferson. "If it weren't for that sniper and some Marine Superman cutting their firepower in half, and some genius kid in DC out-cyberpunching that nasty little punk, you're looking at a thousand dead citizens."

"The colonel came up with a brilliant plan. If you go to the media with another narrative, they will destroy you and it'll do you no good. I'll even tell you what the countermove is. The colonel is so brilliant, he knew that if he let you work up an assault plan, it would be too compromised by ego, turf, overthinking, politics, grudges, and PC considerations. So he played you perfectly, and when you had to act, you didn't have time for any of that bullshit and so what you came up with was simple, direct, and effective, a SWAT classic, the ideal. He wouldn't let you fail; he put you in a position to succeed, which is all any manager can do. You're just not smart enough to see the nuance of the great one's genius."

"Are you trying to be funny?"

"And don't you think the race card will fall out of heaven and land on your skull: you'll be one of those jealous, envious underlings who cannot stand that a black man outperformed them. They will hound you until you are disgraced and your professional life is over. My way, he gets a big DC job and is gone, he thanks and decorates and recommends you, and you are golden forever, whatever it is you choose to do."

"You fucking spin guys, you are the fucking ruination of the world. You take everything that's real and decent and you twist it to some end in some game nobody even knew was on the table," said Jefferson.

"Nicely said, but it is what it is. Welcome to the world we live in, not the world we want to live in. It's a pretty good world for you, Jefferson, don't forget that. You'll get a promotion and the sincere gratitude of Colonel Obobo. It's the best deal anyone will ever offer you."

Nobody had stopped them from approaching, and now they just stood there, as hundreds of people raced by, each with a call to make, a story to tell, a wound to be bound, a loved one to contact. Nobody paid any attention to Mr. and Mrs. Girardi.

They stood there as escapees from the mall flooded toward them.

"Okay," said Mr. Girardi, "showtime."

He threw off his lumpy overcoat to reveal a

nicely tailored double-breasted coat, reached into his pocket, and pulled out a stack of business cards.

"Folks," he said, "Jack Scheister, of the law firm Scheister & Jackell. Folks, you've gone through an ordeal, and somebody should pay for it."

He started handing out cards to people, most of whom were in such a state of shock they took them.

Scheister & Jackell
Attorneys at Law
309-555-2132
24-Hour Law Line
"We sue, they rue."

"Folks," his wife was saying as she handed out the cards, "I'm Monica Jackell. You should be compensated for your time, your pain, your anguish, and we're here to see you get your justice and your cash."

THREE MONTHS LATER

Ray and Molly sat in the bar of a restaurant in Washington DC. They were going to get married shortly and would be flying back to Saint Paul for the ceremony, to which every Hmong in America had been invited. Even old Bob Lee was flying in for this one. McElroy and his wife were coming, as were Nick Memphis, Jake Webley, and Will Kemp. Lavelva would make it if she could get leave, but she was in her third week of Marine Basic, so it was doubtful. But tonight, before the week of marriage craziness started, was just for them.

The order of the night was martinis, vodka variant, slightly dirty, Absolut, no bullshit about shaking or stirring, just whatever the bartender preferred, Ray didn't even know. It was Friday, pretty late, since she worked hard, as did he—recently appointed head instructor of sniper tactics for the FBI under Ron Fields out in Quantico—and she in the legal department of the Department of Energy. If you saw them, you'd see two Asian American yuppies, well preserved, representing diversity, on secure career paths, but not unusual in the cosmopolitan DC restaurant scene.

"Look," said Molly, "it's your sister!"

Indeed it was, on the television. The strikingly pretty girl's face filled the screen over a network insignia and she earnestly reported, "The president today appointed Colonel Douglas Obobo"—and a cutaway showed the handsome police executive shaking hands with the president in the White House media room—"superintendent of the Minnesota State Police, as the new, and first black, director of the Federal Bureau of Investigation. The colonel received nationwide attention on Black Friday last November when he led the response to the terrorist attack at America, the Mall, in suburban Minneapolis"—and the camera showed footage that Nikki's cameraman had actually shot, the vast America-shaped building bleeding smoke and fire into the night as an ocean of ambulances and other emergency vehicles blinked lights around it—"and devised a daring secret assault plan that was credited with minimizing casualties in that horrible event. Only thirty-seven died and fewer than two hundred were wounded, against figures that could have been vastly higher."

Then the president spoke.

"I know of no American who has served his country better in time of crisis—and in time without crisis, in the ordinary ebb and flow of law enforcement duties—than Doug Obobo. He is one of the finest police officials in the nation, without a doubt, and I fully expect him to bring those attributes of courage, intelligence, and creativity—but most of all, empathy and compassion—to our premier federal law enforcement agency."

The two men shook hands as flashbulbs popped.

"That's not quite the way I heard it," said Ray.

"Well, gosh," Molly said, "what do *you* know? I mean it's not like you were *there* or anything," and they both laughed richly, not the first laugh they had shared by any means but far, far from the last.

ACKNOWLEDGMENTS

Most readers will know that there is a mall in Bloomington, MN, similar to the one described here. I indeed visited it for a few days but made no attempt to investigate it and did no actual research there. No inferences should be made regarding that entity's ability to handle a terrorist crisis. *Soft Target* is meant as apocalyptic allegory, not journalism.

Now on to thanks. The biggest share goes to Gary Goldberg, who's become the majordomo of the Steve Hunter empire. Gary has one of those technical brains and an indefatigable gift for figuring out systems, mechanics, programs, the whole gestalt of the machine world that is utterly baffling to me. He was super on this one, and I told him he had done so much work, he deserved some of the royalties, but I wasn't going to give him a cent because it would tarnish the friendship. Hmm, he seemed to swallow that.

Gary thanks Grant Kissel for computer savvy and Dave Bickel for keeping everything plausible.

I have a core of other readers whose responses are always valuable: my friends Lenne P. Miller, Jay Carr, Bill Smart, and Jeff Weber, all of whom pitched in with enthusiasm and suggestions. Needless to say, all failures of nerve, taste, and decorum and all excesses of symbolism, violence, and gore rest with me, not them.

My sister-in-law, Annie Marbella, clued me in on the girl side of the vid game world, for which I am grateful, and my brother-in-law Ken Haas explained the boy side of it to me. BTW, I don't want this to be taken as an anti–vid game screed. Kids, play all you want, blow up shit left and right; as long as your imaginations are working, you're part of the human race and you're not out on the streets robbing old bald guys. Ed De Carlo, the manager of the On Target shooting range and gun shop, talked me through the various intricacies of the trade.

My professional team—superagent Esther Newberg, editor Sarah Knight, and publisher Jon Karp—were as usual supportive and helpful, and Sarah was terrific with her right-on suggestions. Without her, this would be a far dimmer story.

And finally the wife, Jean Marbella: Jeannie, Jeannie, queenie of the martini (once a week, dammit!), brewer of coffee, confidante, laugher (as long as we stay off politics), and reigning zeitgeist of Baltimore journalism, thanks for being there.

Simon & Schuster
Proudly Presents

THE
BULLET
GARDEN

BY STEPHEN HUNTER

Available at SimonandSchuster.com
or wherever books are sold

Please turn the page for a preview of
The Bullet Garden

PRELUDE: CASEY

6–8 June 1944

Roger

"No, no," said Basil St. Florian. "*Bren* guns. We need the Bren guns. It is simply not feasible without Bren guns. Surely you understand?"

Yes, Roger understood but he was nevertheless unwilling.

"Our wealth is in our Bren guns. Without Bren guns, we are nothing. Pah, we are dust, we are cat shit, do you see? Nothing. NOTHING!"

Of course he said "*Rien*," for the language was French, as was the setting, the cellar of a farmhouse outside the rural burg of Tulle, Department of Corrèze, in the region of Limousin, 250 miles south and east of Paris. Basil had just dropped in the night before, with an American chum.

"Do you not see," Basil explained, "that the point in giving you Brens was to wage war upon the Germans, not to make you powerful politically in the postwar, after we have pushed Jerry out. FTP Communists, FFL Gaullists, we do not care, it does not matter, or matter *now*. What matters now is that you have to help us push Jerry out. That was the point of the Bren guns. We gave them to you for that reason, explicitly, and no other. You have had them eighteen months and you have never used them once."

"I will not give you Bren guns," said Roger, "and that is final. Long live the Comintern! Long live the *Internationale*! Long live the great Stalin, the bear, the man of steel! If you were in Spain, you would understand this principle. If you—"

"Dear Roger, listen to the American lieutenant here. Do you think the Americans would have sent a fellow so far as they've sent this one just to tell you lies? This fellow is an actual son of the earth. His pater was a farmer. He raises wheat and cows and fights red Indians, as in the movies. He is tall, silent, noble. He is a walking myth. Listen to him."

He turned to the American and then realized he had, once again, forgotten the name. It was nothing personal; he just was so busy being magnificent and British that he couldn't be troubled by small details, such as American names.

"I say, Lieutenant, what was the moniker again?" He thought it was remarkable that the name kept slipping away on him. They had trained together at Milton Hall outside London for this little picnic for six or so weeks, but it kept slipping away, and whenever it did, it took Basil wholly out of where he was and turned his attention to the mystery of its disappearance.

"My name is Leets," said Leets, in English, accented in the tones of the middle plains of his vast homeland, the Minnesota part.

"It's so strange," said Basil. "It just goes away. Poof, it's gone, so bizarre. Anyhow, tell him."

Leets also spoke French with a Parisian accent, which was why Roger, of Group Roger, didn't care for him, or for Basil. Roger thought all Parisians were traitors or bourgeoisie, equally culpable in any case, and that seemed to go twice for British or American Parisians. He didn't know that Leets spoke with a Parisian accent because he'd lived there between the ages of seven and fourteen while his father managed 3M's European accounts. No, Leets's father was not a farmer, not hardly, and had certainly never fought red Indians; he was a rather wealthy business executive now retired, living in Sarasota, Florida, with one son, this one, in occupied France playing cowboys with the insane, another a naval aviator on a jeep carrier that had yet to reach the Pacific, and still a third 4-F and in medical school in Chicago.

Roger, namesake and kingpin of Group Roger, turned his fetid little eyes upon Leets.

"I can blow the bridge," said Leets. "It's not a problem. The bridge will go down; it's only a matter of rigging the 808 in the right place and leaving a couple of time pencils stuck in the stuff."

But Basil interrupted, on the thrust of an epiphany.

"It's because you're all so similar," he said, as if he'd given the matter a great deal of right proper Oxonian thought. "It has to do with gene pools. In our country, or in Europe on the whole, the gene pool is much more diverse. You see that in the fantastic European faces. Really, go to any city in Europe and the variety in such features as eye spacing, jawline, height of forehead, width of cheekbones, is extraordinary. I could watch it for days. But you Yanks seem to have about three faces between you, and you pass them back and forth. Yours is the farm boy face. Rather broad, no visible bone structure, pleasant, but not sharp enough to be particularly attractive. I fear you'll lose your hair prematurely. Your people do have good, healthy dentition,

I must give you that. But all the plumpness on the face. You must eat nothing but cake. It goes to your face and turns you rather *ballonishish*, and it's bloody hard keeping you apart. You remind me of at least six other Americans I know, and I can't remember their names either. Wait, one of them is a chap called Carruthers. Do you know him?"

Leets thought this question rhetorical and in any event it seemed to tucker Basil out for a bit. Leets turned back to the fat French Communist.

"We can kill the sentries; I can rig the 808 and plant the package, and it doesn't even have to be fancy. It's simple engineering; anyone could look at it and see the stress points. So: pop the tab on the time pencil and run like hell. The problem is that the garrison at Tulle is only a mile away, and the minimum time I can get the bridge rigged is about three minutes, because we have to go in hard. When we shoot the sentries, it'll make a noise, because we don't have silencers. The noise will travel and the garrison will be alerted. Meanwhile, I have to get down and lash the package just so on the trusses. They'll get there before I'm done. So my team will get fried like eggs if we're still rigging when they show. That's why we need the Brens. We've only got rifles and Stens and my Thompson. I need two Brens on the road from Tulle with a lot of ammo to shoot up the trucks as they come along. You can't disable a truck with a Sten. Simple physics."

He went on to explain the ballistic arcana of the circumstance, citing bullet weight, composition, inherent accuracy, muzzle energy and velocity, down to numbers as per cartridge. It was very impressive—if you were twelve. Here it was met with eyes pickled in distraction by all involved.

"Right," said Basil. "Well presented, Lieutenant Bates. Quite fascinating. Now see here, Monsieur Roger—"

"*Non!*" said Roger, spraying them with garlic. He was a butcher, immense and powerful but also garrulous and intractable. He'd fought in Spain, where he was wounded twice. He was almost grotesquely valiant and fearless, but he understood the primitive calculus of the politics: the Brens were power, and without power Group Roger would be at the mercy of all other groups, and that was more important than the prospect of 2nd SS Panzer Das Reich using the bridge to rush Tiger tanks to the Normandy beachhead, as intelligence predicted they would surely do.

"My dear brother-in-arms Roger," said Basil, "the bridge will be blown, that I assure you. The only thing in doubt is whether Lieutenant Bates—"

"Leets."

"Leets, yes, of course . . . whether Lieutenant Leets and his team of maquisards from Group Phillippe will make it out alive. Without the Brens, they haven't a chance, do you see?"

"Phillippe is a pig as are all his men," said Roger. "It is better for them to die at the bridge and spare us the effort of hunting them down to hang after the war. That is my only concern."

"Can you say to this brave young American, 'Lieutenant Bates, you must die, that is all there is to it'?"

"Yes, it's nothing," said Roger, looking like he had a train to catch as he turned to Leets. " 'Lieutenant Bates, you must die; that is all there is to it.' All right, I said it. Fine. Good-bye, sorry and all that, but policy is policy."

He signaled his two bodyguards, who, after rattling their Schmeissers dramatically cinema-style, rose and began to escort him up the cellar steps.

"Well, there you have it," said Basil to Leets. "Sorry, but it looks like your number is up, Lieutenant. You get pranged. Sad, unjust, but inescapable. Fate, I gather. Ours not to reason why, et cetera, et cetera. Do you know your Tennyson?"

"I know that one," said Leets glumly.

"I suppose one could simply not go. I think that's what I'd do in your shoes, but then, I'm not the demo man; you are. I'm the head potato, so I'll supervise quite nicely from the tree line. As for you, if you decide not to go, it would be embarrassing, of course, but in the long run it probably doesn't make much difference whether the bridge goes or not, and it seems silly to waste a future doctor of all the fabled Minnesotas on such a local Frenchy balls-up between de Gaulle's smarmy peons and that giant, stinking, garlic-sucking red butcher."

"If I catch it," said Leets, "I catch it. That's the game I signed up for. I just hate to catch it because of some little snit between Group Roger and Group Phillippe. Stopping Das Reich is worth it; helping Roger prevail over Phillippe is not, and I don't give a shit about red or white guerillas."

"Yet they can't really be separated, can they? It's always so complicated, haven't you noticed? Politics, politics, politics, it mucks up everything. Anyhow, if you like, I'll write your people a very nice letter about what a hero you were. Would you like that?"

As with much of what Basil said, the words were pitched in a key of meaning so exquisite, Leets couldn't exactly tell if St. Florian was serious or not. You could never be sure with Basil; he frequently said the exact opposite of what he meant. He seemed to live in a zone of near comedy where nearly every damned thing was "amusing" and he took great pleasure in saying the "shocking" thing. The first thing he said to Leets all those weeks ago at Milton Hall was "It's all a racket, you know. Our nobs are trying to wipe out their nobs so they can get all the wog gold; that's what it's *really* all about. Our job is to make the world safe for Anglo-American nobs."

Now Basil said, "I can, however, in my tiny British pea brain, concoct one other possibility."

"What's that?"

"Well, it has to do with a radio."

"We don't have a radio."

The radio was lashed to André Breton's body—which, unfortunately, had hit the earth at about eight hundred miles an hour when André's parachute ripped in half on the tail spar of the Liberator that had dropped them the night before. Neither the radio nor André were salvageable, which was why Team Casey was down 33 percent strength before its other two-thirds landed under their chutes a minute or so after André had his accident.

"The Germans have radios."

"We're not Germans. We're the Allies, remember? Captain, sometimes I think you don't take this all that seriously."

"I speak German. What else is necessary?"

"This is crazy. You'll never—"

"Anyway, here's my idea. I cop a German uniform tomorrow and walk into the Tulle garrison headquarters at eleven a.m. With my command presence, I will send Jerry away. Then I will commandeer his radio and put in a call. A fellow owes me a favor. If his groundwork is solid, it just might work out."

"Jerry will put you up against a wall at eleven oh three and shoot you."

"Hmm, good point. Possibly, if Jerry is distracted . . ."

"Go ahead, I'm all ears."

"You blow something up. I don't know—anything. Improvise—that's what you chaps are so good at. Jerry runs to see. While Jerry's got his knickers up his bum, I enter the garrison headquarters, all Savoyed up, Jerry-style. It's easy for me to commandeer the radio, make my call. Five minutes and I'm out."

"Who are you trying to reach on radio?"

"A certain fellow."

"A fellow where?"

"In England."

"You're going to radio England? From a German command post in occupied France?"

"I am. I'm going to dial up Jack Cairncross of the Code and Cypher School at some grotesque country monstrosity. He's some kind of higher pooh-bah there and there are sure to be lots of radios about."

"What can he do?"

"You didn't hear this from me, chum, but it's said he's one of the reds. Same team, just different players, for now. Joe for king, that sort of thing. Anyhow, he's sure to know somebody who knows somebody who knows somebody in the big town."

"London?" asked Bates—er, Leets—but Basil just smiled, and Leets realized he meant Moscow.

Basil

So Basil turned himself into a passable German officer with little enough trouble. The uniform came from an actual officer who had been killed in an ambush in 1943 and his uniform kept in storage by the Maquis against the possibility of just such a gambit. It smelled of sweat, farts, and blood. It was also a year out of date in terms of accouterments, badges, and dinky geegaws, but Basil knew or at least believed that with enough charisma he could get through anything.

And thus, at 11 a.m., as Leets and three maquisards from Group Phillippe prepared to blow up a deserted farmhouse a half mile out of town the other way from the bridge, Basil walked masterfully to the gate of the garrison HQ of the 113th Field Flak Battalion, the lucky air boys who controlled security here in Tulle. The explosion had the predictable effect on the air boys, who panicked, grabbed weapons and other dangerous, frightening (to them) equipment, and began running toward the rising column of smoke. They were terrified of a screwup because it meant they might be transferred somewhere actual fighting was possible.

Basil watched them go, and when the last of several ragtag groups had disappeared, he strode toward the big communications van next to the château, with its thirty-foot radio mast adorned with all kinds of Jerry stylistics; this one had a triangle up top. These people!

It helped that the officer whose uniform he wore had been a hero, as the vivid clutter on his chest indicated. One medal in particular was an emblem of a tank, and underneath it hung three little plates of some sort. The other stuff was the usual porridge, and it all signified martial valor, very impressive to the distinctly non-militaristic Luftwaffers who didn't know tuppence about such stuff but recognized what they took to be the genuine item when it appeared.

Basil got to the radio van easily enough, chased the duty sergeant away by proclaiming himself Major Strasser—he'd seen *Casablanca*, of course, and knew no German had—of Section III-B Abwehr Paris, working for the legendary *Herr Major* Dieter Macht, whom Basil actually knew.

He faced a bank of gear, all of it rather scienced-up in an array of dials, switches, knobs, and gauges set in shiny Bakelite.

The transceiver turned out to be a 15 W.S. E.b., a small, complete station with an output power of 15 watts, just jolly super and what the doctor ordered. The frequency range embraced those used by the British and the mechanics for synchronization between transmitter and receiver were very advanced. Two dials up top, a midpoint dial displaying frequency, the tuner below, and below that buttons and switches and all the foofah of radioland. Had he a course on it somewhere in time? Seems he had, but there was so much, it was best to let the old subconscious take over and run the show.

Die Maschine was very Teutonic. It had labels and sub-labels everywhere, switches, dials, wires, the German gestalt in one instrument, insanely well-ordered yet somewhat over-engineered in a vulgar way. Instead of "On/Off," the switch read literally "Makingtobroadcast/Stoppingtobroadcast Facilitation." A British radio would have been less imposing, less a manifesto of purpose, but also less reliable. You could bomb this thing and it would keep working.

The machine crackled and spat and began to radiate heat. Evidently it was quite powerful.

He put on some radio earphones—the noise of static was quite annoying—found what had to be a channel or frequency knob, and spun it to the British range.

He knew both sides worked with jamming equipment, but it wasn't useful to jam large numbers of frequencies, so more usually they played little games, trying to infiltrate each other's communications and cause mischief. He also knew he should flip a switch and go to Morse, but he had never been a good operator. He reasoned that the airwaves today were totally filled with chatter of various sorts and whoever was listening would have to weigh the English heavily, get interpretation from analysts, and alert command; the whole process had to take days. He decided just to talk, as if from a club in Soho.

"Hullo, hullo," he said each time the crackly static stopped.

A couple of times he got Germans screaming, "You must use radio procedure! You are directed to halt! This is against regulations!" and turned quickly away, but later rather than sooner someone said, "Hullo, who's this?"

"Basil St. Florian," Basil said.

"Chum, use radio protocol, please. Identify by call sign. Wait for verification."

"Sorry, don't know the protocol. It's a borrowed radio, do you see?"

"Chum, I can't—Basil St. Florian? Were you at Eton, '28 through '32? Big fellow, batsman, ginger. I was on the Harrow eleven. June 23, '33. You got a century that day, out for 126 wasn't it?"

"Actually, it was 127, edged it to third slip."

"Ah, right. The wicket was deteriorating a bit, funny bounce. Good showing, though. You had a smashing classic cover drive. Beautiful to watch."

"The god of batsmen smiled upon me that day."

"I was at fine leg, damned good if I say so myself. I dismissed you, finally. You smiled at me. Lord, I never saw such a striker."

"I remember. Who knew we'd meet again like this? Now, look here, I'm trying to reach the code mucky-mucks at that ghastly Toad Hall. Chap named Jack Cairncross. Can you help?"

"I shouldn't give out information."

"Old man, it's not like I'm just anybody. I remember you. Reddish hair, freckled, looked like you wanted to cosh me. Remember how fierce you were; that's why I winked. I have it right, don't I?"

"In fact, you do. All these years, now this. Know which hut he's in?"

"No idea. Can you help?"

"I can get you Bletchley Central. Let me see, yes, via the day code they'd be King-Six-Orange, then. Let's make you Freddie-Seven-Pip. I'm going to have Evers do a patch."

"Thanks ever so much."

Basil waited, examining his fingernails, looking about

for something to drink. A nice bottle, say, of something red from '34, anything would do, '34 was such a fine year. He yawned. Tick-tock, tick-tock, tick-tock. *When* would this Evers fellow—

"Identify, please."

"Is this King-Six-Orange?"

"Identify, please."

"Freddie-Seven-Pip. Looking to speak with your man Jack Cairncross. Put him on, do you mind?"

"Do you think this is a telephone exchange?"

"No, no, but nevertheless I need to talk to him. Old school chum. Need a favor."

"Identify, please."

"I can't remember. Something like Freddie-Pip. Listen carefully: I am in a bother and I need to talk to Jack. It's war business, not gossip."

"Where are you?"

"In Tulle. Tulle, France."

"Didn't realize the boys had got that far inland."

"They haven't. That's why it's rather urgent, old man."

"This is very against regulations."

"Dear man, I'm SOE. You know, the dagger boys. I'm actually at a Jerry radio and at any moment Jerry will return. Now, I have to talk to Jack. Please, play up for the game."

"SOE, public school, weekends in the country, all that then. I hate you all. You deserve to burn."

"We do, I know. Such officious little pricks, the lot of us. I'll help you light the timbers after the war and then climb into them smiling. But first let's win it. I implore you."

"Bah," said the fellow, "you'd best not put me on report."

"I shan't."

"He is, in fact, no longer here. The Scot beggar has left us for the nobs at Six."

"Can you patch me through, then? It's rather urgent." Basil could hear hubbub in the yard. Had the air boys returned?

"I suppose I must, Seven-Pip," said his inquisitor with a tragic sigh.

More clicking and buzzing and whatever magic lurked in the wires and antennae of His Majesty's secret apparatus was again put to the test, until somehow Basil's voice had been repurposed to the rotting old buildings on Broadway.

"Station K. Identify."

"Ah, I think it's something Seven-Pip. Does that help?"

"Observe security protocols, if you please."

"Look here, it's one of your old boys, Basil St. Florian. Everyone at Broadway knows Basil St. Florian."

"I need the code word before—"

"FREDDIE! That's it. Freddie-Seven-Pip!"

Authenticated, Basil waited again until he was shunted at last to some office or other, one hoped close enough to the target.

"Philby."

"Yes, see here, I need to speak with—Kim? Kim Philby, can that be you?"

"It is indeed, Basil. Why, I'd know that voice anywhere! Lord, how I've missed those nights we tried to empty all the gin bottles in Soho."

"What gay lads we were!"

"You're off blowing up Jerry's kitchens, are you?"

"Actually, Kim, I am. And that's why I need a chat with your chap Cairncross."

"That one? The Scot? Dour as haggis in vinegar."

"Can you get him on the blower for me?"

"Of course. But Basil, do call back, anytime. I'd love to hear your adventures. You've much to tell, I'm sure."

In a minute or so, another voice came over the earphones.

"Yes, hullo."

"Jack, it's Basil. Basil St. Florian."

"Who?"

"We met at the Citadel briefing with all the other senior code breakers. I'm with one of the hugger-mugger outfits. Was all banged up. Last year in the war rooms."

"Oh, that. Rather fuzzy, but if you say so."

"Right, Jack. Now, see, here's the thing. I need a favor, do you mind?"

"Well, depending, of course."

"I'm to go with some rough chaps tonight to set off a firecracker under a bridge. Nasty work, but they say it has to be done."

"Sounds fascinating."

"Not really. Hardly any wit to it at all. You know, just destroying things; it seems so infantile in the long run. Anyhow, our cause would be helped if a gang in the area called Group Roger—have you got that?— would pitch in with its Brens. But it's some red/white thing and they won't help. I thought you had Uncle Joe's ear—"

"Who did you say you were? Good heavens, man. People may be listening."

"No inference or judgment meant. I tell no tales, and let each man enjoy his own politics and loyalties as I do mine. That's what the war's all about, eh? Let's put it this way: if *one* had Uncle Joe's ear, *one* might ask that Group Roger in Tulle vicinity pitch in with Brens to help Group Phillippe. That's all. Have you got that?"

"Roger, Brens, Phillippe, Tulle."

"Thanks, old man."

"It's not like you can just ring them up, you know. But I'll give it a whirl."

"There's the lad."

Basil put the microphone down, unhooked the earphones from around his head, and looked up into the eyes of an *Oberleutnant* and two sergeants with machine pistols.

Leets looked at his Bulova. It had been an hour, no, an hour and a half.

"I think they got him," said his No. 1, a young fellow called Leon.

"Shit," said Leets, in English. He was at a window in the upper floor of a residence fifty yards across from the gated château that served as the 113th Luftwaffe Field Flak Battalion's headquarters and garrison. He held an M1 Thompson submachine gun low, out of sight, and wore a French rain slicker, rubbery, and a plowman's shabby hat.

"We can't hit it," said Leon. "Not four of us. And if we got him out, on the surprise aspect of it, where'd we go? We have no automobile to escape."

Leon was right, but still Leets hated the idea of Captain Basil St. Florian of the Horse Guard perishing on something so utterly trivial as a bridge in the interests of one Team Casey that existed out of a misbegotten SOE-OSS cooperative plan, silly, cracked, and doomed as hell. Strictly a show, thought up by big headquarters brainiacs with too much spare time, of no true import. He knew it—they all knew it—and had known it in all the hours in Areas A and F and whatever, disguised golf